"Whoa, t

Tyler put his hands on her shoulders to steady her.

Her heart racing, Carly stepped back quickly. The heated look in his eyes flustered her. She felt trapped.

With a toss of her head, she said, "That sounds like something you'd say to some poor dumb animal. One you were getting ready to brand."

His lazy gaze slid down her from head to toe. "You interested?"

Her mouth went dry. "Don't be ridiculous."

"I notice you didn't answer my question. Are you interested? In wearing by brand?"

"I'm not one of your horses or cows, Tyler."

"I noticed. Believe me. That was one of the first things I noticed about you."

His husky voice sent shivers down Carly's spine. "No, the first thing you noticed about me was that I made Amanda laugh. That's the only reason I'm here, Tyler."

His eyes flashed. "Is it?"

Dear Reader,

Those long days of summer sunshine are just around the corner—and Special Edition has six fabulous new books to start off the season right!

This month's THAT'S MY BABY! title is brought to you by the wonderful Janis Reams Hudson. *His Daughter's Laughter* tells the poignant tale of a widowed dad, his fragile little girl and the hope they rediscover when one extraordinary woman touches their lives.

June is the month of wedding bells—or in some cases, wedding blues. Be sure to check out the plight of a runaway bride who leaves one groom behind, only to discover another when she least expects it in *Cowboy's Lady*—the next installment in Victoria Pade's ongoing A RANCHING FAMILY miniseries. And there's more romance on the way with award-winning author Ruth Wind's *Marriage Material*— book one in THE LAST ROUNDUP, a new cross-line series with Intimate Moments about three brothers who travel the rocky road to love in a small Colorado town.

And speaking of turbulent journeys, in *Remember Me?* Jennifer Mikels tells a passionate love story about an amnesiac woman who falls for the handsome hero who rescues her from a raging rainstorm. Also in June, Shirley Larson presents *That Wild Stallion*—an emotional Western that's sure to tug your heartstrings.

Finally, *New York Times* bestselling author Ellen Tanner Marsh lives up to her reputation with *A Doctor in the House*, her second Silhouette title. It's all work and no play for this business executive until he meets his match in the form of one feisty Southern beauty in the Florida Keys!

I hope you enjoy all our summer stories this month!

Sincerely,

Tara Gavin
Senior Editor

Please address questions and book requests to:
Silhouette Reader Service
U.S.: 3010 Walden Ave., P.O. Box 1325, Buffalo, NY 14269
Canadian: P.O. Box 609, Fort Erie, Ont. L2A 5X3

JANIS REAMS HUDSON

HIS DAUGHTER'S LAUGHTER

Published by Silhouette Books
America's Publisher of Contemporary Romance

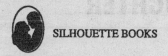

SILHOUETTE BOOKS

ISBN 0-373-24105-4

HIS DAUGHTER'S LAUGHTER

Copyright © 1997 by Janis Reams Hudson

This edition published by arrangement with Harlequin Books S.A.

Printed in U.S.A.

Books by Janis Reams Hudson

Silhouette Special Edition

Resist Me if You Can #1037
The Mother of His Son #1095
His Daughter's Laughter #1105

JANIS REAMS HUDSON

is the author of twenty previous novels, both contemporary and historical romances. Her books have appeared on Waldenbooks, B. Dalton and Bookrak bestseller lists, earned numerous awards, including Reviewers' Choice awards from *Romantic Times* and the prestigious National Readers' Choice Award, and have been finalists for several other awards, including the RITA Award from Romance Writers of America.

When not writing or researching her next novel, Janis devotes much of her time to various local and national writers' organizations. She currently serves as Immediate Past President and National Literacy Chairperson of Romance Writers of America, the world's largest nonprofit genre writers' organization.

Dear Reader,

We've all heard of the old saying that you can pick your friends, but you can't pick your family. That's true, as far as it goes. But families are not bound by blood alone. Sometimes the strongest links have nothing to do with blood ties, but are instead formed in the heart.

No matter how families are formed, they are the lifeblood of our world. Time and again families break apart and struggle to form themselves anew. In any family trouble, the children are both the strongest and the most easily hurt. Children take everything so personally, so literally. A thoughtless word can unintentionally scar a fragile young heart, can silence carefree childish laughter.

There is nothing more precious on earth than the innocent laughter of a child. This story is about a child who does not laugh, the father who aches for her, and the woman who can both heal this troubled family and be healed herself in the process.

It's a story of tears and laughter and love, and comes straight from my heart. I hope you enjoy reading it even half as much as I enjoyed writing it.

Sincerely,

Janis Reams Hudson

Chapter One

"Why do you want to leave her here?"

"I don't want to." Tyler Barnett rubbed his face, then let his hands fall to his lap. "She's only six years old. I don't want to leave her anywhere, but I don't know what else to do. I can't get the kind of help she needs at home. That last therapist terrified her. I was told you were the best. If the only way to help my daughter is leave her with my aunt and have her bring Amanda in for appointments, I'll just have to find a way to live with it."

"I don't think it's in Amanda's best interest for you to leave her here." Dr. Sanders folded his hands atop his spotless desk blotter. "She's obviously still suffering from the trauma of her mother's death. She may very well look on your leaving her here as abandonment."

Tyler clenched his fists against the hopelessness eating at him. "So what do I do? How do I help her?"

"I have a colleague in Cheyenne. Let me give him a call."

Tyler nodded. "Fine. I appreciate it. But keep in mind, Cheyenne's an eight-hour drive from my ranch."

"I understand what you're saying."

"Do you? I said I'd do anything for Amanda, and I meant it. But if I have to shut down my training facilities and move to Cheyenne for several months—or longer—I'll lose my income. Not only will I need to pay for her treatment, but we'd have to have a place to live. Don't get me wrong. I'm not poor. I don't care if her treatment costs me every penny I have. But if my money runs out before she's well, and I have no income..." Frustrated, he shrugged.

"What about insurance?" Sanders asked.

Tyler shook his head. "Amanda hadn't lived with me for two years before her mother died. She was covered on Deborah's policy, but it didn't cover this."

"I see." The doctor frowned. "How far are you from Jackson?"

"A couple of hours."

"Let me talk to that colleague I mentioned and see what we can come up with. If you can stick around for a few minutes, I'll call right now."

Tyler nodded and pushed himself from the chair. "Thank you." The two men shook hands. "I'll be in the lounge with Amanda."

In the hall, Tyler straightened his shoulders and put on a smile. He didn't want Amanda to see the despair and tension eating at him. If Dr. Sanders couldn't help, Tyler didn't know what he would do.

The private, exclusive San Francisco clinic was hushed with quiet. Not the peace-giving quiet of his Wyoming sage flats, but the unnerving quiet of the hundreds of troubled souls who had passed through these halls over the years. The soft whish of his boots across the plush carpet made the skin on the back of his neck prickle.

At the end of the hall, Amanda and a young woman wearing a white lab coat over blue jeans were the only people in the waiting room. From her perch on the edge of a child-size chair, Amanda, her back to the hall, leaned toward the woman kneeling at her feet. Both were engrossed in whatever they were doing with their hands. The woman laughed. She was a cute little thing with short, straight hair the same light golden chestnut shade as one of Tyler's favorite stallions.

Then Tyler heard another sound that stopped him in his tracks and backed the breath up in his lungs. It squeezed his heart and flooded his eyes. Had he imagined it? Did he want to hear it so desperately that his ears had invented the sound to soothe his soul?

But, no, there it was again, soft and faint, but oh, so real. His heart kicked in with a giant thud against his sternum, and his lungs expanded to suck in air. Heat and ice rippled side by side down his spine. Light-headed, almost dizzy, Tyler sprinted the rest of the way to Amanda's side and dropped to his knees. As he reached to touch her dark, precious head, his hand shook violently. "Amanda, honey?"

Amanda whipped her head around toward him, her blue-green eyes, the mirror image of his own, big and bright and filled with delight. Her lips parted in a silent smile; her eyes questioned.

Tyler scooped her up in his arms and stood. "Oh, baby, baby, you did it!" He hugged her tight, his eyes squeezed shut.

After a long, silent prayer of thanks, he opened his eyes and pulled back enough to see her face. "You laughed." He planted a big kiss on her nose. "Oh, baby, you laughed out loud."

Amanda's eyes widened. Her lips moved. *I did?*

But no sound came. She put her hand to her throat and tried again. Nothing.

Disappointment stabbed sharp and quick, but Tyler ignored it. She had laughed. He'd heard her. This was more than the vague mumbling he'd heard one night in her sleep, which had assured him her inability to speak was not phys-

ical. This had been a wide-awake, broad-light-of-day, un-
selfconscious laugh. If she did it once, she would do it
again. He refused to let doubt and disappointment mar the
moment.

"Yes," he told his daughter with an uncontrollable
smile. "You laughed. I heard you."

The child opened her mouth and worked her throat again.
When nothing came out but breath, her brows drew together in an agonized expression.

"Don't worry, honey. It may take awhile, but your voice
is coming back. It really is. Now," he said, tweaking her
nose to take her worry away. "What was so funny that I
heard you laugh clear down the hall?"

With a silent giggle, Amanda pointed to the doctor or
technician, whoever she was, still kneeling before the now-
empty chair, watching the two with curiosity. The young
woman's hands seemed trapped in a tangle of string.

"She made you laugh?" he asked Amanda.

Amanda grinned and nodded vigorously.

Even that small, seemingly ordinary action thrilled Tyler
and brought a lump to his throat. Since Deborah's death,
expressing an opinion of any kind was unusual for his too-
docile daughter.

Tyler studied his child's face, the relaxed happiness he
saw there that had been missing for so long. "I promised
we'd find somebody who could help you. You think maybe
she's the one?"

Amanda's eyes widened with sheer delight. This time she
nodded so hard her teeth clicked.

"Okay." Tyler let her slide down his leg until she
reached the floor. "I'll see what I can do."

Amanda ran to the young woman's side and tugged on
her arm until the woman stood. While the woman tried to
extract her fingers from the web of string, Amanda dragged
her forward.

"I'm Tyler Barnett," he said, extending his hand.
"Amanda's father."

Still focused on the struggle to free her fingers from the string, the young woman muttered a distracted, "Hang on."

Her voice, soft, quiet, unexpectedly sexy, sent a warm tingling down Tyler's spine, surprising him.

"There." She pulled her fingers free of the tangle and met his gaze.

She looked young, he thought at his first full glimpse of her cute face. Mid-twenties at the most, with hair shorter than his, and eyes so big and brown they nearly swallowed her face.

But there was something in those eyes, something not young, not cute. Their expression spoke of...sadness? Was that what he saw?

He shook his head. Whatever was there was none of his business.

She shook his hand. "Carly Baker."

Her firm, no-nonsense handshake was at odds with her pixie looks, her sad eyes and her soft, sexy voice. Yet as businesslike as her grip was, it could not disguise how tiny her hand felt in his, how soft and smooth and warm. Thrown off balance by the contrasts, Tyler released her slowly.

"I don't know how you did it, but I'll pay you to come home to Wyoming with us and do it again."

The woman named Carly Baker blinked slowly. "Do what?"

For a moment, just one brief instant, even Tyler wasn't sure what he was asking. But the child at his knee was never far from his thoughts. He took Amanda's hand. "Make her laugh out loud again."

The woman tilted her head, her eyes narrowed with suspicion. "You're kidding."

"I'm not. That's essentially the first sound she's made in six months. She obviously responds to you. I'm offering to hire you to work with her. I'll make it worth your while."

Eyes still narrowed, she asked, "How much?"

The new pickup and enclosed horse trailer would have to wait another year or two. "Would fifty thousand lure you away from this place?"

Her eyes flew open wide. "Now I know you're kidding."

Hell, Tyler thought, how much did a few weeks of a child psychologist's time cost these days? "All right, seventy-five," he offered, kissing the new barn goodbye.

"You're a patient here, right?" the woman asked, one eye narrowed. "Suffering from delusions?"

"Look," Tyler said, feeling her slip away from him. He needed her. Amanda needed her. He would just have to forgo buying that mare he'd looked at last week. Another horse would come along later. Maybe not as promising as Magnificent Cutter, but if he had to sell his right arm to help Amanda, he'd do it.

He took a deep breath. "Whatever you've got, my daughter needs it. I'll make it a hundred thousand. Without selling some things I can't afford to sell, that's every dime I've got in the world."

The woman blinked. "If you're not a patient here, you should be."

"He's not crazy, Carly."

Tyler and Carly turned to find Dr. Sanders leaning against the wall, looking as though he'd been there several minutes.

"And I think," the doctor added, "that you should take him up on his offer."

Carly rammed her hands, one of which still clutched a wad of string, into the deep pockets of her lab coat. "I think you're just as nuts—"

"Before you get into that," Dr. Sanders said, holding his palm out to stop her. He called to a woman heading down the hall toward them. "Stephanie, do you have a few minutes?"

The woman smiled. "Of course, Doctor. What can I do for you?"

Dr. Sanders reached a hand toward Amanda, and the girl took it. "This young lady," he said, "has had about all the tests she can stand for one day, but I still need the results from one more. Could you take her next door to the Baskin-Robbins 'laboratory' and find out just how much ice cream she can eat without making herself sick? With her father's permission, of course," he added, turning toward Tyler.

Tyler wasn't about to argue. Not with the gleam of pleasure in Amanda's eyes at the thought of ice cream, nor with the obvious support Dr. Sanders was offering in getting Carly Baker to cooperate.

"How 'bout it, funny face?" Tyler tweaked her nose. "Are you up to the test?"

Amanda looked from him to Dr. Sanders to the woman named Stephanie. Stephanie held out her hand and winked at her. Amanda looked back at Tyler with a shy smile.

"Well, okay," he said with feigned worry. "If you're sure you're up to it."

Amanda gave a careful nod and went off with Stephanie.

Carly Baker sat in one of the two armchairs before Eric Sanders's desk. The man named Tyler Barnett tugged on the legs of his brown Western-style slacks and sat in the other. He looked hard. The chiseled features of his tanned face, including that hawklike nose and square jaw, his broad shoulders, flat stomach, even his callused hands, all looked carved from seasoned oak. Everything about him appeared rugged, solid and unyielding. Except when he'd smiled at his daughter.

Carly couldn't forget that natural tenderness she'd glimpsed. It hadn't fit with her first impression of him as he came down the hall. His dark, shaggy hair—proclaiming he probably wasn't a corporate executive—tumbled down onto his furrowed brow and hung over the back of his collar. Frowning, he had threaded his long fingers through the slightly wavy mass and shoved it back. He'd looked deeply troubled. Until he'd seen Amanda. As far as Carly was concerned, any man who could smile like that at his daughter deserved the benefit of the doubt.

Still, his ridiculous…proposition, for lack of a better term, was something to doubt. Rational people simply did not walk up to total strangers and offer them a hundred thousand dollars. Not that a nice hundred grand wouldn't solve all of her current problems.

"What did you do to make her laugh?" Dr. Sanders asked her.

With a wry grin, Carly pulled the wad of tangled string from her pocket. "I was showing her how to make a cat's cradle. I mangled it so badly, there wasn't much else to do but laugh."

Sanders smiled and shook his head. "I really think you should consider Mr. Barnett's offer." He placed his clasped hands in the center of his immaculate desk pad. "With your background, you could be of real help."

"I'm in enough trouble already without adding taking money under false pretenses to my credit. What are you trying to do, land me in jail?"

"Don't be ridiculous," Dr. Sanders said.

"Besides," Carly added, "you know I'm not trained to help Amanda."

"Whoa, there." Tyler Barnett eyed them both. "Maybe I've been a little hasty. Would one of you like to explain about jail? I was under the impression that Ms. Baker was part of the staff here," he said to Dr. Sanders.

Carly chose to answer for herself. "Must have been the white coat that fooled you. I'm just a lowly volunteer."

Barnett eyed her carefully, making her feel as though she were under a giant microscope. "Why does he think you can help Amanda?"

Carly shifted in the chair and shrugged.

"She's not aware of Amanda's background," the doctor said, "so she doesn't realize just how much she could help."

Carly felt a sinking sensation in the pit of her stomach.

"Are you saying she and I have something in common?" she asked Dr. Sanders.

"May I?" Dr. Sanders asked Barnett.

Barnett nodded.

"Amanda's mother was killed in a car accident several months ago. Amanda hasn't spoken since."

Carly closed her eyes and took a deep breath. She didn't need any further explanation. She could only guess what Tyler Barnett felt at the loss of his wife, but she knew exactly what the child was going through. Feelings crawled through her memory one by one. Old, shadowy nightmares of guilt and anger, betrayal, pain, loss.

"Now you see why I think you can help?" Dr. Sanders said softly. "Who better than you, Carly? Who else can understand why she can't talk?"

Carly felt Tyler Barnett staring at her. She opened her eyes, but wouldn't look at him. She'd overcome the problems from her childhood. She understood fully what she had done to herself and wasn't necessarily uncomfortable with the subject. She just wasn't sure she was ready to discuss it with this hard-looking stranger. The tenderness she'd seen in him seemed reserved solely for his daughter.

"I take it that means you experienced something similar," Barnett said.

Carly looked at Dr. Sanders. "You started this. You might as well do the explaining."

"All right." He turned to Barnett. "The reason I think Carly can help Amanda is, first of all, Carly has helped several children here at the clinic over the years."

"You're exaggerating. I haven't done anything."

"What about Jeff Hawkins, just last month?"

"All I did was talk to him while he waited for his appointment with you."

"Yes, and the first thing he said to me was that he didn't hate his baby sister anymore. I'd been working with him for weeks without getting anywhere. There are others she's helped, too," he told Tyler. "Children just seem to respond well to Carly."

Dr. Sanders frowned and glanced down at his hands briefly. "The other reason I think she can help, particularly in Amanda's case, is that Carly's father died when she was nine. She developed severe stomach problems. After dozens of tests and probably gallons of Pepto Bismol, her doctors could find no physical explanation. Through counseling, she was able to deal with her guilt—"

"Guilt?" Barnett asked.

"Children often assume a great deal of responsibility for things that happen around them. It's not uncommon for a child to blame him- or herself for divorce, an accident, the death of a sibling or a parent. The more traumatic the incident, the greater the guilt. 'If only I'd been better, Daddy wouldn't have gone away.' That sort of thing."

"You think that's what Amanda's doing? Blaming herself?"

"I think it's a possibility. Then there's the sense of betrayal some children feel when they lose a parent. Sometimes there's anger. There's always pain. We won't know for certain what Amanda is going through until we can get her to tell us what she's feeling. That's where therapy comes in. And that's also where I think Carly can help."

"I'm no therapist, for heaven's sake," she protested.

"No, but there's not exactly an abundance of child psychologists in the Wyoming wilderness," Dr. Sanders said. "I'm waiting on a phone call right now about a colleague who's moving from Cheyenne to Jackson. As I understand it, that's still quite a distance from Mr. Barnett's ranch. Amanda's not going to be able to see him as often as I'd like. The way she responds to you, you could fill in the gap, talk to her about what you went through, let her know she's not alone with whatever she might be feeling."

"Isn't that a little unorthodox?" Carly asked.

Dr. Sanders smiled. "It might be, but I believe Mr. Barnett is right in thinking you can help her. And admit it. You could use the money."

Carly shook her head. "I can't take the kind of money he's offering. I'd feel dishonest."

"Well, now, there's a first," Barnett said. "A woman with a financial conscience."

Carly arched a brow at Dr. Sanders. "You want me to work for a man with an attitude like that?"

Barnett threaded his fingers through his hair. "Sorry. I meant it as a compliment. Will you take the job?"

"You made the offer when you thought I was something more than a volunteer. I can't hold you to that."

"Then name your price. What do you think Amanda is worth?"

Carly stiffened. "I wouldn't dream of putting a price on a child's welfare. All I would be doing essentially is baby-sitting."

Barnett shrugged. "Call it whatever makes you comfortable. All I want to know is, will you do it? You'd be living on a ranch in the middle of nowhere. No big city nearby, no nightlife or fancy stores."

Carly waved away those concerns. She hadn't had a nightlife or shopped in a fancy store in months, and hadn't missed either. "That wouldn't matter to me. I could use the peace and quiet."

Barnett gave her a half smile. "You'll probably go stir-crazy in less than a week. That's one reason I'm offering so much money."

"I can't take that kind of money. I don't know anything about you, and you expect me to just ride off into the sunset with you?" She looked to Dr. Sanders. "What if he's an ax murderer, for heaven's sake?"

The doctor grinned. "He's not. I checked."

Barnett raised a brow.

Dr. Sanders shrugged. "I thought of suggesting Carly when I first looked at Amanda's file. I made a few calls."

"Find anything dastardly in my background?" Barnett asked with a definite drawl in his voice.

"Not hardly, unless you mean hard work, loyalty and honoring your word more than most people honor a written contract."

Carly watched, fascinated, as a slight blush stained Barnett's cheeks.

He looked back at her. "He says I'm trustworthy, and I swear I'm not an ax murderer. So do we have a deal?"

As much as she needed money, Carly could not bring herself to accept his offer. It was too good to be true. There had to be a catch somewhere. A big one. Miracles like this just didn't happen to her.

"You need a job," Dr. Sanders reminded her.

"I know. But don't you think he should know why I need one?"

Dr. Sanders rolled his eyes. "Don't start with that."

"Are *you* an ax murderer?" Barnett asked with a slight twitch to his lips.

"No," Carly countered, "but I eat little children for breakfast."

Barnett's smile widened. "I don't think so."

"Are you willing to gamble your daughter's welfare on it?"

The way he stared at her, they might have been alone in the room. She could practically feel his eyes probing into her mind, reading her thoughts, her feelings. Her secrets.

"Yes," he said softly. "Because I don't think it's a gamble at all. You wouldn't hurt a child if your life depended on it."

"This is ridiculous," Carly said, trying not to scream. "I can't take a hundred thousand dollars for baby-sitting."

He stared at her another minute before speaking. "Do you cook?"

Carly blinked. "Why?"

"Do you cook?" he repeated. "And I don't mean anything fancy. Can you cook good, hearty food for working men? Meat and potatoes. Bacon and eggs. That sort of thing.''

It was Carly's turn to smile. What would he say if she told him she cooked meat and potatoes every day? That it was her job? But she supposed slinging hamburgers onto a grill and dunking French fries into a vat of hot grease down at the Burger Barrel wasn't exactly what he had in mind. ''Yes, I can cook.''

''Can you keep house? Dust, vacuum, mop, do laundry?''

''Why?''

''I'll pay you five thousand dollars right this minute, if you agree to come home with me. At the ranch, I'll pay you one thousand dollars a week to cook for Amanda, my father, four ranch hands and me, plus keep house. And another thousand a week to spend time with Amanda.''

''I was right the first time,'' she told him. ''You're out of your mind.''

''Is it a deal?''

Carly rose from her chair and headed toward the door. Her knees shook at the thought of all that money she was walking away from. ''I'm not the person you need. You don't know anything about me.''

''What do I need to know?''

''You need to know why I spend my days volunteering instead of earning a living.''

''Carly,'' Dr. Sanders said, a note of warning in his voice.

She ignored him. Barnett would change his mind when he knew the truth.

''You need to know,'' she said, reaching for the doorknob, ''that the person you want to entrust with the care of your home and your child is not only not qualified for the job, but lost her last job, which she'd held for eight years, because of embezzling.''

Chapter Two

The eight-year-old Chevy died just as Carly pulled into her driveway. Fighting the sudden loss of power steering and power brakes, she ground her teeth together and mashed on the brake pedal with all her might to halt the car before it rolled through the low brick wall separating the parking area from the backyard. With inches to spare— two or three at least—the car stopped.

She put the car in park and closed her eyes. If she didn't get the carburetor worked on soon, she might not be so lucky as to have the car stall in her parking space. Next time, it might happen on the freeway, or on the Golden Gate Bridge on her way to Vallejo to visit her mother. A shiver ran down her arms at the thought of getting stranded on the bridge.

Damn that Tyler Barnett for dangling a hundred thousand dollars in her face when she so desperately needed money. If he'd made any kind of reasonable offer, she would have been more than tempted to accept. But a hundred thousand dollars? She simply couldn't take it. Not that much money. She would never be able to live with herself. She would feel like the thief she'd been named.

With the classifieds tucked under one arm, she climbed out of the car and headed slowly for her apartment, not at all eager to find out how many bills had come in today's mail. Since she had lost her bookkeeping job at Blalock's, the bills had been piling higher by the day. The minimum wage she earned at Burger Barrel came nowhere near covering her rent, car payment, insurance, utilities and groceries. Maybe there would be a better paying job in today's paper. Something that wouldn't require a reference.

Fat chance. *She* wouldn't hire a bookkeeper without a reference. No one would. No one except a crazy cowboy from Wyoming.

Not that Tyler Barnett looked crazy. On the contrary, he looked like a rugged individualist who knew what he wanted from life, and watch out, Bub, to whoever tried to stop him. He looked competent, confident. And, she reluctantly admitted, he looked damned good, with his hard features and piercing blue-green eyes.

"Yeah, and remember what happened the last time you fell for a pretty face," she muttered under her breath.

But then, Tyler Barnett's face couldn't really be called pretty. Appealing, yes. Rugged, handsome...sexy. But not pretty. And, in the long run, it wouldn't make any difference, because she would never see him again.

Inside the dim hall, she pulled the mail from her mailbox, purposely refraining from flipping through the envelopes until she was inside her apartment. The restraint didn't help much. The envelope directly under her thumb as she clutched the stack was from her landlord. Nob Hill landlords who divided their mansions into apartments were notorious for wanting their rent on time. She felt her stomach knot.

All the way up the stairs to her second-floor apartment, she refused to look at the rest of her mail. Mildly surprised and wildly relieved to find the lock on her door hadn't yet been changed, Carly dropped the mail on the coffee table, then went to her bedroom. With firm determination, she ignored the stylish Evan Picone and Liz Claiborne suits now shoved to the back of her closet and changed into her mud brown polyester Burger Barrel uniform.

Afterward, with only twenty minutes left before she had to leave for work, she sat on the couch and picked up the mail.

So damned thoughtful of the landlord to remind her she was two months behind on her rent, and the third was coming due next week. Did he think she didn't know?

An electric bill. At least it wasn't overdue. Yet.

The contents of the third envelope tied another knot in her stomach and added a touch of nausea for good measure. If she didn't make two car payments by the end of the week—which was today—her account would be closed and her car repossessed. She had until five o'clock.

She swallowed and glanced at her watch. Five thirty-two.

With shaking hands, she swiped at the moisture on her heeks. If she lost her car, she would have to give up volunteering at the clinic. Her schedule at Burger Barrel would not allow her enough time to accommodate the bus schedule. Then, too, her mother would never let her live down having her car repossessed.

Give up, a voice in the back of her mind taunted. *Admit you can't make it.*

Try as she might, denying that voice had been getting harder over the weeks. Today, with all this fan mail from her creditors, it was nearly impossible.

Maybe the voice was right. Maybe she should just go to her mother and stepfather and admit they were right. Admit that at the tender age of thirty, she couldn't make it on her own. Let them support her until she found a decent job.

"Yeah," she muttered as she tossed the mail aside. "And listen to my mother tell me how I should have married James when I had the chance."

James, so perfectly clean-cut handsome.

James, attentive, devoted.

James, the serious one, so careful with his money, so sweet, so loving.

James, so old-fashioned, so considerate of her reputation, that he'd gone to elaborate lengths to keep their "engagement," their entire relationship, a secret, to the point of making her swear she wouldn't even tell her best friend.

James, who'd coerced and teased her computer password at work out of her.

James, the embezzler who'd used her code when transferring thousands of dollars over the past several months into a dummy account.

James, as shocked as the rest of her co-workers to "learn" Carly had stolen from the company.

James, who spent the day she was being accused of embezzling announcing his engagement to Becky Blalock, the boss's daughter and Carly's best friend since grade school.

That was the man Carly's mother thought she should have married.

"If you had married him," her mother said, "he wouldn't have used your password, and you wouldn't have lost your job."

Mom had just a tad bit of trouble with reality.

A bitter taste filled Carly's mouth. She should have known better than to let James enter her mind when her stomach was already churning. That her mother still thought, after what that creep had done to her, that Carly should have married him, made her want to scream.

Instead of screaming, however, she took a deep breath, counted to ten, then let it out. It didn't help much, but it reminded her it was time to go to work.

She slipped the shoulder strap of her purse over her head, then grabbed the stupid mud brown tam that went with her uniform and headed out into the sounds of late-afternoon traffic. Cars honked, people laughed and shouted, a cable car two blocks west clanged its bell. The city was alive all around her, softened by the approach of evening fog.

Halfway down the front walk, she stopped. At the curb before the elegant old mansion that housed her apartment, a man was helping a little girl out of the passenger side of his car.

Tyler Barnett.

Carly felt like groaning. What was he doing here?

But then, she knew the answer. He had obviously come to convince her to change her mind and accept his offer.

Carly smiled as Amanda stepped from the car and straightened the short, ruffled skirt of her pink dress. The child was a little angel, and Carly had fallen for her at first sight. Fallen hard. She ached deep inside for the pain a girl so young had suffered. Would yet suffer, if she was to get her speech back.

Carly felt her heart soften. "Hi, Amanda."

Amanda waved and flashed two adorable dimples. Then she cocked her head and studied Carly closely.

"What is it?" Carly asked.

Amanda closed one eye and tapped her eyelid with a finger.

"I'm afraid I don't know what that means," Carly said.

"Never mind," Tyler Barnett said. "It's just some of Amanda's own brand of sign language."

"Oh." Against her will and better judgment, Carly's gaze drew to Amanda's father.

Amanda tugged on his arm and put her finger to her closed eyelid again.

"It's okay," he told her. "It's none of our business."

"I'll probably regret this," Carly said, "but what's none of your business?"

Instead of answering, he gave a perturbed frown.

Amanda tugged on his arm, harder this time, and repeated her gesture.

Tyler heaved a sigh. "All right." With more than a hint

of resignation and wariness, he looked at Carly. "Amanda wants to know why you've been crying."

Carly's cheeks burned. With a nervous laugh, she averted her gaze. "Oh, you know. One of those sad old movies was on TV."

He looked as if he didn't believe her, then shrugged. "There," he told his daughter. "See? Nothing's wrong. She was just watching a sad movie, that's all."

A soft touch on the back of Carly's hand had her looking down into serious young eyes. The child's eyes, like her father's, looked as if they could see into Carly's soul.

Carly forced a smile. "So, did you pass your ice-cream test?"

Amanda grinned and nodded.

"Okay," Tyler told his daughter. "You got to say hi, now go wait in the car for me while I talk to Ms. Baker." The words that could have been harsh were, instead, soft and loving.

Amanda waved goodbye and went back to the car, looking over her shoulder at Carly several times on her way.

Tyler Barnett folded his arms across his chest and widened his stance, as if ready for battle.

Carly's choices were few. She could make a run for it, she could turn and go back inside, or she could face him. Raised flower beds flanked both sides of the sidewalk all the way down the yard. Crawling over them to escape Barnett's presence would be the height of indignity, and was out of the question, as was retreating back up the sidewalk to her apartment.

Barnett looked beyond her shoulder at the house behind her. "It's beautiful," he said, surprising her.

Carly followed his gaze to the three-story, age-smoothed stone mansion. "Yes. It was converted to apartments years ago. There's always a waiting list. I was lucky to even get in."

And would be luckier still, if she didn't get kicked out, she knew.

But she couldn't think about her overdue rent. Tyler Barnett still stood militantly before her, and she needed to get going. She took the offensive. "What do you want? I'm late for work."

"You're walking?"

"It's only a few blocks."

He smirked. "The Burger Barrel, huh?"

"It's a living." Her cheeks stung at the lie.

"I'll bet."

Carly chewed on the inside of her jaw and kept quiet, hoping he'd take the hint and leave. He didn't.

"Dr. Sanders explained what happened at your last job," Barnett said. "I don't believe you took any money, and if you did, I don't care. I'm not asking you to be my banker, and the family silver hasn't been polished in so long, you wouldn't have it if I gave it to you. Amanda and I want you to come home with us."

"How did you find me?"

"You're in the phone book."

Carly frowned at the obvious answer. It had been a stupid question, anyway.

Tyler uncrossed his arms and shifted his feet. "I promised Amanda I'd take her on the cable cars tomorrow before we go home Sunday. We'd both like it very much if you'd come with us."

"Stand at that corner," Carly said pointing a half block down, "and one will be along in a few minutes."

He was shaking his head before she finished. "I checked the guidebooks. That one just goes up and down this one street. We want to see more than that—Lombard Street, Fisherman's Wharf, Union Square. All the tourist stuff. You could be our guide. I'll even throw in lunch."

Carly shook her head. "You don't give up, do you?"

He leveled his gaze on her, drilling her with those piercing blue-green eyes. "She needs you."

"She needs a trained psychologist, not an out-of-work bookkeeper."

"Ms. Baker—Carly—Amanda has never responded to a stranger the way she did to you today. Never. And except for the time I heard her mumble in her sleep several months ago, she has not once, not one single time, uttered a sound since the night her mother died. Until today. With you."

Carly opened her mouth, not sure what to say, when he held up a hand to hush her. "Come with us tomorrow. Spend the day getting to know us."

"Mr. Barnett—"

"Please."

His quiet, husky plea did something to her insides. She shuddered. Before she knew what she was doing, she whispered, "All right." What could it hurt, after all? Dr. Sanders trusted him enough to suggest she go to Wyoming with him. Surely a day playing tour guide in a crowded city would be safe enough.

His smile was slow and powerful. Devastating in its brilliance and the way it affected her respiration.

Maybe not so safe.

"Thank you," he said. "We'll be here at ten."

Tyler put his key into the ignition and watched in his rearview mirror as Carly crossed the street and disappeared into the crowd on the sidewalk. He let out a long, slow breath. Progress. Slight, but forward. Tomorrow he would convince her. Somehow.

And he was beginning to care less and less just how he got her to come home with him. She had to help Amanda. She *had* to.

When he and Amanda pulled up at the curb the next morning at ten, Carly was sitting on the front porch steps waiting for them. Tyler felt his breath give a slight pause. He didn't normally go for sassy-looking pixies, but Carly Baker was so damn…cute. That was the word for her. Cute.

Looking at her, he could practically feel the life and energy humming just beneath her surface. It was tamped down now, weighted, no doubt, by the trouble on her last job Dr. Sanders had told him about. Tamped, trapped, dimmed, but only temporarily.

Then she stood and started down the sidewalk toward his car, and the word *cute* flew right out of his head. Fire-engine red high heels and a matching miniskirt made those shapely, golden legs look a mile long. The exaggerated sway of her hips as she walked the downhill slope of the sidewalk made his pulse leap. Her oversize red shirt, unbuttoned to reveal a plain, scoop-neck white top beneath, looked as if it would fit him better than it did her. The baggy garment that all but concealed her small breasts somehow gave her a fragile air, made her look as if she might break if handled roughly.

In direct contrast, the giant gold loops dangling from her ears almost to her shoulders looked as bold as all get-out.

Cute was long gone. Strolling down the sidewalk between riotous beds of flowers, looking like a wild crimson rose among scraggly weeds, Carly Baker was nothing short of dynamite. So damn sexy she took his breath away.

He got out of the car and helped Amanda out the passenger door, then turned to greet Carly. Whatever he'd thought he'd seen in her eyes the day before was gone. No hint of sadness or pain now. Her big brown eyes glowed with the sharp light of determination, maybe defiance.

"Whew." He grinned. "You're gonna wow 'em in Wyoming, and that's a fact."

It was the heat in his eyes that made Carly wonder if she'd made a mistake wearing these clothes. She had needed a lift, and her red outfit always made her feel good. She hadn't considered what he would think.

Then she gave a defiant toss of her head and decided to hell with him. She had dressed this way for herself. If he chose to let himself get worked up...

His eyes darkened to a turbulent green.

When was the last time she'd had this effect on a man?

It must have been a long time ago, because she couldn't remember it. James had certainly never looked as if his only thought was to drag her to the nearest dark, private place and catalog her erogenous zones.

But then, James had never made her heart pound with just a look, either. Suddenly her self-confidence, which had been severely wounded of late, took wing and soared.

And why not? Why not see if she still had what it took to keep a man interested for more than a few minutes? After today, she would never see Tyler Barnett again. What could a little flirting hurt? He was going back to Wyoming the day after tomorrow. Her bruised ego could use the boost of a ruggedly handsome man's interest for a few hours. And Tyler Barnett more than filled the bill.

Western clothing on a man wasn't all that rare a sight in San Francisco, but on this man, the effect threatened something inside her that had never felt threatened before. His deep brown boots were polished to a high sheen and looked hand-tooled and worth more than her car. There was nothing remarkable about his brown dress slacks, unless she counted the silver oval belt buckle big enough to choke a moose.

His starched, white Western shirt accented the deep tan of his face and hands. The pearlized snaps teased a woman with how easily she could—

Down, girl, she told herself sternly. To get her mind off the snaps on his shirt, she raised her gaze. "Love your Stetson."

He tugged on the brim of his white hat. "Bailey, but thanks."

"What's a Bailey?"

Tyler chuckled. "The brand of my hat."

"Oh. Obviously, what I know about Western hats wouldn't fill the brim."

"Come to Wyoming, then, and learn."

She just grinned and shook her head.

The hat in question looked like an extension of the man.

He hadn't worn it yesterday, and she hadn't missed it. But now, seeing it shade his eyes against the late-morning sun, she realized the hat belonged on him.

Carly realized something else just then, too. She and Tyler were standing on the sidewalk ogling each other like a couple of teenagers with raging hormones, completely ignoring the reason they were together in the first place. Feeling guilty, she looked down at the child holding Tyler's hand.

"Hi, there. My, don't you look pretty?" And she did. Another frilly dress, this one yellow, decked out in ruffles and lace, with a giant bow at the back of her waist. "A perfect little lady."

Amanda peeked up through long bangs and smiled.

"Are you two ready to go?" Tyler asked.

Glancing up at him, Carly noticed the sudden sadness in his eyes as he gazed at his daughter. But it was none of her business. After today, she'd never see the Barnetts again.

"I'm ready." She pulled the shoulder strap of her red leather purse over her head and settled the bag on her hip.

With Amanda between them, they turned their backs on the California-Van Ness cable car clanging up the street and walked three blocks north to catch the Powell-Hyde line.

"How can you walk in those things?" Tyler asked, glancing down at Carly's high heels.

"I'm used to them."

He smirked. "I'll bet they see a lot of miles at Burger Barrel."

Carly was determined to have a good time today. She was not going to get defensive about her job slinging hamburgers. Especially since she didn't have the job, as of last night. She'd been "released from employment."

She forced a smile. "Yes, and they look terrific with brown polyester."

On Washington they got lucky and were able to squeeze

onto the first cable car that came along without having to stand in line.

Carly surprised herself by enjoying her role as tour guide. Tyler surprised her by seeming to enjoy himself, too. She hadn't thought a Wyoming cowboy would find much to like about a crowded city.

But he and Amanda eagerly took in the sights up Hyde Street, over Russian Hill. The car stopped at Lombard Street and Carly got the distinct impression that if Tyler'd had a camera, he would have taken a picture.

"Look at that street, Amanda," he said. "That thing's got more curves than a mountain switchback. And look out there. That's called Coit's Tower. And behind it is San Francisco Bay. Did you ever see water so blue?"

His eyes, Carly thought with poignancy, looked every bit as young and excited as Amanda's, every bit as blue as the bay. When was the last time she'd seen a grown man enjoy himself so thoroughly?

The cable car lurched into motion, throwing Carly against Tyler's chest. It felt like running into a stone wall. One of his hands covered hers where she gripped the brass pole tightly. With his other hand he held on to Amanda and steadied her.

If Carly had been asked, she never would have guessed the texture of rough calluses against the back of her hand could excite her. She wouldn't have dreamed the mere motion of a man's head dipping slowly toward hers could set her on fire. And she would have flatly denied how much she wanted a virtual stranger to tilt his head just a little bit more, so she could slip in beneath the brim of that white hat and taste his lips.

Shocked at her own thoughts as much as by the sudden flare of heat in his eyes, Carly leaned back. It was a damn good thing she wasn't going to Wyoming with Tyler Barnett. The man was positively lethal. But, oh, it felt good to know she had the same effect on him.

A moment later, Tyler lifted Amanda up against his chest

so she could see the Golden Gate Bridge coming into view, and the tension was broken.

They got off the cable car at the Victorian Park turntable and crossed over to Ghirardelli Square. Amanda urged them toward a street performer in clown makeup. She watched, wide-eyed, as he twisted and bent and shaped balloons into animals. The young man spotted her enrapt gaze and gave her an exaggerated wink, motioning her over with the long orange balloon in his hand.

She looked up at her father, blue-green eyes wide and pleading.

"What are we waiting for?" Tyler asked. "Let's go."

He led them to the silent clown, who proceeded to bend and shape the orange balloon until, with a flourish, he presented Amanda with the results—a two-foot-tall giraffe.

Amanda bounced up and down, clapping her hands and grinning. She hugged the giraffe to her chest just tight enough to make Carly wince in anticipation of a loud *pop*, but the balloon animal proved tough enough.

Tyler slipped some money from his pocket and told Amanda to drop it in the large plastic cup at the clown's feet.

"She's adorable," Carly said with a smile.

"Yeah." Tyler's smile disappeared. He gave Carly a direct, probing look. "And she needs help. She needs you."

Carly bristled. He was not going to make her feel guilty. "Was I mistaken? I thought today was for fun. That you weren't going to do any arm-twisting."

He took a deep breath. "Right. No arm-twisting."

Amanda returned and took Tyler's hand.

"Okay, Ms. Tour Guide," he said to Carly, "what's next?"

Carly led the way past The Cannery and its current complement of street musicians, along another couple of blocks on Jefferson to Fisherman's Wharf.

"This," Carly said dramatically, "is the second most

popular tourist attraction on the West Coast, second only to—''

"Don't say it," Tyler cried with an exaggerated shudder. "Don't say what?"

"You were about to say the *D* word, the name of that place down in Anaheim. The place of big ears and small worlds.''

"Yeah, so?''

"So, a certain young lady gets the most pitiful, pleading look in her eyes every time she sees or hears anything about that place.''

Carly grinned. "Give you a hard time, does she?"

Tyler rolled his eyes.

"So why don't you take her?''

"No time on this trip. Maybe next time.''

They spent more than an hour seeing the sights and smelling those wonderful smells along Fisherman's Wharf. The sea, fresh fish, hot bread, garlic from one shop, cinnamon from the next. A full banquet of aromas.

Tyler was afraid Amanda would get tired or bored, but she seemed happy enough clutching her orange balloon giraffe. He held her free hand and tried to take in the scenery, the hundreds of people, the unique atmosphere, but found it more than difficult to keep his eyes off their tour guide. Carly seemed to be working extra hard at being cheerful. He wondered why. If she had her way, she'd never see him again. Why should she care whether she was so damned bubbly every single minute or not?

With Amanda's help, Tyler bought his dad and each of the hands a T-shirt in one of the dozens of shops along the street.

Afterward, Carly followed her nose and pulled them to a steamy sidewalk kitchen for a snack of fresh crab and hot bread.

"Where to next?" he asked her.

She smiled brightly. "You can't leave town without seeing Union Square. Come on."

He wondered if she did it on purpose, if the high heels were responsible, or if that incredible sway to her hips came naturally. She had him feeling like a stallion locked away in the stud stall, with an in-season mare prancing by and twitching her tail.

Damn. He'd definitely been alone too long the day a cute, sad-eyed pixie at least ten years his junior could turn him inside out.

At the turnaround for the Powell-Mason cable car, they had to stand in line. Finally they made it onto the third car and rode past North Beach, up over Nob Hill again, and down to Union Square. Here, at last, was a small patch of open ground. Tyler hadn't realized how hemmed in he'd been feeling until he spotted the open-air plaza of Union Square.

Of course, it wasn't much of an open space, surrounded as it was by huge buildings: the St. Francis Hotel, Macy's, Saks, Neiman Marcus, Gumps, Sears, Blalock's and a dozen other famous names.

They started across the plaza and were almost to the tall monument in the center when Carly, walking on Amanda's other side, stiffened and came to an abrupt halt.

Carly stared at the couple walking toward them and felt the crab she'd eaten less than an hour ago threaten to rise. James and Becky. Seeing them together, holding hands and laughing, hurt unbelievably, and it shouldn't. She should have been used to the idea by now.

Poor little rich Becky Blalock, heir apparent to the Blalock fortune. When Walter Blalock retired in a few years, Becky would take over the department store where she and Carly had both worked these past eight years.

The two girls had been best friends since third grade, when they'd gotten caught passing notes making fun of Eugene Amsterdam's cowlick. Through the years, Carly and Becky had shared their secrets, shared Becky's father after Carly's had died, learned about life together, about boys.

From the way things were turning out, neither of them had learned much, it seemed, about men. Not men like James.

For Becky to fall for James's sweet lines as easily as Carly had didn't seem all that strange. After all, Becky hadn't known he'd been seeing Carly for nearly a near. But for Becky to believe Carly would steal from Blalock's was a blow from which Carly feared she might never recover.

Becky and James stopped a few feet away. Becky smirked. "Well, well, if it isn't Little Miss Traitor. Little Miss Embezzler." Her malicious grin widened. "How's that hamburger job of yours these days?"

The crab in Carly's stomach took another leap. The truth was right there in Becky's eyes. Either Becky or her father had gotten Carly fired.

Carly blinked to clear her vision and nudged Amanda's shoulder. "Let's go." And she fled.

When Tyler swung Amanda up in his arms to keep pace, Carly forced herself to slow down. "Sorry," she muttered.

"Do you want to talk about it?"

"No."

Across the square, they headed up the street for the five-block walk back to Carly's apartment. When they came in sight of her driveway, Tyler said, "Looks like one of your neighbors is having car trouble."

Carly looked up to see a tow truck backed up to a green... *Oh, God.* The truck was backed up to her car!

She sprinted up the driveway to the man who was hooking a chain underneath her back bumper. "What are you doing? That's my car. I didn't call for service."

The man rose up slowly and turned. He was short, barely taller than her own five foot two, with a thick chest, long arms and short neck. "Are you Carly Baker?"

That sick feeling came back, with a vengeance. She nodded.

"The bank sent me to pick the car up."

She tried to swallow, but nothing happened. "You can't be serious."

"Dead serious, ma'am. I'm to pick up $672.27, or this car."

"But...but you can't take my car," she cried.

"Yes, ma'am, I'm afraid I can." He pulled a sheaf of papers from his shirt pocket. "It's all legal."

Tyler watched the blood drain from Carly's face, knowing full well that when she realized he was right beside her, she would wish him to hell and back for witnessing her humiliation. Still, he could help her, if she'd let him. If she would quit being so damned stubborn and take the job he offered.

"Give us a minute," he told the man.

Carly jerked toward Tyler, surprised, horrified to find him there. He leaned down and spoke to Amanda, but Carly couldn't hear for the buzzing in her ears. The bank was repossessing her car. It couldn't be real. It couldn't.

Amanda skipped over to the small yard beyond the parking spaces. Dark curls and yellow ruffles bounced in the sunlight.

Tyler took Carly's arm and felt her trembling. "Come with me." He led her to the back porch of the building, where he could see both Amanda and the man with the tow truck. Sitting on the top step, he pulled Carly down next to him. "If you don't mind my asking, how did you manage to get yourself in this mess?"

Carly scowled. "Wasn't hard at all. I trusted a man." With special emphasis on the last word.

Tyler chose to ignore her sarcasm, and ignore that he was about to ask her to trust another man, one she hardly knew. He nodded toward the tow truck. "Do you have the money to pay him?"

She tossed him a glassy-eyed glare. "Oh, sure. I just haven't made my car payments because I like ruining my credit and getting nasty notes in the mail. It's none of your business. Besides," she added under her breath, "if I had any money, I'd put it toward my back rent to keep from getting evicted at the end of the month."

Tyler took a deep breath. "I have a solution for you."

"I said," she growled, "it's none of your business."

Okay, Barnett, it's now or never. Time to fish or cut bait.

He tugged up the left leg of his slacks until he could reach the top of his boot and pull out the pouch. Switching legs, he repeated the procedure. He tossed the two small zippered bank bags onto her lap one at a time.

As each one landed with a quiet *whap,* Carly flinched. Not from the weight—the bags were light—but more from what she instinctively knew they contained. Her stomach tightened even while her fingers begged to grab the contents of the bags and run. "You don't play fair, do you?"

"I'm not playing. That's the five thousand I promised up front. In cash."

A cold shiver raced down her spine. "I don't take charity, Mr. Barnett."

"It's not charity." She'd never heard a voice so cold, so hard. "It's a job," he said tightly. "Keeping house, cooking and looking after my daughter, Ms. Baker. Two thousand dollars a week, with the rest of the hundred thousand I promised when Amanda starts talking."

Carly tucked her fingers beneath her thighs to keep from touching the bank bags. The solution to all her problems lay in her lap and in his words. With the five thousand, she could catch up all her bills. Even pay some off altogether. With the income from the job he was offering, she could pay off the rest in no time and have enough left to live on for years.

What are you waiting for, you fool? Take it.

Yes, what was she waiting for? If he was dumb enough to dangle that much money in front of her, she should be smart enough to take it.

But to accept his oh, so tempting offer under the pretense

of being able to help Amanda, when she didn't really know the first thing about children...how could she do it?

How could she not?

"Six months, Carly," Tyler said. "Give me six months of your time, and the money, all one hundred thousand of it, is yours."

Chapter Three

The runway of San Francisco International Airport sped past the window at Carly's right shoulder in a blur.

What had she done?

In the face of losing her job and the threat of having her car repossessed, she'd done the unthinkable. She had sold the next six months of her life to a stranger. She had accepted Tyler Barnett's job, his money, and the responsibility for his daughter's welfare. She'd sublet her apartment to her downstairs neighbor's sister, used her $5,000 advance from Tyler to catch up her bills, listened to her mother rant and rave and, at 3:11 this afternoon, just twenty-four hours after having a set of bank bags flopped onto her lap, had boarded a plane for Wyoming. And she'd done it for personal, selfish reasons rather than a genuine desire to do the job for which she'd been hired.

Not that she didn't want to help Amanda Barnett if she could—Carly just didn't know if she would be any good at it. She looked over at the bright-eyed child in the next seat and prayed for guidance.

Their plane hadn't even leveled off at cruising altitude before Amanda was yawning. Tyler flipped up the armrest between his seat and Amanda's, adjusted her seat belt and urged her to curl up with her head in his lap.

Watching the tenderness this strong, rugged man displayed for his tiny daughter tugged at something deep inside Carly. She remembered her own father and the special bond they'd shared, the wrenching loss she'd suffered, the hole in her life left by his dying. The guilt.

Was Dr. Sanders right? Was Amanda suffering a similar guilt over her mother's death? Carly would have to talk to Tyler, find out what had happened. But not on an airplane with a seat and a six-year-old between them, where they would have to yell at each other to be heard above the engine noise.

A stewardess offered Tyler a pillow and blanket for Amanda, and he made Amanda as comfortable as he could. Carly raised her own armrest and took the child's feet onto her lap.

"You don't mind?" Tyler asked.

Carly shook her head. "She'll be more comfortable. What happened to her giraffe?"

Tyler rolled his eyes, shook his head and grinned wryly. "He popped. For a while there, I was worried I was going to have to buy him a seat on the plane."

Amanda shifted her head away from the change in her daddy's pocket, then snuggled under the thin airline blanket with a sigh. Carly's hand on her ankles felt good. She was glad Carly was going home with them. She just hoped Carly and her daddy wouldn't be too disappointed when Amanda still wasn't able to talk. They didn't understand that it wasn't up to her.

* * *

Carly spent most of the flight staring out the window, wondering, worrying about how to deal with Amanda. And how to deal with Amanda's father. She kept picking up conflicting signals from him. Friday while he played tourist he'd been open and friendly, casting her an occasional admiring glance. More than once she'd caught him checking out her legs. The attention he had paid her had given her feminine ego a much-needed boost.

But the minute she'd accepted his offer, he'd become all business. For that, she was grateful, for she was determined that their relationship be a business one. Never again would she mix business with pleasure, the way she had with James.

After consideration, she realized she didn't need to wonder about how to deal with Tyler Barnett. He was her employer, just as Walter Blalock had been.

The thought brought a wry smile. Walter Blalock was fifty-five years old, balding, with flappy jowls and a potbelly.

Tyler Barnett was...the stuff of female fantasies.

They changed planes in Denver for the second and last leg of their flight to Jackson Hole, Wyoming, the nearest airport of any size to Big Piney and the Bar B Ranch. Because they landed after nine-thirty that night, all Carly was able to see of Jackson Hole was a smattering of lights.

Tyler stowed their luggage in the bed of his dusty, battered pickup, and they headed out through the pitch-black night for the last one hundred or so miles to the ranch.

Once again, Amanda curled up in the seat and went to sleep.

"Poor thing." Carly smoothed the child's hair back from her face. "She's worn-out."

"Yeah. Flying always makes her sleepy."

"Tell me about her."

He was silent a moment, in the darkness of the pickup.

Then, quietly, he said, "She's the best thing that ever happened to me."

Carly swallowed against the emotion that rose in her throat. "Does she have any brothers or sisters?"

He shook his head. "No."

The old pickup barreled down the two-lane highway. Carly stared out at the blackest nothingness she'd ever seen. No lights in sight anywhere. Was that a portent of things to come?

She took a deep breath and told herself to stop being ridiculous. Everything would work out.

But not, she knew, if Tyler Barnett didn't get a heck of a lot more talkative about his daughter. "I need to know about her background. What her life has been like, how she lost her mother, everything you can tell me. It's important."

"I know," he said, his voice grating. "All right. But to understand everything, I have to start at the beginning."

"That would probably be best."

"How tired are you?" The glow from the dash lights showed a grimace on his face. "This is liable to get pretty boring. I'd hate to put you to sleep."

Carly smiled, as she was sure she was meant to do. "I'll risk it. Just talk, Barnett."

"Okay. First you have to understand about Deborah and the ranch. When Deborah and I got married, we really thought we could make a go of it. At least, I thought I could. Looking back, I think she had some idea that ranch life was a hell of a lot more glamorous than it is. The Bar B is a working ranch. A family ranch. My dad runs the cattle operation. I don't have anything to do with that anymore, except to help out at the busiest times, like branding and haying and the fall roundup. My end nowadays is horses."

"What kind, racehorses?"

He shook his head. "Cutting horses, mostly. Breeding. Training. Making the circuit."

"Is it just you and your father?"

"No. I'm the oldest of four. Robert and Joe, my two brothers, each manage a station on the outlying parts of the ranch. Sandy's the youngest. She and her husband, Greg, manage the other station."

Carly frowned. "I hate to sound ignorant, but what's a station?"

Tyler's lips quirked. "Ever watch an old Western and hear the talk about line camps?"

She nodded. "Sure."

"Same thing, except now they each have a house, raise their families there. Each station is like a ranch within a ranch, and each station manager is responsible for a certain section of country, of fence, a certain number of cattle."

The implications of a ranch that size were startling. "The Bar B is that big that you need three stations?"

"One of the larger outfits around, but not the largest, by any means. We cover twenty-five thousand deeded acres, not counting the government land we lease for summer grazing."

"Twenty-five *thousand?* Is that as big as I think it is?"

"How big do you think it is?"

"I don't know, but it sounds enormous."

He nodded. "That's as good a word as any. It's almost forty square miles. The entire San Francisco Peninsula is less than fifty, and San Francisco itself covers just the tip."

"That's...that's staggering. You sure your name's not Rockefeller or Trump?"

Tyler's chuckle sounded grim. "Not hardly. The horse end of the business does all right, but there's not much money in cattle these days. If it wasn't for the oil and gas, I doubt we'd have a dime to spare."

Carly rubbed her brow. Oil and gas? Good grief. No wonder he could afford to pay her such an outlandish salary.

"Anyway," Tyler said, "while you've got more than a million people on that peninsula of yours, in our forty square miles we've got barely a baker's dozen. Five houses, a few barns, and the rest is sagebrush and cattle.''

"How do you know so much about San Francisco?"

He flicked her a narrow-eyed glance. "Ah, shucks, ma'am," he said in an exaggerated drawl that dripped with sarcasm, "even a big, dumb cowpoke like me can read."

A little sensitive, are we? she thought. But she bit her tongue on the words. Instead she prodded him to continue with what he'd been saying. "So you brought your wife here?"

Tyler was quiet a moment, staring down the tunnel of light cast by his headlights. "Yeah. She started making noises right off about moving, hiring a manager to handle my end of the ranch. She never understood that you don't just hire someone to—never mind. I won't get into that. By the time Amanda was four, Deborah had had all she could take of the isolation, the lack of things she was used to in Chicago. Art, theater, shopping, parties. When we split, we both agreed that a four-year-old girl needed her mother more than she needed her father, so Amanda went with her."

"That must have been difficult for you."

He cleared his throat. "Yeah, well, I've had better times."

His raw voice left an ache in her chest. She'd seen for herself how much he loved his daughter. She couldn't imagine the pain of having a child taken away. "Did you get to see Amanda very often?"

"Whenever I wanted, as often as I could get away long enough."

"How often?"

His hand flexed on the steering wheel. "I made the trip about every two or three months. I noticed the change in Amanda the first time I went."

"Change?"

He braced his elbow on the door and rubbed the backs of his fingers across his chin. "At the ranch she was always a little tomboy, following everybody around. Insisted on wearing jeans, boots, a hat. Said she was determined to be a cowboy. Guess that didn't go over too well in Chicago.''

Carly nodded in understanding. ''She would have felt out of place with the other kids there.''

Tyler shook his head. ''Maybe, but there really weren't many other kids in her life. Deborah moved back in with her parents in their huge mausoleum of a house where they dress for dinner and never raise their voices, and have an army of servants waiting on them hand and foot.''

It sounded lonely to Carly. ''No room for cowboys, huh?''

''No. Not for cowboys, or pint-size tomboys, or even little girls, really. That's when Amanda started wearing all these frilly dresses.'' He fingered the lace ruffle at the hem of her skirt. ''Not that I don't like them. She looks like a little angel dressed up like this. But I guess she got so used to ruffles and lace, she hasn't been in a pair of jeans since I brought her home.''

''How long ago did you bring her back?''

''About three months ago.''

''Was that when she lost her mother?''

Tyler shook his head. ''No, Deborah died more than six months ago. I had finally talked her into letting me bring Amanda home with me for a few weeks. I flew back to Chicago two days later to pick her up, but when I got there I learned that Deborah had been killed in a car wreck the night before.''

''And no one bothered to call and tell you?'' Carly cried.

With his jaw tensed, Tyler shook his head. ''They couldn't, really. She'd left Amanda with her parents and gone to a party. The accident happened at around four in the morning. Her folks didn't get word until later in the day. By then I was on the plane. My guess is, until the police showed up, they probably thought she was up in her room sleeping late.''

"And Amanda hasn't spoken since? Why didn't you bring her home right then?"

"I stayed with Deborah's folks for the funeral. When we realized Amanda wasn't talking, we took her to her pediatrician. He said there was some slight damage to her vocal cords from crying so hard when she realized her mother wasn't coming back. He suggested that moving her back to Wyoming just then might be too traumatic."

"And then?"

"I came home."

His words, his tone, were matter-of-fact, but the bunching jaw and his grip on the steering wheel hinted at what it had cost him to leave Amanda in Chicago. Carly had seen the way he looked at his daughter. It must have torn him to pieces to come home without her. "What happened after that?"

Tyler glanced down from the road to his daughter's face resting on his thigh and stroked her hair. "I went to see her once a month. It was my third visit before I finally decided to talk to the doctor myself about why she couldn't speak."

Slowly he lifted his hand from his daughter's hair and wrapped it tightly around the steering wheel.

"What did the doctor tell you?"

"He told me her vocal cords had healed just fine weeks earlier. He had suggested to the Tomlinsons that Amanda should see a child psychologist. They didn't believe him. They wouldn't accept that she had an emotional problem. To them, that was...something to be ashamed of."

Carly swallowed the hot retort that rose in her throat at the idea of Amanda's grandparents ignoring her needs in such a callous manner.

"Anyway," Tyler went on, "that was the day I packed her up and brought her home."

"And she hasn't spoken at all?"

For a long moment, the only sound was the hum of tires

on pavement and the occasional splat of a bug against the windshield.

Finally Tyler answered. "Her first night here, I slipped in to check on her. She mumbled in her sleep."

"So you knew she really *could* talk."

"I knew there wasn't anything wrong with her voice. We tried a therapist down in Rock Creek a couple of times, but every time she came out of her session, she'd be upset and withdrawn for days. I heard about Dr. Sanders from a friend of a friend, so, off we went. And there you were."

Yes. *And now, here I am. In the middle of I don't know where, with a troubled, angry man and his troubled, silent daughter. And I'm supposed to help Amanda.* Carly searched a sky blacker than anything she'd ever seen and asked for guidance. She had a feeling she and Amanda were both going to need it.

"Don't blink anytime in the next ten seconds," Tyler warned with a terse smile, "or you'll miss town."

Carly looked up from gazing at Amanda's sleeping face and saw a handful of buildings, a half-dozen streetlights. "Town?"

"The thriving, four-square-block metropolis of Big Piney, Wyoming. Population around four hundred. Closest town to the ranch."

Carly's lips twitched. "I'm beginning to get an idea of what went through your wife's mind."

Tyler frowned. "Ex-wife."

Before Carly saw anything she would dignify with the name "town," Tyler made a right turn. The sign at the corner read State Highway 350. "Town" disappeared behind them, with only blackness stretching out ahead into forever.

Somewhere around ten minutes later by Carly's guess, the pavement ended. Over the thunder and clatter of gravel thrown by the tires against the undercarriage of the pickup, she said, "I could have sworn that sign back there said this was a state highway."

"It did," he answered grimly. "Welcome to Sublette County, Wyoming."

"You say it like you don't much care for it."

"It's my home."

That told Carly absolutely nothing. She remembered his comments in Dr. Sanders's office. "You don't think I'll like it here."

He kept his gaze steady on the gravel road. "No, I don't. It takes a special kind of woman to live out here."

"Well." His words stung sharper than they should have. "I guess that tells me what you think of me."

"For what I'm paying you, you don't have to like it. You only have to help Amanda."

Feeling as though she'd been put firmly in her place, Carly braced herself against the jostling of the pickup on the deteriorating road by jamming an elbow against the armrest. "How much farther?"

"About another ten miles."

She looked down at the child sprawled loose-limbed across both their laps. "I can't believe she can sleep through all this."

He glanced down and frowned slightly at his daughter, but didn't comment.

Carly stared out the window, knowing it was too dark to see anything, doubting, from what Tyler had said, that there was anything to see in all these lonely miles. Since turning off at Big Piney she'd counted four utility lights, each marking the location of a house—the only houses for miles around. At home she would have called them streetlights; here, there were no streets.

Oh, boy. What had she gotten herself into? She was perhaps beginning to understand why Tyler had offered her so much money to come up here with him. And she thought she understood, too, some of what Deborah Barnett had felt upon coming here, realizing she was expected to spend the rest of her life in the middle of nowhere.

"Is anything out there?"

Tyler cast her a sideways glance. "Not much. Cattle, but I'm sure that's not what you meant. If we keep on this road we'll end up in the Bridger-Teton National Forest."

"If?"

"We'll be turning off soon."

Finally, past midnight, and what seemed like hours after the pavement had turned to gravel, Tyler slowed and turned off across a cattle guard onto a rutted dirt road. They drove underneath a modest wooden arch that read Bar B Ranch, A. J. Barnett.

"A.J.?" she asked.

"My father."

Minute after minute, Carly kept expecting to see the ranch house, a utility light, anything to indicate someone lived nearby. There was nothing except a barbed wire fence stretched tight between wooden posts marching down each side of the road. All the fence appeared to be keeping in was the sagebrush revealed by the headlights of the pickup. It proved no barrier at all to the jackrabbit that dashed across the beams of the headlights and under the bottom wire.

Then the road curved around the base of a low hill, and there, finally, stood the buildings of the Bar B Ranch—she hoped. The utility light revealed a two-story white frame house, another smaller house, two barns, several other buildings of various sizes and corrals.

Carly swallowed. This was it, then. The place where she would spend the next six months of her life.

The road split, one lane leading around to the front of the house. Tyler took the other and parked next to another pickup and a Blazer near the back door, where a light shone through a window.

The sudden quiet, after the racket of all that gravel,

seemed deafening. Tyler's voice startled her. "Before we go in, I want to say one thing."

"You mean we're here?" she asked with feigned innocence. "You're sure you don't want to drive for another couple of hours?"

He narrowed his eyes and studied her a long minute. In the dim light, his mouth looked grim, his face hard.

"I'm joking," she told him. "You know, a joke? Like, ha ha? Why did the chicken cross the road, et cetera?"

He didn't so much as blink.

"You do have jokes in Wyoming, don't you?"

Tyler continued to stare at her. "Just remember, you gave your word."

"Of course I—"

"Six months, or until Amanda talks—whichever comes first."

"If you're so convinced I'm not going to last, why did you hire me?"

"Because I didn't have a choice," he snapped back. "Right now you're the only chance Amanda's got."

"Why, thank you." Carly batted her eyes. "I always wanted to be someone's last resort."

Suddenly Tyler slumped and scrubbed his face with both hands. "I'm sorry. I didn't mean…"

"Forget it." It was clear that Tyler was beyond exhaustion and eaten up with worry for Amanda. Carly apparently wasn't in much better shape; otherwise she wouldn't be upset over his stating the simple truth. She was, at least for now, Amanda's only help. "I'll do whatever I can for Amanda. I'll give her my best."

"Your best is all I'm asking. It's more than she's had so far. And if Dr. Sanders comes up with a therapist within even a semireasonable driving distance, maybe between the two of you, it will be enough."

The house was cloaked in that middle-of-the-night quiet that spoke of tiptoes and whispers. The rooms, what Carly could see of them with most of the lights off, were big and airy and gave off a homey feeling of comfort.

Amanda never woke as Tyler carried her upstairs to her room and put her to bed. Carly offered to help, but he declined rather gruffly. While he changed his sleeping daughter's clothes and tucked her in, Carly looked around.

Her charge's bedroom was a little girl's paradise. The furniture was French provincial, antique white trimmed in gold. A pink ruffle dangled from the canopy arching over the bed, with a matching dust ruffle below. A fluffy comforter with huge pastel flowers covered the mattress.

Dozens of dolls and stuffed animals perched along shelves and across the top of the chest of drawers. The dresser held an array of little-girl things—matching comb and brush set, a porcelain bowl filled with colorful barrettes and a delicate ballerina music box.

Carly frowned. This was the room of a little cowgirl? Not hardly.

"What is it?" Tyler asked, keeping his voice low.

Carly forced her frown away and shook her head. "Nothing."

Leaving the door to Amanda's room partway open, he showed Carly to the corner bedroom at the far end of the hall. He flipped on the light and motioned her inside.

The room was large and airy and old-fashioned, the furnishings obviously well cared for by loving hands. Carly loved it on sight. A small nightstand with a lamp sat beside a big double bed with a shiny brass headboard. Blue gingham covered the bed and both windows.

Across from the bed sat an early-American-style dresser and chest, and an old rocking chair that looked like a well-cared-for family heirloom.

"This will be your room," Tyler said from the doorway. "The bathroom next door is yours and Amanda's. I'll bring up the luggage."

Carly tossed her purse on the seat of the spindle-back rocker. "I'll help."

Mild surprise lit his eyes. "Suit yourself."

When all their bags were upstairs, Carly asked, "What time will you want breakfast?"

Tyler waved a hand in the air. "Don't worry about breakfast. You're here for Amanda. Everything else is secondary."

"Yes, I'm here for Amanda. But you're paying me for other things as well. What time do you want breakfast?"

He gave a shrug that spoke of irritation. "Suit yourself. We eat at six. Counting you and Amanda, there'll be eight of us—"

"Eight?"

"Smitty, Willis, Neal and Tom, our hands, eat with us. Then there's Dad, Amanda, you and me, but Amanda will sleep late. You'll have to keep hers warm or fix her something later."

Carly nodded. "Fine. Anything in particular I should fix?"

One side of his mouth curved down. "You're taking this cooking thing pretty seriously."

"Considering how much you're paying me, I think I should."

He shook his head. "We'll eat anything, just make sure there's plenty of it. And we'll drink all the coffee you can make. And since you're so determined to take care of all this stuff, you'll need to keep a pot going all day, too. My dad will love you for it."

Tyler closed the door to his room and leaned against it with a sigh of exhaustion and relief. He'd done it. He'd gotten Carly Baker to the Bar B. He refused to let himself feel guilty for taking advantage of the financial mess she'd gotten herself into. He knew if she'd had any alternative, she would have stuck it out in San Francisco and given him a polite, "Goodbye and good luck."

Now, if only he could keep her here until Amanda was well again. Carly reminded him so much of Deborah it was scary. Not in looks, certainly. Deborah, with her long, platinum blond hair and slow, graceful movements, had been the epitome of glamour and class.

Carly undeniably had class, too, but hers was a lively, exuberant type. Maybe it was her age; she looked about twenty-five. Young enough to grab life by the tail and hang on. She must be older, though, because she'd mentioned going to college before working at Blalock's Department Store for eight years.

Whatever, she was still a city girl, used to the hustle and bustle, the crush of people, the restaurants, shopping, theater, libraries, all those things she wouldn't find anywhere near the Bar B. Would she stay the six months she'd agreed to?

Hell, he thought with a rueful chuckle. She didn't have much choice. Her only way out would be to steal one of the ranch vehicles and drive to the airport in Jackson Hole. He gave serious thought to hiding all the truck and car keys, but she wasn't the type to resort to theft, no matter what they'd said about her at Blalock's.

Carly's alarm went off at the ungodly hour of 4:30 a.m. Thirty minutes later, her hair still damp from the shower, she groped her way downstairs to the kitchen, appalled that people actually got up this early on a regular basis. The things she did for money. Her nose led her to the pot of coffee someone had already made.

Steaming mug in hand, she toured the kitchen. It was big, with cabinets, counters, sink and stove, all in white, taking up one long wall.

A huge old-fashioned chrome-legged table and chairs for eight took up the other side of the room. Memories of her own childhood growing up around the chrome-legged table in her mother's kitchen teased her, warmed her. There was something undeniably comforting about those old tables.

A mudroom, with a huge chest-style freezer at one end and a sink at the other, led out to the back door. The wall

next to the door into the kitchen bore a long row of pegs,
for hats and coats, she assumed. Next to the mudroom was
a laundry room, the size of which indicated she'd be doing
a great deal of laundry. Then came a small bathroom off
the corner of the kitchen. Beside the bath was a huge walk-
in pantry that held the equivalent of the inventory of a small
grocery store. She would evidently be doing as much cooking as washing.

Beyond the pantry stood another door, this one leading
to a large formal dining room. She didn't take the time just
then to examine it. Breakfast, she assumed, was normally
served at the kitchen table. If not, it would be today.

Now. What to fix.

...just make sure there's plenty of it.

"You got it, boss," she whispered. She might have felt
more up to the task, but the sky outside the window over
the sink was just turning from black to gray. It was the
middle of the damn night.

Then again, for what he was paying her, she would just
have to get used to the hours.

That in mind, she pulled open the refrigerator door and
went to work.

Out of habit, Tyler knocked each foot against the top
concrete step to dislodge as much straw and muck as possible before pulling open the back door. The smell of bacon
frying teased his nostrils and made his stomach growl. Eager for the taste of someone else's cooking at his own
breakfast table for a change, he stepped into the mudroom.

He hadn't prepared himself for the early-morning sight
of her, and he should have. But how could he have known
how right Carly Baker would look standing in front of the
stove in his kitchen? She shouldn't look right. She should
look like a fish out of water, with those shiny, skintight
leggings, a floppy sweatshirt and fuzzy house shoes with
eyes on the tops and teeth at the toes. Damn if she didn't
look cute. And right. As if she belonged.

He must have made some sound, for she jerked her head toward him. Then her gaze flew to the clock on the counter.

"You're not late," he said, reading the sudden panic in her eyes. "I'm early."

Carly forced a calming breath into her lungs. Her heart had no reason to suddenly start pounding as if she'd just finished a five-mile jog. He wasn't about to fire her if breakfast was late, and as he'd said, he was early.

But silently she admitted the sudden jump in her pulse had nothing to do with the clock or breakfast. It had to do with the sight of Tyler Barnett standing in the doorway looking more rugged, more totally *male* than any man she'd ever seen.

Gone were the dress slacks and shirts. Worn, faded jeans hugged his lean hips and thighs and looked as soft as butter. The shearling jacket made his shoulders look a mile wide. Highly polished boots had been replaced by old scuffed ones. His hat shaded his eyes, but she caught the steady gleam she had seen occasional glimpses of the day she'd worn the miniskirt.

Whatever that look meant, her body responded with tingling skin and racing blood.

As if suddenly aware he'd been standing motionless too long, he stepped through the doorway into the kitchen.

Only then did Carly notice the stainless-steel pail he carried. "What have you got?"

He swung the pail up and set it on the counter, then went to the pantry and retrieved a wide-mouthed glass gallon jug. "Milk," he said.

Carly peered over the edge of the pail and saw bubbling white foam. "Come on," she said, placing a hand against the pail and feeling warmth. "Everybody knows milk is cold and comes in cartons."

Tyler let out a surprised laugh. Then he cocked his head and peered at her through narrowed eyes. "You're kidding, right?"

She gave him her most innocent blink. "About what?"

He pursed his lips. "How does the milk get into the cartons?"

"From a machine at the dairy."

His eyes narrowed even more. "Where does the machine get it?"

Carly blinked again, then widened her eyes. In a voice filled with dawning wonder, she said, "You mean...from cows?"

He stared for a long moment. "You *are* kidding, aren't you?"

She couldn't help it then, she laughed. "Only halfway. I've never seen fresh milk before."

"Here, hold this." He placed a cloth over the mouth of the big jar and motioned for her to hold it in place. Then he poured the warm foamy milk into the jar, straining it through the cloth.

He stood so close she could feel his breath on her forehead.

The pail emptied, but he didn't move.

Carly slowly raised her eyes. His face was only inches above hers. She struggled up past his rugged jaw and those perfect lips that seemed to be reaching toward hers, over the blade of his nose with its slight hump on one side. Funny, but she'd never noticed that hump before. She wondered if he'd broken his nose.

Then she inched her gaze up to meet his and held it there, unable to look away. As she watched, the bright blue-green eyes changed, the green overpowering the blue.

His eyes held no questions, no promises. Just heat. Shocking, unexpected heat. He leaned down another fraction of an inch. She felt herself straining toward him.

Behind him, the back door flew open.

Chapter Four

Deep voices carried in from the mudroom. Rattled by both the look in Tyler's eyes and by the intrusion of others, Carly turned sharply away and stepped to the stove. With jerky motions, she dumped a skilletful of two dozen scrambled eggs into a large bowl. As she pulled two dozen pancakes from the oven where they'd been keeping warm, she heard boots and voices and running water in the mudroom. She loaded the table with food, and as she filled everyone's coffee cup, Tyler started the introductions.

His father, Arthur Barnett, stood shoulder to shoulder, head to head, with Tyler's six-foot height. The resemblance between the two men was obvious. Carly now knew what Tyler would look like in the years ahead. More lines on his face, put there by age, worry, laughter and weather, and thick hair so white it drew her gaze again and again.

The elder Barnett spoke little, but managed to tell her how glad he was she had come to help his granddaughter.

Next came Smitty Hodges, whose age she guessed to be

early to mid-sixties. He stood maybe an inch shorter than the Barnett men, as skinny as a beanpole, with more gray than brown in his thinning hair and long, droopy mustache.

"How-do, ma'am," he offered with a serious face.

Willis Hodges, Smitty's nineteen-year-old grandson, was all legs and Adam's apple, shy smiles and blushes.

"Don't pay any attention to the kid, here. He doesn't get out much. Probably doesn't know what girls are for. Howdy. I'm Neal Walters, and I do."

Carly shook the proffered hand, but refused to fall into the obvious trap of opening her mouth. Neal Walters was somewhere in his mid-thirties, around five-nine, with a thick, short neck and burly shoulders. His medium brown hair was cut military-short, and his great big toothy smile crinkled the corners of his brown eyes.

But there was something else in those eyes, too. Something arrogant and predatory that made Carly's shoulders tense.

Beside her, Tyler shot Walters a hard glare.

Carly turned with relief to the last man. Tom Two Feathers was younger than her by several years, in his mid-twenties maybe, with a beautiful, deliberately sexy smile and a mischievous twinkle in his black eyes. Both his smile and his eyes invited a return smile, rather than the unease she'd felt a moment ago with Walters. High cheekbones, coppery skin and straight black hair made him look as Indian as his name indicated.

"Welcome to the Bar B," he said politely.

By the time Carly saw to everyone's needs and took a seat with the men at the table, an hour's worth of cooking had disappeared. There wasn't a single thing left for her to eat. She lowered her gaze and sipped her coffee. For today, she would wait and eat with Amanda; tomorrow, Carly vowed to fix more food.

More than once as the men sipped their final cups of coffee and talked about the work planned for the day, Carly caught Tyler giving her a peculiar look. She couldn't tell

what was going through his mind, but he looked almost...
surprised.

And he was surprised. That chair at the opposite end of
the table from his had been empty for more than two years.
The last person to sit there had been Deborah.

When Tyler had brought Deborah home as his bride,
she'd been given the place of honor at the foot of the table,
the place his mother had occupied until her death. His father had given his seat at the head of the table to Tyler,
and moved his belongings from the big master bedroom
upstairs to the small one he now occupied downstairs next
to the office. Arthur had said that Tyler, as oldest son,
would be the head of the family when Arthur retired. Now
that Tyler had a wife, there was no sense in not making a
few changes right off.

To look up now from his breakfast and see a pixie with
sparkling eyes and short dark hair, where once Deborah had
sat, blond, elegant, cool, took Tyler by surprise. Mostly, he
figured, because, dammit, he liked looking up and seeing
Carly at the foot of the table. And yeah, that surprised him.
It wasn't that he shouldn't enjoy the sight of her, but more
that it shouldn't matter to him. She wasn't there to please
his eyes. She was there for Amanda. No other reason.

Besides, Carly was a city girl. Probably wouldn't take
well to sagebrush and isolation.

As she got up and refilled her coffee cup, Arthur pushed
his chair back from the table and rose. "Darn fine breakfast,
Miss Baker."

Carly turned and beamed at him. "Thank you. But call
me Carly, please."

Arthur gave her a sober nod. "I didn't know doctors did
this sort of stuff." He waved his cup toward the sink full
of dirty dishes.

Carly gave a light laugh. "I don't think they do. I'm not
a doctor."

"Therapist, then."

Carly shot Tyler a look, assuming he simply hadn't had

time to explain the situation to his father. "No therapist, either. I'm just a layperson."

Arthur Barnett blinked at her.

"No formal medical or psychiatric education," she added.

The look that came over the older man's face was cold enough to freeze an Eskimo. He turned to the four hands. "Head on out. We'll be along in a few minutes." To Tyler, he said, "I'll see you in the office. Now."

Stunned by the man's sudden change in manner, Carly gaped at Tyler.

"Don't worry about it," he told her in a clipped voice. "He's just surprised. He must have assumed..."

"He must have assumed a great deal. What did you tell him about me, anyway?"

"Not much. I haven't had time."

With that, he turned and followed his father into the office just off the living room. Carly heard the door close with a faint *snick*.

She had carried fewer than half the dishes to the sink when the yelling started. She didn't want to listen. Not really. But Arthur Barnett's booming voice carried through the walls in snatches she simply could not ignore.

"...said she came from that clinic...you let me think...then what the hell good is she?"

Carly's hands shook so badly she had to set her load of dishes down to keep from dropping them.

"*How* much? Good God!...gold digger...after nothin' but money...*off this ranch.*"

Carly pressed her hands to her flaming cheeks and felt her stomach knot. Lord, she knew she shouldn't have come here. She left the kitchen at a trot, thinking to get upstairs to her room where she couldn't hear the voice, the nasty remarks that sliced into her.

On her way to the stairs, she had to pass through the living room. There, Mr. Barnett's voice rang loud and clear through the closed office door at the opposite end of the room.

"If you had to bring a woman here, you damn well should have brought a wife, someone local, not some useless, money-grabbing city girl who doesn't know a cow from a mule. When the hell are you gonna get married again and give me grandchildren?"

"I'm not some stallion to be put out to stud." Tyler's voice was cold with fury. "And as for grandchildren, you've got plenty."

"Not from you, I don't."

Slowly, as if his words had to fight themselves out of a strangled throat, Tyler asked, "Are you disclaiming my daughter?"

"Don't be a horse's ass. Of course I'm not. But Amanda's just a girl. You need *sons*, dammit."

Tyler's answer was a low, unintelligible growl.

Carly reached the bottom of the stairs, intent on taking them as fast as she could. Instead she froze. There at the landing where the steps took a ninety-degree turn, stood Amanda, eyes big and way too bright, lower lip trembling.

"That does it," Carly muttered. In an instant she forgot her own feelings in favor of Amanda's. The girl had obviously heard every damning word from the office. Amanda had enough to deal with without adding more weight to her young shoulders. Without a thought to the consequences, Carly whirled and marched across the living room, threw open the office door and barged in.

Tyler and his father jerked toward her unannounced, uninvited entrance. She closed the door firmly behind her, fire racing through her veins.

Arthur Barnett bristled. "This is a private conversation, young lady."

"It might be, if you weren't conducting it at the top of your lungs." She ignored Tyler and marched on his father, keeping her voice low. "Right now there's a very troubled six-year-old girl standing on the stairs hearing every word you shout. Amanda has enough problems without having to listen to her own grandfather sneer and say she's not worthy of being his grandchild because she's *just* a girl."

"How dare you come in here—"

"Oh, I dare all right. Your son hired me to look after his daughter and help her overcome whatever is eating at her so much that she can't even talk. You're entitled to feel about her any way you want. But so help me, as long as I'm here you'll keep your stupid, hurtful thoughts to yourself, or I'll sew your lips shut. You will *not* cause that child more harm. Do I make myself clear?"

The man's eyes narrowed to slits. His nostrils flared. "Get out."

"I'm going. There's a very hurt little girl out there who needs me."

"You be off this ranch in an hour or I'll throw you off myself."

"I'll leave this ranch when he—" she flung an arm toward Tyler "—tells me to go. Until then, you're stuck with me."

The elder Barnett opened his mouth to say more, but Carly spun for the door.

Tyler watched her storm out in a huff of righteous fury. He never would have thought she had it in her to blow up like that. Sort of made his own rage at his father pale by comparison.

Funny, but she certainly hadn't defended herself that day in Union Square, yet here she was, taking up for his daughter like a she-cat defending her cub.

"Get rid of her," came his father's choked command. "Get rid of her right now."

Tyler arched a brow and pursed his lips to keep from smiling. Not many people had ever bested Arthur Barnett the way Carly had. "Oh," he said slowly, his eyes narrowed, "I don't think so."

Carly found Amanda curled up on her unmade bed, ruffled sundress, lace-trimmed socks, patent leather shoes and all, crying her eyes out. Her silent sobs pierced straight to Carly's heart and drained away her anger. "Oh, sweetheart." Carly lay down beside her and Amanda crawled into her arms.

And that's how Tyler found them a few minutes later.

"That's it, baby, cry it all out," Carly crooned.

Tyler sat on the edge of the bed, heartsick that Amanda had heard the venom that had spewed from his father's lips. The thing was, Arthur had meant what he'd said, but not in a hurtful way.

"To my dad," he said with a frown, "men and women have different functions in life. Men raise the stock, take care of the land and provide for the family. Women raise and care for the family. In Dad's book, each role is vital for survival, but they're not interchangeable. A man has his place, and so does a woman. And those places, and their accompanying responsibilities, are different. Separate."

Tyler shook his head. How could he make a heartbroken six-year-old girl understand that her grandad hadn't meant to hurt her?

And how was Tyler himself supposed to deal with someone else holding his daughter while she cried? Yet, once again, the word *right* came to mind. The woman and child looked right together.

A dangerous thought. A stupid thought.

He put his hand on Amanda's back and rubbed gently, feeling her sobs slowly ease. He glanced at Carly.

With a finger to her cheek, he wiped away a tear. "You take your job seriously, don't you?"

She shrugged and gave him a wry smile. "When I hurt, I cry. I stay healthy that way. Heck, sometimes I cry when I'm happy."

Tyler studied those dark brown eyes. "I don't guess this was a happy cry."

"No." She looked down to find Amanda staring up at her with tear-swollen eyes and a runny nose. "This was a hurt cry, wasn't it, Amanda? You heard what your grandad said, and it hurt your feelings, so you cried.''

Amanda gave a jerky nod.

"Good for you.''

Amanda reached up and touched Carly's damp cheek, a question in her eyes.

"You want to know why I was crying?''

Amanda nodded.

"I was crying because I know your grandad didn't mean to hurt your feelings. He was mad at me, and maybe at your daddy, and he said things he didn't really mean.''

Amanda looked wary. Intrigued.

"Everybody does it,'' Carly said. "I'll bet you've done it, too. I know I have.''

Carly wondered at the sudden mixture of pain and panic that filled the child's eyes.

"You get mad or get your feelings hurt and you say something you don't mean without even realizing it. Next thing you know, you've made somebody else mad, or hurt their feelings.''

Amanda looked surprised.

"She's right, sweetpea,'' Tyler said. "Grandad didn't mean what he said. He loves you. And when he gets home tonight, I'll bet he tells you so. Meanwhile, boy, you girls are lucky.''

Carly sniffed and wiped her cheeks. "How's that?''

"Girls get to cry. Us guys, well, everybody'd call us sissies if we cried.''

"Oh, yeah? So what do you do if you can't cry?''

Tyler shrugged and grinned. "If I'd been Amanda, I'd probably have run downstairs and kicked Grandad in the shins.''

Carly blinked and bit back a laugh. "Let's not resort to violence, please. I think sticking out her tongue would have sufficed.''

Amanda looked from one adult to the other as if she thought they were both crazy.

Tyler laughed. "Ah, come here, sugar." He pulled Amanda into his arms and gave her a big hug, complete with sound effects.

The action reminded Carly so much of her own father, a lump formed in her throat.

"You two girls gonna eat breakfast, or loll around in bed all day?"

"Are you hungry?" Carly asked Amanda.

Amanda nodded shyly.

"Well, then, what are we waiting for? But you'll have to help me. The *men* ate everything I cooked. They didn't leave us even a bite. *That's* worth sticking your tongue out for."

If only she would, thought Tyler. If only Amanda would do *something* besides sit around and be the perfect little lady, never expressing an opinion, never playing outside, never raising the very devil the way she used to, always being so damned docile.

Except, of course, when it came to wanting to go to Disneyland. Or not wanting to put on jeans. With any luck, Carly would be able to help with the latter.

He shook his head and let out a sigh. "Dad's making sandwiches for himself, Smitty and Tom, since they're checking fence today. Willis and Neal will eat in town while they're running errands. I'll be the only one around for lunch, and I can build my own sandwich. If you're still determined to cook, we'll all be in for supper at seven."

"We'll be ready and waiting," Carly answered.

The sudden heat in his eyes sent a shiver racing down her arms.

After breakfast, Amanda helped Carly clean the kitchen, but only after the child donned an apron—one that swallowed her—to keep her dress clean.

From the kitchen window, all Carly could see of the ranch was the huge barn directly opposite, across a stretch of bare ground. Suddenly she was anxious to see this place called Wyoming. Yet she didn't want to go out and chance running into Tyler, not after that last look he'd given her up in Amanda's room. The look that made her think he was thinking about leaning down and kissing her.

No, she didn't want to run into Tyler just yet. Not until she stopped wishing he *had* leaned down and kissed her. Stopping that wish might take awhile.

However, if she wasn't willing to go out back and face him, that didn't mean she had to confine herself to the house.

After exchanging her house shoes for a beat-up pair of Reeboks, Carly, with Amanda in tow, stepped out the front door. This side of the house sported a long, shaded gallery with a swing hanging by chains at one end and a grouping of three white wicker chairs at the other. Two steps led down to a sidewalk that cut a swath through the lush green front lawn. On one side, a huge cottonwood stretched to the sky and shaded half the yard. The gravel driveway at the end of the grass circled wide, then rejoined itself near where it split at the side of the house.

But beyond the yard…oh, my. Carly stepped from beneath the shade of the wooden porch into the blazing July sun and stared, entranced. Beyond the yard she saw… forever. A forever sky, bright turquoise blue, so big and clean it seemed impossible. A forever land, timeless, infinite in scope, dotted with sagebrush and stretching out flat here, rolling gently into low hills there, on and on as far as she could see to the east and south, and until the dark, looming mountains took over in the west. The occasional well pump didn't detract one whit from the beauty.

"The mountains to the west," came Tyler's low voice, "make up the Wyoming Range."

Her gaze strayed back to the sage-covered plains. Awestruck by the sheer, stark magnificence of what she saw, Carly swallowed. "It's so…powerful, so…breathtaking."

"Not everyone sees it that way. To most, it's just another high desert."

She turned toward him then and saw his eyes, the wariness, and knew instinctively he was speaking of his wife—ex-wife. "I pity them, then. They're fools. This is... magnificent."

Her gaze pulled away from Tyler back to the land as if drawn by a magnet. The utter simplicity and vastness surrounding her spoke volumes about the type of man who would call this place home. A strong man, and quiet. A private man, who wanted nothing more from life than what he could wrestle from it with his own two hands and the sweat of his brow. A stubborn, determined man, who would fight for his right to live on this vast open plain on his own terms.

She could only assume, from what little she knew and what lay before her, that Tyler Barnett was such a man.

"What have you got this time?" she asked with a nod toward the plastic bucket he carried.

He looked into the bucket, then pursed his lips. "After your reaction to the milk this morning, I don't know if you're ready for this."

"Hey, after the milk, I'm ready for anything."

He held the bucket out toward her, and Carly peered inside to find what looked to be more than two dozen large eggs. She grinned. "I wondered how you afforded breakfast around here. But what's that brown stuff all over them? Looks like dried mud."

Tyler laughed. "Guess again. And while you're guessing, remember where eggs come from. *Precisely* where they come from, and I don't mean egg cartons."

"Oh."

"Yeah, oh." He set the bucket in the shade of the front porch, then said, "Come on, Amanda. Let's show Carly around."

Carly wondered at the look of challenge in his eyes. Was he waiting for her to be offended over realizing there was a glob of chicken droppings on probably every egg in the bucket? Did he expect her to change her mind and decide she hated the ranch? She couldn't help but wonder what Deborah Barnett's reaction to the Bar B had been.

Tyler and Amanda led Carly around to the north side of the house. Here was an entirely different world from the rolling plains of sage to the south. Tyler pointed out enormous fields of hay stretching out on either side from a thick line of willows.

"Is that a stream?" she asked.

"Middle Piney Creek." He pronounced it *crick*. "The life's blood of the Bar B."

Yes, she thought, water would be scarce in this high, arid land, regardless of how green the nearby mountains looked or how lush the hay in the fields. With the house situated on a slight rise she could see irrigation ditches threading through the fields.

Two large barns, one for stallions and one for mares and geldings—"It's quieter around here that way," Tyler explained—were separated by a maze of corrals that wrapped around three sides of each building. Beyond the corrals, horses and a few cattle dotted fenced pastures of short grass. Closer in, there were sheds, tractors, a large garage, a chicken house with enclosed yard and the small house Carly had seen last night.

"That's the old house," Tyler told her. "The men live there."

Beyond the "old house," Tyler pointed out his indoor arena. "It's not huge," he said, "but it lets me work the horses during the winter."

Not huge? The red-and-white metal building looked enormous to Carly.

"And this gentleman," he said, leading Carly to the only corral fenced in white steel pipe and cable, whereas the others were enclosed with wood, "is Prancer."

"Tyler, he's magnificent."

And he was, in looks, in carriage. The bay quarter horse stallion's coat gleamed like polished mahogany as he pranced along the corral fence before them, head high, small ears twitching, his black mane and tail rippling like heavy silk with his every movement. Beneath that glossy coat, well-developed muscles bunched and flexed.

"I see where he gets his name," Carly offered with a smile.

Tyler chuckled. "Yeah. His real name is Loves to Prance. And he does."

Something over her shoulder caught Tyler's attention.

Carly turned and followed his gaze to see a plume of dust snaking toward the ranch. A moment later the sun reflected off an orange pickup bouncing along the gravel road, dust shooting up behind it like a rooster tail.

"Tammy," Tyler said.

Carly waited for further explanation, wondering at the soft affection in his voice. The way he said the name started an ache in her chest. Whoever this Tammy was, Tyler obviously cared about her.

"She's probably coming over to meet you, show you around."

"Why? Who is she?"

"Tammy Harris. She and her husband, Timmy—"

With the mention of a husband easing the ache in her chest, Carly smiled. "Tammy and Timmy? You're kidding."

Tyler smiled. "Yeah, everybody teases them about their names. They're our nearest neighbors, five miles back toward town. Tammy's been looking after Amanda and taking care of the house for the past few months."

"And I just did her out of her job. Terrific. Does this Tammy person have any violent tendencies?"

Tyler laughed and shook his head. "She'll be glad to see you. She's got a baby due in a few weeks. Taking care of two houses was getting to be too much for her. She had to quit whether I found anybody to take her place or not. I called her from San Francisco and told her you were coming." He eyed the pickup again. "Looks like Tim's with her."

Tyler led Carly and Amanda across the dry, hard-packed ground to the back of the house, where the orange pickup rolled to a stop next to Tyler's truck at the back door.

Tammy Harris couldn't have been a day over eighteen. Long, wavy red hair, freckles scattered across her nose and cheeks and a wide, friendly smile big enough for two.

Tim, who didn't look much older, if at all, was tall and lanky, with a shank of sandy brown hair hanging down on his forehead from underneath his hat.

Tyler introduced them, and they all made their way into the kitchen for a cup of coffee.

"Tammy was bound and determined to get over here today and meet the new woman," Tim said with a shy smile for Carly. "But she's not supposed to drive anymore till after the baby comes, so I knew I'd better get her over here before she nagged me to death."

"Oh, go on with ya." Tammy gave him a playful swat on the arm. "You were just as curious as I was, and you know it. Now that you've seen Carly, you'll be hightailing it over to my daddy's to tell all my brothers there's a new woman in the county."

Tim's face turned the shade of a vine-ripened tomato. "I'll not be doin' any such thing." Then he grinned. "Not without making sure Tyler hasn't already got his brand on her."

Carly choked on a mouthful of coffee.

"Way to go, Tim, you've embarrassed her."

Carly coughed to clear her throat. "Yes," she said. "I think you have." She chanced a quick look at Tyler and found him staring at her with a look of amused challenge.

"Sorry, ma'am," Tim said with an unrepentant grin. "But look at Tyler," he told Tammy. "I was right. Looks like your brothers are out of luck."

Just when Carly thought it couldn't get worse, Amanda tugged on Tyler's arm.

"What is it, sugar?"

He let Amanda lead him to Carly's side, where the girl

pressed her finger to Carly's hip and made a hissing sound between her teeth. Then she looked up at Tyler, her brow furrowed in wrinkles.

Tyler chuckled. "No, I'm not really gonna brand her. It's just a figure of speech. Tim was only kidding." But the look Tyler gave Carly just then was hot enough to sear flesh.

"Way to go, Tim," Tammy muttered again.

Tyler spent the rest of the afternoon trying to forget the blush on Carly's cheeks when Tim spoke of branding. He and Carly had walked outside to see Tim and Tammy off. The minute the orange pickup had driven away, Carly had hustled that shapely fanny of hers back into the house and set to work cleaning the kitchen as though her life depended on it.

Tim's teasing had brought one thing home to Tyler, though. Carly was attractive, single and female—a rare commodity in Sublette County. Other men would find out she was here on the Bar B, and they'd come sniffing around.

The thought should have amused him. It didn't.

"Feeling a little territorial, are we?" he asked himself beneath his breath.

Yeah. He was feeling a little territorial.

Before Tammy and Tim had arrived to spoil the moment, Carly had surprised him. Damn near knocked him off his feet, in fact. In his wildest dreams, he had never expected lively, city-bred Carly Baker to like this quiet land he called home, yet he couldn't deny her reaction this morning. The look of wonder in her eyes had nearly stopped his heart. For a minute there, one fantastic, blood-rushing minute, he had thought—hoped?—that look had been for him.

"Dream on, buddy."

At the harsh sound of Tyler's voice in the quiet barn, the gelding whose hoof he was filing snorted and tried to jerk his leg free.

"Easy, fella. Just talking to myself. Almost through here. A little more, and…there." He released the hoof and stood back, running a hand along the animal's flank. "All done."

He put his rasp away in the tack room and led the horse back out to the corral. The sound of his dad and the others driving in from a day of checking fences reminded him that it was suppertime.

After the way Carly had lit into his dad that morning, Tyler wondered what would happen when the two came face-to-face again. He guessed he didn't need to worry about her. She could sure enough take care of herself.

Still, he didn't want to give the pair any time alone together. Given half a chance, if this morning was anything to go by, his dad and Carly were liable to snatch each other bald-headed.

Chapter Five

Carly stood at the kitchen sink and washed her hands, trying to think if there was anything she'd forgotten for dinner. But concentrating on the meal was next to impossible, knowing that at that very moment, Tyler was upstairs in the shower. Wet. Naked. His muscled body slicked with soap.

Lord, what was happening to her? She never used to be obsessed with men. Even James had never occupied her mind the way Tyler did, and she'd been in love with James. Hadn't she?

The sound of voices drew her gaze to the window. The rest of the men were closing up the barns and other buildings for the night.

Beside her, Amanda looked up anxiously.

"It's your grandad. He and the others will be in for supper in a few minutes. Is the table all set?"

Amanda gave her a glum nod.

"Hey, why so sad?"

The child's eyes cut toward the window.

"You're not still thinking about what your grandad said this morning, are you?"

With a small frown, Amanda nodded again.

"Ah, honey, I told you he didn't mean it."

Young shoulders lifted in an ancient sigh.

"You don't believe me, do you?"

No response, except for downcast eyes.

Carly held her breath and decided to gamble. It was nothing more than the old buzzard deserved for saying a nasty thing like that about his own granddaughter. She knelt in front of Amanda. "What do you wanna bet I'm right, that he didn't mean it?"

A half shrug.

"Okay, here's the deal. If you're right, and he did mean it, I'll make your bed for the next week."

Ah-ha, a spark of interest. Well, okay, not interest, exactly. Amanda was looking at her as though she thought Carly had lost her mind.

"And if I'm right," Carly went on, "you have to make my bed for the next week."

Amanda's eyes filled with doubt, but she nodded.

"So, it's a deal?"

This time Amanda grinned.

"What's a deal?"

The sound of Tyler's deep voice had both females turning toward the door to the living room. Before Carly could do more than acknowledge how her heart leaped at the sight of him, boots scraped on the step outside the back door. An instant later, the door opened and Arthur Barnett stepped into the mudroom.

He stood still a moment, just beyond the door to the kitchen, and eyed Carly as if he thought she might turn rabid and bite at any second.

Good. The ol' buzzard ought to be a little jumpy around her. He could say what he wanted about her, but she wouldn't stand for his mean talk about Amanda. Not while Carly had breath in her lungs.

Still, she'd already told him what she thought. Her next move was for Amanda's peace of mind. Carly waited until Mr. Barnett hung his hat on a peg in the mudroom, then, fighting a big smile—oh, he was going to hate her for this—she took Amanda's hand and met him as he stepped into the kitchen.

"Good evening, Mr. Barnett. Amanda and I have a bet going that only you can settle."

He cast a cautious, questioning glance at Tyler, who shrugged in return. "What kind of bet?"

Carly softened her voice and laced it slightly with sympathy. "It's about this morning."

Mr. Barnett stiffened. His cheeks flushed and the corners of his mouth turned down.

"I bet Amanda that you didn't really mean what you said about her being *just* a girl, that it was only one of those things people say when they're mad about something else. One of those things nobody really means. I bet her that you still love her."

After casting Carly a sharp, narrow glance, the man squatted before his granddaughter. "She's right, you know," he said with a nod toward Carly. His voice was rough with emotion. "I didn't mean a word of it. Ah, shucks, shortcakes, you know you're my best girl, don't you?"

Amanda gave him a shy smile.

"Come on then, and give your poor ol' grandad a hug so he'll know you're not mad at him."

After Amanda complied, he invited her to help him wash up for supper. As she headed out the door ahead of him, he turned back to Carly. "In the future, I'll thank you to leave me to do my own apologizing."

"In the future, I hope there's no need," Carly shot back.

Arthur Barnett glared at her a final moment, then left the room.

Carly waited, her breath held, for Tyler to comment on how blatantly she'd stuck her nose into family business.

He stalked across the room toward her, slowly, deliberately, his dark eyes holding her motionless. Oh, Lord, he must be too angry for words.

She clenched her fists at her sides. "I know I took an awful chance. I don't blame you for being upset. But I had to get him to apologize to her. I...I'm sorry."

He stopped mere inches away. Dampness from his shower still clung to his dark hair. She smelled the fresh scent of soap, the clean woodsy fragrance of his aftershave. He radiated heat and power. If he wanted, he could probably pick her up and snap her in two with his bare hands.

"I—I'm...sorry."

Those bare hands rose and clasped her shoulders, but gently rather than cruelly. His head dipped low, and before she realized his intent, his smooth, firm lips brushed hers.

Carly sucked in a sharp breath. A soft melting sensation started in the pit of her stomach and spread outward, taking her completely by surprise and stilling any protest she might have made, had she been capable of thought just then.

"Thank you," Tyler whispered, brushing her lips a second time with his. Then he released her shoulders and straightened, his eyes never leaving hers.

She shivered at the sudden loss of his touch. "F-for what?"

"For handling that the way you did." He stepped back, giving her room to breathe, to think. "He really does love her, you know."

"I—I'd hoped I was right about that."

Voices approached from just beyond the back door. The men were on their way in.

Tyler stepped casually to the counter and poured himself a cup of coffee. "So, what was the bet for? What did you win?"

Trying to ignore the trembling in her knees, Carly cupped out her bottom lip and blew a stream of air upward to fluff her bangs. "Amanda now has to make my bed for the next week."

"You've got a six-year-old doing housework?" His voice was full of skepticism.

Carly carried the bowl of mashed potatoes to the table. "Making beds isn't 'housework.' Besides, it'll give her something to occupy at least a little of her time until I can get her out of those dresses and into more practical clothing so she can play outside."

"I wish you luck on that one," he said with feeling.

"I'm not going to rush it just yet. She needs a little time to get used to me, and to recover from today, I think."

Carly could use a little time of her own to recover, she thought as she loaded the dishwasher after supper. But she wasn't getting it. Neither the kiss nor the man would go away.

The kiss lingered in her mind like a haunting dream.

No, more like an unsettling revelation. She hadn't known she could feel so much from such a brief contact. And with a man she barely knew. A man who was her employer, no less.

It was scary. Unthinkable. Unacceptable.

But it had happened.

Perhaps she could have brushed the memory aside, if only the man had cooperated. But Tyler Barnett was not cooperating. Every time he had looked down the length of the table at her during supper, his bright eyes had said, *I kissed you.*

Sometimes they said, *I'm going to do it again one day.*

And always, the message that disturbed her just as much, *You liked it, too. You'll like it even more next time.*

There wouldn't be a next time, Carly vowed. She hadn't come to Wyoming to get mixed up with a man. She'd come to Wyoming *because* she'd gotten mixed up with a man.

The wrong man. She wasn't about to make that mistake again.

Branding, indeed. Her cheeks still stung at the thought.

Tyler Barnett would just have to get his kisses somewhere else. Carly Baker was not available.

With that resolve firm in her mind, she gave the dishrag a hard twist and turned to wipe the table. And ran smack into Tyler's broad chest.

"Whoa, there." He put his hands on her shoulders to steady her.

Her heart racing, Carly stepped back quickly and ran up against the counter at her back. The heated look in his eyes flustered her. She felt trapped.

With a toss of her head, she said, "That sounds like something you'd say to some poor dumb animal. One you were getting ready to brand."

His lazy gaze slid down her from head to toe, then back up, making her skin tingle. "You interested?"

Her mouth went dry. "Don't be ridiculous."

"I wouldn't dream of it."

"Back off, Tyler."

"I notice you didn't answer my question."

"What question was that?"

"Are you interested. In wearing my brand."

She gave another toss of her head, hoping to look defiant. "I'm not one of your horses or cows."

"I noticed. Believe me. That was one of the first things I noticed about you."

His husky voice sent hot and cold shivers down her spine. "No, the first thing you noticed about me was that I made Amanda laugh. That's why I'm here, Tyler. That's the only reason I'm here."

His eyes flashed. "Is it?"

"That, and the money. I needed the money."

As she watched, his jaw squared and the spark of heat in his eyes cooled. "Yeah, right. The money."

"That's right. The money."

"Then get back to earning it," he told her sharply.

Stung, she brushed past him and attacked the table with the dishrag.

Tyler ground his teeth and swore to himself. When he looked up, his father was standing in the doorway to the living room. Watching.

Carly crossed the living room, heading toward the stairs and bed, when Arthur Barnett's voice stopped her.

"Miss Baker?"

Steeling herself against whatever he planned to throw at her this time, Carly slowly turned to face him. He sat in a recliner next to a sofa. Tyler, she thought, was in the office.

"What can I do for you?" she asked.

"First thing tomorrow you can move my things upstairs, and yours down here into my room."

"No."

Carly flinched at the harshness, the suddenness of Tyler's voice from the office doorway.

Arthur frowned sharply. "She shouldn't be upstairs with you."

"She's not upstairs with me." His words were for his father, but his eyes were on Carly. "She's upstairs with Amanda. That's where she stays."

"You know it's gonna be all over the county how we've got an unattached female living here with two bachelors. Six if you count the men. There's bound to be talk."

Carly smoothed her hands down her thighs. "I don't mind moving down here, Tyler."

"I mind," he said firmly.

"If it makes your father feel better to have me downstairs—"

"I didn't hire you to please my father. I hired you for Amanda. I want you close to her." Something flared in his eyes. "Unless you're uncomfortable with the idea of sleeping just down the hall from me."

She hadn't been. She hadn't even thought to worry about where they slept in relation to each other. But now…

Carly straightened her shoulders. She'd be damned if she'd let him know he made her uneasy. Theirs was a business relationship, nothing more. And her business was Amanda.

"Of course I'm not uncomfortable. The room is lovely," she added, deliberately misinterpreting his words.

Tyler gave a slight nod, then looked at his father. "It's settled, then. She stays where she is."

When Arthur didn't comment further, Carly assumed the subject was closed. "Good night." With trembling knees, she turned away and headed up the stairs.

Tyler watched her go.

So did his father. "You're making a mistake, son. A big one."

Tyler ran his fingers through his hair. "What is it with you? What have you got against my bringing someone here who can help Amanda?"

"Not a damned thing. But is that why you really brought her here?"

"What the hell's that supposed to mean?"

"You know what it means. I see the way you look at her, like you can't wait to get your hands on her. How's that supposed to help Amanda? How is *she* supposed to help Amanda at all? She said herself she's no doctor."

"Dad, she made Amanda laugh. Out loud."

"You told me that. You also told me, and I can see for myself, that nothing's really changed. Amanda still can't talk. You also told me that high-priced doctor in San Francisco recommended her."

"He did." Tyler told his dad what he knew of Carly's background.

Arthur frowned heavily. "I still don't think she can help."

"That's obvious," Tyler said softly. "No offense, but

it's not your decision. Amanda is my daughter. I'll do whatever I can to help her."

Arthur shook his head. "I know you will. I want her to be able to talk, too. But I heard that Baker woman—"

"Her name is Carly," Tyler declared.

"I heard her tell you she came because of the money. The last woman you brought here nearly bled this place dry. You get mixed up with this one, mark my words, she'll do the same."

"I'm not going to 'get mixed up with this one,' as you put it."

But he wanted to. He knew it as sure as night gets dark. There was no way in hell Carly Baker could live under his roof, sleep mere feet away from him night after night for six months, without his wanting her.

Oh, yeah, he wanted to get mixed up all right.

The question was, would she get mixed up with him? Would a city-bred girl from Nob Hill want anything to do with an ordinary rancher who lived in the middle of nowhere and went around smelling like a horse most of the time?

Over the next few days, he had his answer, but it wasn't the one he wanted. Every time he got near Carly, she backed off like a skittish mare. In the kitchen she kept the full length of the table between them whenever possible. If he ran into her in another part of the house, her defense was a dust rag, a vacuum, or Amanda. Outside—hell, she never went outside, as far as he could tell.

By Thursday, he knew he had to do something. The way she jumped and flinched when he got near was starting to make *him* jumpy. After his dad rode out with Smitty and Neal, and Tom and Willis were cleaning stalls, Tyler went back to the house and found Carly at the kitchen sink. Alone. Amanda wasn't up yet.

"Did you forget something?" she asked, her voice sounding thin.

"You tell me," he said slowly.

"I—what do you mean?"

"Tell me if I've forgotten how to act around a woman without scaring her."

Her hand resting on the edge of the sink twitched. "Scaring her? Why would you scare someone?"

"That's what I'd like to know. What am I doing that scares you so much?"

"What makes you think you scare me?"

"Oh, I don't know." He strolled toward the counter. "Maybe the way you're backing away from me right now, when all I'm after is coffee."

She stopped in midstep and tossed up her chin.

"Then, too, maybe it has to do with the way you try to avoid me, the way your voice quivers when you can't."

He searched her face, finding it stiff, her eyes downcast. "Hell," he said, frustrated. "You can't even look me in the eye anymore."

After a long, uncomfortable silence that Tyler refused to break, Carly's shoulders slumped. "You're right," she whispered. "I guess I can't."

He took a short breath. "Mind telling me why?"

Carly felt his gaze on her and shivered. "Maybe...it's the way you look at me." She glanced at him and saw surprise flit across his face.

"How do I look at you?"

Oh, Lord, she'd left herself open for that one. Now what? How did she answer him? "Like...like..."

"Like I like what I see?"

She jerked her gaze away and felt her cheeks sting.

"Like you're a desirable woman?"

A lump lodged in her throat. She wasn't going to let him do this to her. She wasn't going to be flattered and lied to and led on by a man again. Straightening her shoulders, she raised her head. "Come on, Tyler, it's not necessary. You got me here. I took your job. I'll do everything I can to help Amanda. There's no need for the false flattery."

He stopped in the act of reaching for the coffeepot. "False flattery?"

She shrugged and looked away. "You know what I mean."

"No," he said softly, "I don't think I do."

With jerky motions, Carly faced the sink and turned on the water to rinse out the dishrag. She was making a fool of herself. Maybe she had been misinterpreting those looks he'd been giving her. Maybe that hadn't been heat she'd seen in his eyes after all.

"Talk to me, Carly."

She turned off the water and whirled toward him. "Why are you doing this? Why can't we just...just stick to business?"

"Business? On a ranch this size, this isolated? This isn't an office, for crying out loud. I didn't hire you to do my filing."

"All right," she cried. "Friends, then. Can we just be friends and forget all this...this other stuff?"

He finally grasped the coffeepot and filled his cup. "I thought we were already friends."

After wringing the excess water from the dishrag, Carly moved to the table.

"Friends tell each other when something's wrong," Tyler said.

Instead of answering, she started wiping the table with perhaps more vigor than was necessary. She had to do something to keep from looking at him.

She heard his boots scrape lightly across the floor, the slight jingle of a spur. Good grief, what was she doing in the wilds of Wyoming with a man who wore *spurs?*

And he was walking toward her. Stalking her.

She skittered around the table.

Tyler swore beneath his breath. "Would you light a minute and tell me what the hell you meant by false flattery?"

With the secure width of the table between them, she paused. "All right. I mean all those hot, lingering looks you keep giving me, trying to make me think you're... you're interested in me.''

"Well, hell," he cried, slamming his cup onto the table and sloshing coffee onto the just-wiped surface. "I *am* interested in you."

That stopped her cold. Bewildered, she looked into his eyes. There she read frustration and puzzlement, but also a straightforward, frank attraction she couldn't deny. He really was interested in her.

How had it happened? Why...?

"And that makes you nervous as hell," he said softly. "I can see it in your eyes. But I see something else in your eyes, Carly."

She immediately lowered her gaze.

"I'm not the only one who's interested. You're interested right back, and that makes you even more nervous."

With her heart pounding a rapid drumbeat in her chest, Carly shook her head. "Tyler, this is crazy. I don't want you to be attracted to me. I don't want to be attracted to you."

"I think it's a little late for that. Funny thing about feelings. They don't care what your mind wants. They just sort of happen on their own. I'm not going to hurt you, Carly," he added softly.

A shudder ripped through her. "Aren't you?"

Tyler thought about Carly's parting words, uttered just before she'd fled the kitchen and left him feeling like a jerk. Why had he pushed her so damned hard?

But then, he knew why. What he was feeling was too strong for simple attraction. It was bone-deep, gut-wrenching want. His blood rushed and his jeans got tight just thinking about her.

If she had any idea what he really felt, she'd panic. She was close to that already.

But why? Why would his wanting her, her wanting

him—because she did, and hadn't even tried to deny it—
why would that scare her so badly?

Maybe, he thought, trying to calm himself, it had something to do with Mr. Junior Executive back in San Francisco. Was she still carrying a torch for that sleek little
puppy?

Surely not, or she wouldn't get that hungry look in her
eyes when she looked at *him*.

But then, she was a woman alone in a strange place, no
friends, only a half a dozen old cowboys and a troubled
child for miles around. She was totally dependent on Tyler.
On his goodwill, his word.

When those thoughts fully registered, his eyes widened.
Hellfire, no wonder she was skittish. She was, essentially,
completely at his mercy. What woman wouldn't be leery?

Frowning, he slipped into the corral and slowly approached the new mare that had arrived that morning for
training. "Easy, girl. That's it—whoa, easy. I'm not going
to hurt you."

I'm not going to hurt you, Carly.

Aren't you? she'd asked in return.

"No," he crooned to the mare, to himself, to Carly.
"No, I won't hurt you. I just want to be friends. For now,
let's just get to know each other. How does that sound,
huh?"

The mare twitched her ears back and forth, but stopped
her fidgeting. Still wary, she nonetheless responded to his
easy tone and stood still for his petting.

It was Friday night before Tyler got the chance to talk
to Carly alone again, and even then he had to ask her to
come to the office with him. He didn't miss her instant
tension when he closed the door and sealed them in relative
privacy.

"Have a seat." He motioned toward the old wing chair
before the desk, while he took the swivel chair on the other
side.

Carly sat, her shoulders tensing until she saw him pick up a pen and start writing in a large ledger-size checkbook.

Behind Tyler stood a floor-to-ceiling bookcase filled with everything from Shakespeare to books on veterinary medicine. At right angles to the bookcase hung a glass-enclosed display case. Earlier in the week Carly had thoroughly inspected all the huge silver buckles mounted against black velvet inside the case, as well as the gold, bronze and silver statues on the shelves next to it.

Carly knew virtually nothing about horse shows or rodeos, but the name Loves to Prance appeared on an impressive number of buckles and trophies. Grand Champion of this, National Champion of that, Reserve Champion—whatever that was.

The stallion was apparently an American Quarter Horse Association Champion. A framed newspaper clipping claimed he was also a National Cutting Horse Association Triple Crown Champion.

Other horses had won awards, too. Names like Sweet Little Sugar, Miss Sage, White Sox, Sugar's Prancing Bingo and Sage Duster were engraved on many of the buckles.

Tyler's name, too, appeared on more than a few buckles and trophies, as did his father's.

Tyler's voice startled her. "Your first week's salary." He tore the check from the book and handed it to her across the desk.

Carly took the check carefully, not willing to let her fingers touch his. "Thank you." She started to rise.

"One more thing."

She froze, her gaze flying involuntarily to his. His eyes were open and calm, no threatening heat, no secrets.

"I think you had the right idea yesterday when you said we should be friends."

Surprised, Carly let herself sink back onto the chair. "You do?"

"Yeah." He gave a slight grin. "So how about it? Can we be friends?"

Carly felt relief rush through her. If it was tinged with disappointment, it didn't matter. His friendship was what she wanted, what she needed. Her smile came easily. "I'd like that."

Tyler returned her smile, feeling as though he'd just accomplished a major feat. He liked seeing her relax around him. "So would I." He leaned back in the chair and laced his fingers together behind his head. "So, now that we're friends, maybe you'll tell me what you're going to do with all that money."

Her smile twisted. "I'd like to say I'm going to save it up and hire an attorney to get my old job back."

Much as he didn't want to think about her going back to San Francisco, he forced himself to ask, "But?"

She shook her head. "I want my job back, but I don't want to have to push my way back in. I don't think I'd have the nerve."

Despite himself, Tyler chuckled. "Anybody who can take on my father the way you've done is not lacking in nerve."

"That was different." She waved away his compliment, if that's what it had been. "That was for Amanda."

"Yeah, and I wondered while you were telling him off why you didn't do that to those two in Union Square that day."

Carly gave a harsh laugh. "It would have been a waste of breath. Becky wouldn't have listened to anything I said. She seems to have completely forgotten we've been best friends nearly all our lives. And James already knows I didn't take the money."

"He knows, and you were dating him, and he's not sticking up for you? You're better off without him."

"I know that now. I just wish I'd known it before I let him worm my computer password out of me."

Tyler slowly straightened in the chair. "*He* did the embezzling?"

Carly's mouth quirked. "I don't see how it could have been anyone else."

"Did you tell your boss this?"

"With no proof? When the audit uncovered the problem the same day James and Becky—the boss's daughter, mind you—announced their engagement? Who would have believed me?"

"Their engagement? I thought he was dating you."

"This is embarrassing. I think I've said enough."

"Oh, no you don't. You can't leave me hanging. We're friends, remember? Tell me."

She sighed. "All right, yes, James and I were dating. For about a year. But nobody at work knew. I was his supervisor, and he was up for a promotion at the end of the year. He said he didn't want…oh, God, this is ironic. He didn't want anyone to think he was using me."

Tyler could see her struggling not to cry—or scream, he couldn't tell which—and it twisted something inside him. He wanted to take her in his arms and hold her, promise her no one would ever hurt her again. At the same time, he wanted to get his hands around Mr. Junior Executive's neck and squeeze. Hard.

The sheer force of his reaction startled him. Yeah, he was attracted to Carly. Yeah, he liked her. But in reality, he barely knew her. He'd always believed in minding his own business and letting other people mind theirs. With Carly, he didn't seem to be able to maintain that distance and objectivity. Didn't seem to want to.

The picture in his mind made him ache for her. Carly, so young and full of life, ready to fall in love. What's-His-Name, James, slick and cunning and greedy, preying on her. Probably swearing his undying devotion while telling her their secrecy was for her own good, the bastard.

To have him end up engaged to her best friend would

have been devastating on its own, without having all signs point to her regarding the embezzlement.

"So, what are you going to do?" he asked quietly.

"I'm going to forget about it for now and go to bed." She rose from the chair and reached for the doorknob. "Good night, Tyler. Thanks for listening."

He managed a slight smile. "That's what friends are for."

Chapter Six

Because they had agreed to be friends, Carly let Tyler talk
her into going to church with him, his dad and Amanda
that Sunday.

"We start haying next week, so this will be the last
chance I'll have to get to town for a while. I want to show
you around so you'll know where things are in case you
need something. Besides, the rest of the family will be
there, and they're anxious to meet you."

He could have talked all day and not said that. She would
have felt better. The idea of meeting the rest of his family
had her gnawing the inside of her jaw.

"Just do me a favor, will you?" he'd asked Saturday
night, a laughing twinkle in his eyes. "Please don't wear
that red miniskirt to church, or they'll kick me out for
drooling all over you."

He said it in such a friendly, teasing manner that it was
impossible for her to take offense. Besides, he seemed to
have taken this friendship thing to heart. He was just trying

to make her feel good by boosting her spirits, make her feel attractive. And dammit, it had worked. She had smiled all the way up the stairs on her way to bed.

But going to church with the Barnetts turned out to be something else Carly could have done without. They arrived after everyone else was already seated. The small white frame building sat on a corner across from a gas station. Cars overflowed the tiny gravel parking lot and lined the uncurbed street.

Inside, sunlight streamed through the stained-glass window behind the pulpit and cast patterns of colored light across the hardwood floor.

Despite the crush of people filling the pews, every sound seemed to bounce and echo from wall to wall. Whispers hung suspended in the sun-streaked air between the floor and ceiling, paper crackled, people shuffled and rearranged themselves in their seats and cleared their throats. Even above the powerful strains from the organ, where a blue-haired lady played a mournful rendition of "Bringing in the Sheaves," the sounds carried. Tyler's and Arthur's boots thudded. Amanda's Mary Janes tapped. And careful though she tried to be with each step, Carly's high heels struck the old oak floor like rifle shots.

Heads turned, eyes stared and questioned. Hands covered mouths as people leaned toward one another to whisper, to wonder about the stranger in their midst.

When Carly would have slipped quietly into an empty spot in the back pew, Tyler, following his father, led her and Amanda to the second row from the front. As half of it had been left conspicuously empty while the other pews were full, she assumed these were Tyler and Arthur's usual seats.

That meant several of the people surrounding them were probably Barnetts, too, but Carly didn't dare turn her head to look. She could feel the sharp speculation in the air, the eyes on the back of her head.

Were they thinking, like Arthur, that she was some little

gold digger out to take Tyler for his money? No, they probably didn't even know who she was. In which case, they were undoubtedly wondering about that, about why she was with Tyler.

She remembered the censuring, hostile looks Arthur had given her lately. They were the same as those she'd received in the offices at Blalock's after the money had turned up missing. Hard. Cold. Speculative.

Carly stared straight ahead and tried to ignore the feeling of paranoia growing in her chest.

Amanda smiled up at her, and Carly forced herself to smile back, all the while counting the seconds until she could get away from this place, these people.

After the services, it took ages to get back down the aisle and out the door. Tyler and Arthur stopped to greet nearly everyone. Carly tried to hang back, but Tyler wouldn't have it. Amid the crush of people pouring from the pews, he took her by the arm and pulled her up beside him, while Amanda held his other hand.

He introduced her without explanation, merely saying, "This is Carly Baker." She couldn't guess which among the people she met were the ones she'd felt staring at her. Simply knowing what some of them probably thought made her want to cringe.

Men, women and children alike greeted Tyler with warm friendliness. But when they turned their gazes on Carly, she could see the speculation in their eyes. Who was she? What was she doing here? What was she to Tyler?

All in all, the trip down that aisle toward the door and freedom was one of the longest in Carly's life.

Outside, in the blinding sunlight and stifling heat of noon, it got worse. Tyler introduced her to his family. She met Robert and his wife Karen, Joe and his wife Barb, and the baby of the family, Sandy, and her husband, Greg. There were four children ranging in age from two to six among the couples, but Carly couldn't tell which child belonged to whom.

Then there was a Barnet cousin, Frank, who lived in Big Piney with his wife Bev and their daughters. Emily was seven; Laurie, six.

They were all polite enough, but again Carly could see the speculation, the censorship in their eyes.

Before heading for home, Tyler drove Carly past the grocery store, the café, feed store and bank, so she would know where they were should she need them. She was so intent on keeping tears of mortification at bay, she didn't even bother to ask him what the devil he thought she might need at the feed store.

That evening when Amanda was getting ready for bed, Carly started what she referred to as her "jeans" campaign. She sat behind Amanda on the edge of the canopied bed and brushed out the child's long, dark hair. "Is there anything in particular you'd like to do tomorrow?"

Amanda shook her head.

"All the men will be out working in the hay fields. Your daddy told me. I'll have to take lunch out to them. Will you help me? It'll be like having a picnic."

Amanda turned her head just enough to give Carly a shy smile and nod.

"Good. I've got a feeling I'm going to need all the help I can get. You'll probably need to wear jeans. I wouldn't want you to ruin—"

Before she could finish, Amanda was shaking her head.

"You don't want to wear jeans?"

Amanda shook her head again.

Carly continued pulling the brush through the girl's hair. "I suppose I can understand that. Your dresses are so pretty. I guess that's why you don't play outside, huh? Because you don't want to ruin your dresses?"

Pulling her hair free of the brush, Amanda turned on the bed to face her. The troubled look on the girl's face made an ache bloom in Carly's chest, but she did her best to ignore the pain. It was time to do a little gentle probing and pushing. "Did your mommy buy you all those pretty dresses?"

With an anxious look that spoke volumes, Amanda nodded.

"She liked you to be all dressed up and pretty, didn't she?"

Another nod. Big blue-green eyes, so like Tyler's, filled with emotion.

Carly wanted so badly to pull Amanda into her arms, to cradle her against her chest and soothe away the hurt. Instead she probed deeper. "You miss your mommy, don't you, sweetheart?"

Her lower lip trembling, Amanda nodded again.

"I'll bet if you could talk, you'd tell me you like to wear the dresses because they make you feel closer to her, now that she's gone, and that you know she'd like to see you dressed up. Would I be right?"

Amanda nodded.

"I wonder..." Carly used her fingers to fluff Amanda's bangs. "Do you remember when you and your mommy lived here on the ranch, before you moved to Chicago?"

This time the nod came with a slight smile.

"Did you wear dresses all the time back then, or did you wear jeans to play in?"

Amanda cocked her head to think.

Carly knew she would have to phrase her questions more carefully so the girl could answer yes or no. As she started to do just that, Amanda reached out and poked a finger against Carly's thigh. Her jean-clad thigh.

"You wore jeans?"

A vigorous nod this time.

"And you played outside?"

Yes.

"I'll bet your mommy didn't mind you wearing jeans to play in, did she?"

The brightness in Amanda's eyes dimmed. She studied the knee of her flowered pajamas and gave a small shrug.

Carly took another shot. "I'll bet if your mommy was here now, she wouldn't mind if you wore jeans to play outside. I think she'd understand, don't you?"

No response.

"You want to give it a try tomorrow and wear your jeans? You could run and play and do all sorts of things, and you wouldn't have to worry about getting one of your pretty dresses dirty or torn."

The child looked up with pleading, tear-filled eyes and shook her head.

Carly stroked a hand down Amanda's head. "Ah, honey. It's hard, isn't it? I know just how you feel. In fact, I shouldn't have even asked you to give up your dresses for jeans. Not when I still can't eat ice cream."

With a curious frown, Amanda cocked her head.

Carly took a deep breath. She didn't particularly enjoy opening a vein and bleeding in front of someone, but this time it was important. It would, she believed, help Amanda. Still, it took a long moment for the words to come.

"I was nine when my daddy died," she said softly. "I remember that day so well."

Amanda stared at her, wide-eyed.

"I had thrown a fit after dinner because there wasn't any ice cream for dessert. Daddy decided to get me some." She pressed her lips together and waited for composure. Even without closing her eyes, she could see her father's irritated grin, see him toss his car keys in the air and catch them, see him head out the front door that last fateful time. "He had a heart attack while he was at the store. He never came home again. I haven't been able to eat ice cream since."

By the time Carly finished the story, both she and Amanda had tears trickling down their cheeks.

"Look at us," Carly managed to say with a choked laugh. "Here we are, crying again, this time over blue jeans and ice cream."

Amanda gave a tremulous smile and wiped her cheeks with the flat of her palm.

"There you two are."

Tyler's voice from the doorway made them both jerk.

"Ah, jeez, you guys." He wore a pained look. "Not again. You trying to flood the place? What's wrong?"

"Flood the place," Carly said to Amanda with disgust. "What does he know? We're just letting go of a little sadness, that's all," she told Tyler. "We've got to let it out now and then, so it won't choke us. Right, Amanda?"

Amanda gave Tyler a shy smile and nodded.

"And it feels good to get rid of all that sad ol' stuff, doesn't it?" Carly asked.

Again, Amanda nodded.

Tyler shook his head and gave them a wink. "Well, if it feels good, you two go right ahead and cry all you want. Cry buckets and buckets if you want."

Amanda gave a breathy giggle.

"Nah." Carly grinned. "We feel about as good as can be right now. We probably won't need to cry again for, oh, maybe a whole day or two, right, Amanda?"

Amanda giggled again and nodded.

Carly smiled and kissed the girl's nose. "You have sweet dreams, honey. I'll see you in the morning."

Amanda gave her a smile in return, and Carly left to give the girl and her father time for their private good-night. Feeling a little shaky after her confession about the ice cream, she headed for the coffeepot in the kitchen. A few minutes later, Tyler joined her there and poured himself a cup.

"Did you make that up?" he asked.

"Make what up?"

"That business with the ice cream."

Carly raised her brows. "Eavesdropping, were you?"

"Shamelessly. Do you or don't you eat ice cream?"

She gave him a sad smile. "Afraid not. That's the one thing I haven't been able to conquer."

He gave her a crooked smile. "I didn't know ice cream was something to be conquered."

"Not the ice cream itself. The guilt. If I hadn't demanded my ice cream, my daddy would still be alive."

Tyler eyed her while taking a sip of coffee. "That's ridiculous, you know."

"Of course I know, in my head. But somewhere down inside, the little girl in me still thinks I don't deserve to eat ice cream anymore."

"Like Amanda doesn't deserve to wear jeans and play outside?"

"Exactly."

"Great. How are you supposed to help Amanda, when you haven't been able to help yourself?"

Carly didn't care for his sarcastic tone, but she really couldn't blame him for it. "Maybe," she told him softly, "Amanda and I can help each other."

"Is she going to give the jeans a try?" he asked softly.

"Not yet," Carly said. "I didn't really expect her to give up her dresses so easily. To her, that's the same as giving up her mother. It's going to take her some time to realize the one has nothing to do with the other. But at least now, maybe she'll think about it."

Tyler grinned. "Maybe you should make another bet with her. If she'll wear jeans, you'll eat ice cream."

"Cute, Barnett. I don't think you want to witness a replay of what happened the last time I tried to make myself eat plain vanilla."

"What happened?"

"I tossed my cookies—or in this case, my ice cream— all over the kid who dared me to eat it."

He rolled his eyes. "You're right. I'll pass on that."

Tyler hated haying. Not because it was so damned exhausting—everything on the ranch was hard work. Cutting, raking, baling and stacking ton after ton of hay used a different set of muscles than most of the work he normally did, and he came home sore every night, but it was the

soreness of honest labor. Haying wasn't harder than everything else, only a different kind of hard.

It wasn't the rush to get the hay baled and stacked before
the rain came that he hated. A rancher was always at odds
with nature, racing it, fighting it, praying for it to help him
out for once instead of work against him. The race against
the rain was just part of the challenge.

It wasn't sitting hour after hour on a damned tractor
when he much preferred to be on the back of a horse that
made him hate haying, either, although it came close.

No, it wasn't any of those things that made Tyler detest
haying season. It was the damned chaff. God, but he hated
getting those tiny, prickly, itchy bits of hay inside every
single inch of his clothes. Most particularly he hated getting
the damned stuff down the back of his shirt. It made him
itch and squirm, turned his mood black and his language
foul. Every year it took him a good week and a half to
settle down and live with it. Even then, he spent each day
grinding his teeth until he could shower off.

But this year, as if the chaff wasn't enough, Tyler had a
whole new reason to hate haying. It kept him away from
Carly. He didn't realize at first why his mood was more
foul than usual. After all, it wasn't as though he spent much
time with her during the day. But he was used to working
in the barn and corrals with the horses, the house always
within sight, used to knowing Carly was only a few yards
away. Knowing that if he could think up a good enough
excuse, he could walk to the house and see her any time
he wanted.

And it wasn't as though haying kept him away from the
house all day. It could have, probably should have, but he
couldn't afford to let his prime cutting horses, nor the
horses he was training for others, go an entire month without working. So he spent the mornings haying and the afternoons working and training the horses.

As compromises went, it wasn't ideal—not for getting
the hay in on time, not for getting the best results from the

horses—but it was necessary. A ranch was only worth as much as its hay, and at a need of one and half tons per cow, it took a hell of a lot of hay to see the fifteen hundred or so head of cattle remaining after the fall sale through a Wyoming winter.

But he didn't like not being able to see Carly when the mood struck him. Not that he'd allowed himself to stop work every time he felt like seeing her. Still, he had known she was near. That fact had helped him keep his head on straight.

He wondered how much longer he could keep a rein on his emotions around her. He had agreed to be friends, and he liked being her friend, but he wanted more. Dammit, he wanted a hell of a lot more.

He wanted to touch her without seeing caution crowd the laughter from her eyes. He wanted to taste her, hold her, kiss her. And even then, he knew he would want more.

After haying. He would give her until after haying was over. Then he would see if they could be more than friends.

Carly felt the rush of haying season in the very air around her. Every morning the men hurried through breakfast to get to the fields by sunup. When she loaded the pickup with food and drove it to them at noon, she felt their strained patience with the need to stop and eat.

At night, when they finally came in around eight-thirty or nine, she felt the rush of their thoughts—would the clouds building in the west dump rain on the fresh-cut hay and force them to wait until it dried before they could bale? Yet even though their thoughts flew, their bodies were weighted down with exhaustion.

And poor Tyler, trying to help with the haying in the morning, work his horses in the afternoons and evenings, then catch up on paperwork after supper, and still spend time with his daughter.

It was too much. He was trying to do the work of two men. At least in one area, she could help him if he would let her. With determination, she poured him a fresh cup of coffee and marched to the office, where he sat hunched over the computer keyboard. A pile of invoices sat next to him, along with the ledger-style checkbook.

"More coffee?" she offered.

Tyler looked up with a surprised smile. "Yes. Please." His fatigue was evident in the way he slumped in the chair and rubbed the back of his neck. "Any interruption to this chore is appreciated."

"You're not having fun?"

He reached for the coffee and shot her a wry look. "I detest bookkeeping."

"Actually," Carly said, "I rather enjoy it. I could do it for you, if you want. That is…if you…trust me."

"Why wouldn't I trust you?"

Carly felt her cheeks sting, but refused to lower her gaze. "Because of Blalock's."

"What does Blalock's have to do with whether or not I trust you?"

"Come on, Tyler, you know—"

"Did you steal from them?"

"Of course not!"

"Then why are we talking about them?"

"Because I just offered to do your bookkeeping," she snapped back.

"Yeah." For a moment, his eyes lit. Then he sat back and rubbed his neck again. "But it wouldn't be fair. I'm not paying you for bookkeeping."

"No, but what you are paying me for doesn't fill a whole day. And what to you is a chore, to me would be a treat. I'm really very good at it, you know."

A slow grin spread across his face. "If you're sure you don't mind."

"If I did, I wouldn't have offered."

"Well, before you change your mind, come stand behind me and watch while I finish these entries."

Pleased that he'd agreed to accept her help, Carly

rounded the desk and stood behind his high-backed desk chair. The computer program he used was not one she'd seen before, but it was a straightforward accounting program. She knew she wouldn't have any trouble with it.

While explaining the ins and outs of the software and how he wanted items listed, Tyler kept rubbing the back of his neck.

Finally Carly brushed his hands aside. "That's enough to get me started. You can show me the rest tomorrow night." She put her fingers to the sides of his neck and massaged.

Tyler let out a loud breath. "God, that feels good."

His neck and shoulder muscles were so tight she had to really work at them. It was several minutes before she felt them begin to loosen.

Tyler closed his eyes and let his head drop forward. It felt so damned good to have her touching him. Her small hands were warm and gentle, yet kneaded his tight muscles with surprising strength.

With his eyes closed, he acknowledged how much he wanted to feel her hands on other parts of him—all the other parts of him. And if he didn't stop thinking like that immediately, he would likely do something stupid, like repeat his thoughts aloud.

"You're amazing," he said.

"How's that?"

"You give a great massage, you're a terrific cook, the house is always neat and clean, Amanda adores you and I..." He let his words trail off, appalled at what he'd almost said.

"And you?" she prompted softly, her hands working their way down his back.

I have the hots for you. But he couldn't say that. No way. It was too crude. It was too...accurate. It was too soon.

"And you?" she prompted again.

"And I," he said leaning his head back to look at her, "am glad you're here."

She smiled. "So am I."

"Are you?" He turned his chair to face her. The motion pulled his shoulders out of range of her hands. "I know you didn't want to come here, wouldn't have come if you'd had any other choice."

"I know," she said. "But I'm still glad I came."

And she *was* glad, Carly admitted to herself. She was glad the decision had been taken out of her hands and that she'd been forced to come home with Tyler and Amanda. She liked living on the Bar B.

She liked taking care of Amanda and the big old house. She liked cooking for hungry men who appreciated her efforts. It beat the dickens out of slinging hamburgers for hurried customers, or cooking for one, which, more and more over the past few months, had consisted of microwaving a lonely frozen dinner.

She liked the huge, vast landscape that went on forever outside the house. She liked the smell of horse and hay and fresh air that clung to Tyler when he came in every night.

And she liked Tyler Barnett. Truly liked him. She enjoyed his company, his smiles, his laughter. The love in his eyes for his daughter moved her every time she saw it.

If only…

Famous last words. If only she could forget the way his lips had felt brushing against hers. If only she could deny how badly she wanted his strong arms around her. If only…if only she wasn't starting to care entirely too much for a man she would never see again once her work with Amanda was finished.

Chapter Seven

Carly's taking over the bookkeeping didn't keep Tyler completely out of the office, but it cut the hours he normally spent there more than in half. He did still have to take care of his breeding and training records, but when it came to paying bills, all he had to do these days was sign the checks Carly wrote for him. The new routine allowed him more time at night with Amanda than he would otherwise have had during haying.

It also gave him more time with Carly.

And his dad. Arthur's mood, when it came to Carly, seemed to have mellowed somewhat. At least the man was no longer openly hostile toward her.

"Ha. That's my railroad," Arthur said to Carly. "Pay up, city slicker."

No, Tyler thought, not hostile at all.

Carly paid up, but she had rolled doubles, so she took another turn. Tyler was so busy watching the fierce concentration on her face that he didn't pay any attention where her game piece landed until after Amanda had rolled. By then it was too late.

"You cheated," he cried.

Carly gave him a snooty look. "I did not. You stared right at my piece. It's not my fault if you own so many properties you can't remember which ones they are."

Amanda grinned at him, while his dad gave him a disgusted look.

"I know which ones I own," Tyler grumbled. "My brain just forgot to remind me, that's all."

"Yeah." The expression on Carly's face changed, as though some bright idea had just crossed her mind. She gave Amanda a quick look, then glanced away. "The brain can play all sorts of tricks on us."

She was being so deliberately casual, Tyler wondered what was going on in *her* brain. To see where she was headed with the topic, he said, "Yeah, the brain is a strange thing."

She straightened a stack of yellow bills on her side of the playing board. "It sure is. I've read a couple of books about it." She glanced at Amanda again. "Did you know your own brain can keep secrets from you?"

Tyler felt a prickling sensation along the back of his neck. Whatever Carly was up to had something to do with Amanda. "What kinds of secrets?" he asked as offhandedly as he could manage.

"Oh, you know, like where you put something so you'd be sure to find it later. Of course, usually you can never find it, but your brain knows where it is. It just keeps it a secret from you."

"And maybe," Arthur asked cautiously, "when you say something you really hadn't planned to say, or didn't mean, your brain knows why you said it, even if you don't?"

"Exactly," Carly cried. She fluffed Amanda's bangs with her fingers. "Why, I'll bet Amanda's brain even knows why her voice doesn't work. Her ol' noggin's just keeping it a secret, that's all."

All the animation in Amanda's face drained away. She looked at Carly with such sadness in her eyes, Tyler wanted to cry.

"Hey," Carly said to her softly, "it's all right, honey. Brains do this sort of thing all the time. All we have to do is figure out why it's keeping the secret, then maybe it will tell us why you can't talk. Once we know that, well, everything will be a snap. We'll know what to do then."

Amanda shook her head slowly, her eyes still on Carly.

"No?" Carly asked. "No, you don't think your brain will tell us the secret?"

Amanda shook her head harder this time. No, that wasn't what she'd meant.

"You mean you think your brain doesn't know the reason you can't talk?"

Amanda's brow furrowed with frustration as she shook her head again. She jabbed her chest then her head with her forefinger.

"I don't understand, honey."

Amanda repeated the gesture again, pointing to her chest then her head.

Tyler felt his pulse race. His mouth went dry. "Amanda, are you trying to say that you know why you can't talk?"

She turned her big, sad gaze on him and nodded her head slowly up and down.

"Can you tell us?" Carly asked softly.

Amanda's answer was to point at the ceiling.

Tyler looked to Carly and his dad. Both shook their heads.

"We don't understand, sweetpea," he said.

Amanda heaved a sigh and frowned. At least while concentrating on how to communicate with them, she didn't look so profoundly sad. That was something, anyway, Tyler thought.

Her gaze darted around the room, then lit on the small bookcase under the stairs. She jumped up and ran to it, then returned lugging the big black family Bible, which she dropped on his lap.

"I don't get it," Arthur said.

Amanda frowned harder, then pressed her palms together as if in prayer.

"You prayed for your voice to come back?" Carly guessed.

Amanda shook her head.

"The reason you can't talk has something to do with the Bible?" Tyler asked.

Yes, Amanda nodded emphatically. She hefted the Bible off his lap and carried it to the floor, where she started flipping through pages.

What the devil—oops, Tyler thought. Poor choice of words, considering. But what in the world was she doing? She hadn't learned to read yet. She was only six, would start first grade at the end of the month.

The thought of Amanda being old enough to go to school momentarily distracted Tyler, until he realized what she was doing.

The Bible was one of the old King James versions, complete with gold lettering long since worn away from the pebbly leather cover, which itself had been rubbed almost smooth generations ago. Inside the front cover, in a variety of handwriting styles, rode the list of births and deaths in the Barnett family, starting with the birth of Tyler's great-grandfather, in the spidery scrawl of his great-great-grandmother.

The other thing this Bible contained aside from scriptures was pictures. Elaborate, elegant drawings of several of the major events in the Bible, like Noah and the Ark, the Sermon on the Mount, Christ on the Cross.

And the picture where Amanda stopped. The one of an old bearded man in long, flowing robes. Holding the earth in his cupped hands.

Amanda pointed at the picture and looked up solemnly.

Carly sucked in a breath. "Amanda? Do you mean...you can't talk because God won't let you?"

Tyler felt his chest tighten.

Lower lip trembling, Amanda nodded.

Tyler squeezed his eyes shut and, inappropriate though it was, thought, *Ah, hell.*

"Amanda?" Carly waited for the girl to look at her. "Why won't God let you talk?"

Tyler scowled. If she had an answer, Amanda couldn't explain, not without being able to talk. But she surprised him.

She pointed a finger at herself, then rubbed the other forefinger across the first one, in a "shame on you," or in this case, "shame on me" motion.

"Ah, baby," he said, reaching for her.

Carly motioned him back, her eyes on Amanda. "You did something bad, so God won't let you talk anymore? Is that it?"

A tear spilled down one cheek as Amanda nodded. Then another tear came, and another.

To hell with Carly and her questions. She'd really broken through to Amanda tonight, and he was glad, but that was enough for now. His daughter was hurting.

Tyler scooped Amanda into his arms and hugged her tight. "It's all right, baby, it's all right. We'll fix it, I promise. God never stays mad for very long, you know. Especially not at pretty little sweetpeas. It'll be all right."

Carly swallowed around the lump in her throat. So. God was punishing Amanda. It all fit. So classic, it could have been in a textbook. Or straight from Carly's own past.

It didn't matter that Amanda was wrong about God. It wasn't God who thought she'd been bad, it was Amanda herself. It would have to be Amanda's own forgiveness of herself that lifted the silence from the child's life. But now that her feelings of guilt were out in the open, they could be dealt with.

The battle wasn't over, not by a long shot. But this skirmish had been a milestone. The rest would come. In time.

Tyler carried Amanda upstairs. Amid her tears and silent hiccups, he helped her get ready for bed then lay down beside her and held her until long after she'd cried herself to sleep.

God, but he wanted to cry, too. What could a baby like Amanda have possibly done to make herself feel so damned guilty?

Nothing. There was absolutely nothing Amanda could have done to justify what she was unwittingly putting herself through.

Yet in her mind, he knew, she was guilty of some terrible sin. It was plain that she believed she'd been so bad she didn't deserve to talk again. She hadn't hesitated in letting them know, once Carly started asking the right questions, that God was punishing her. Not for the first time, Tyler wondered what his little girl's life had really been like in Chicago.

She must have been told, more than once, that God punished bad little girls. Where would she have learned that? In church? At home?

Not from Deborah, that was certain. Deborah had never been much of a churchgoer; she'd only gone to church at Big Piney out of duty, because the rest of the family went.

Deborah's parents?

He sighed. He didn't know them well enough to answer his own question, but he didn't think they were into preaching.

With another sigh, he rose from Amanda's bed and quietly made his way back downstairs. His dad had turned in, but Carly was sitting at the kitchen table with a cup of coffee.

Amanda wasn't asleep. She heard her daddy go downstairs, heard his deep voice, Carly's quiet answer. She didn't want her daddy to be unhappy, and he said he wanted her to be able to talk, but she wasn't sure she ever would. Besides, she had learned that what grown-ups said wasn't what they meant.

"Play that new piece you learned on the piano for your grandfather, Amanda."

But Mother hadn't meant it, because Amanda had been only halfway through the song when Mother had stopped her. "That's enough, dear. Run along to your room, now."

And her mother had always told her to talk, but she never really meant it.

"This is your uncle Frank. Say hi to him, Amanda."

"Say hello to Jerry, honey."

"Your daddy's on the phone. Come talk to him."

But every time, her mother hadn't meant it, not really. Every time Amanda had spoken to all those people, her mother had come right back a minute later and told her to be quiet.

Amanda had always tried to be good, she really had. She had tried and tried to do what Mother told her. Except for that last time. That one last time.

"No, you cannot call your father. You don't need to talk to him. He'll be here tomorrow to get you."

"But, Mother, I—"

"Be quiet. I have a party to go to, and I'm going to be late."

"I only wanted—"

"One more word out of you, young lady, and I'll just drive off and never come back. I don't want a little girl who can't be quiet when she's told."

"But, Mother—"

"Good night, Amanda. I'm leaving. And don't you dare try to call your father while I'm gone."

"I hate you!" Amanda had cried. "I hate you, I hate you!"

She hadn't meant it, of course, but she had been so *mad*.

Mother *never* let her call Daddy. Amanda had only wanted to make sure he was still coming for her. What if he got busy and forgot she was waiting for him?

Just like she waited for her mother later that night. And waited. And waited.

But her mother had said she wouldn't come home again if Amanda wasn't quiet. Mother had kept her word. She drove off that night and never came back. Never would come back. All because Amanda hadn't kept quiet.

Amanda swallowed hard at the memory and squeezed her eyes shut tight. She didn't want her daddy or Carly or Grandad to hear her cry again. She had cried enough that next day when they told her Mother wasn't coming home again. Had cried so hard her throat had hurt. She loved her mother, wanted her to come home. She hadn't meant those awful words she'd yelled at her. She hadn't!

But when she had tried to tell Grandmother and Grandfather the next day how sorry she was for saying such a terrible thing, her voice had been no more than a hoarse croak. She had tried again, and the croak had grown fainter and fainter, until no sound came out at all.

Then had come the doctors, one after the other, poking at her, prodding her, poking long, fat sticks down her throat. They all said she would talk again as soon as her throat was well. But Amanda knew better. She had been so bad, yelling at her mother like that, that she knew God wasn't going to let her talk. Not for a long, long time. Maybe never again.

When Tyler came down from putting Amanda to bed, Carly ached at the pain she saw in his eyes. He walked to the counter, where he braced both hands and hung his head. She couldn't stand to see him hurt. She left her seat and went to him, reached out for him.

He turned and pulled her fiercely into his arms and buried his face where her neck met her shoulder. "God, how could this happen?'' His voice was ragged with emotion. "How could she possibly think…''

"It happens," Carly said softly, her arms holding him tight. It felt good, holding him against her, feeling him hold her. So good. His solid strength surrounded and supported her. Yet, in the quivering of his arms she felt his need to be held.

He turned his head and pressed his lips against her neck. Carly felt herself grow weak with longing.

Tyler tasted and nibbled, and tasted again, unable to get enough. He wanted, needed more of her than just her arms. He wanted her mouth against his, her bare skin beneath his hands. He needed her caring, her wisdom, her patience. "Carly.''

She heard the plea as he trailed openmouthed kisses up her neck and along her jaw. She should stop him. She should pull away and put distance and sanity between them.

But when his mouth took hers so fiercely, she tasted his need and was lost. When was the last time anyone had really needed her? Right here, right now, this strong, capable man made her feel essential to his very survival by the way his hands splayed possessively across her back, the way his tongue lured hers, the way he moaned, sounding desperate and needy and yearning. For her.

And she gave. With her arms and mouth and heart, she offered him everything he asked for, and more. She kept giving until he tore his mouth from hers and gasped for breath, his eyes closed, expression tortured.

Carly pressed her head against his chest. His hand came up to keep her there. He laid his head against hers and held her close. They stood that way for long moments, letting lungs and heart rates ease, letting sense return. The only sound was the low hum of the refrigerator in the corner.

Finally Tyler squeezed her once, hard, then loosened his hold and raised his head to look at her. "So what happens now? We still have no idea what it is Amanda thinks she's done that's so terrible.''

Carly wasn't offended by his failure to mention what had just happened between them. Indeed, she was grateful. His pain for Amanda had brought him into her arms. She understood his need to talk about his daughter, just as she had understood his need a moment ago for solace.

Carly sighed. "I know." He was right, they still didn't know what made Amanda believe she'd committed a terrible sin.

Reluctant to lose his touch, yet knowing he no longer needed her in that way, Carly stepped from his embrace. The loss of his warmth made her shiver. "Finding out what she thinks may be next to impossible."

"Because she can't tell us," Tyler said flatly.

"Right. But she doesn't have to tell us, not exactly."

"What do you mean?"

She met his troubled gaze squarely. "All she has to do is forgive herself. It doesn't matter if we never learn the whole truth. She has to believe she's not as bad as she thinks she is."

Tyler looked lost, hurt. Angry. "How do we do that?"

"Patiently," Carly told him. "One step at a time."

Tyler, however, was not a patient man. Amid memories of how Carly had felt in his arms, how she had tasted on his lips, the honest, generous way she had offered herself to him, he couldn't help but think of what had driven him to her that night.

Amanda felt guilty about something. He needed to know what. The next afternoon, after Carly reported what they'd learned to Dr. Sanders, Tyler called his former in-laws and told them what had happened.

"What I want to know is, why does she think God punishes bad little girls?"

"Oh, my word," Earline Tomlinson said faintly. "Nesta."

Tyler felt the muscles across his shoulders knot. "Who," he said slowly, "is Nesta?"

"She was our housekeeper until shortly after Deborah... after Deborah's accident. She was forever saying things like that."

"Things like what?"

He heard Earline swallow. "Things like, if you don't wash your hands before dinner, God will get you. That sort of thing."

Tyler ground his teeth. "You let an employee talk that way to your granddaughter?"

"Oh, my word, Tyler, that was just Nesta's way. We never, none of us, thought anything of it."

"Well, think about it," he snarled. "Think about what Amanda could have done that she could think was bad enough for God to never let her talk again."

"I can't...can't imagine anything. She was always so good, so sweet. I'll...I'll talk to Howard. Maybe he'll remember something...oh, my word, Tyler, I'm so sorry. But I'm so glad you've found this out. We were wrong not to get Amanda into counseling. I see that now. We just never believed it could be anything like this."

Tyler let out a sigh of frustration.

"Wherever you found such a good therapist for her, I'm pleased. So pleased."

Because he had no reason not to, Tyler told Earline Tomlinson about Carly. And immediately wished he hadn't.

"Living with you? Treating Amanda? And she's not even a doctor? Tyler, what is going on out there? Have you lost your mind?"

"Whatever is going on," he answered, "it's working. Amanda's not talking yet, but she is coming out of it, Earline. Carly's good for her."

"Even so..."

He knew he'd regret it, but he asked anyway, "Even so, what?"

He listened to Earline dance around various vague objections for several minutes before she finally came out with it. "And living with you? No, I can't think that's a good idea at all. What type of impression is that leaving with Amanda?''

"You're way off base, Earline. I've got to get back to work. You and Howard see if you can remember anything Amanda might have done that she'd think was bad. If you come up with anything, give me a call."

As quickly as possible, Tyler hung up the phone. Why hadn't he kept his mouth shut about Carly?

With a curse, he slapped his hat on and headed out the back door. His marriage might have been short-lived, but in-laws, it seemed, were forever.

For days after that kiss in the kitchen, Carly lectured herself. It had been an isolated incident, not likely to ever be repeated. She understood that Tyler had been especially vulnerable that night. Any warm pair of arms, any set of feminine lips offering comfort would have done. It hadn't been personal. He hadn't needed *her*. She'd merely been available.

Finally, slowly, her arguments started sinking into her hard skull and she was able to stop reliving that kiss.

Except, of course, for odd moments now and then. Like when she caught the sound of Tyler's voice from somewhere outside. Or when he stepped into a room where she was. Or when she closed her eyes. Or when...

Damnation, Carly Sue, just stop it. Tyler hadn't meant anything by kissing her. They were friends, that was all, and he had needed a friend that night. She was glad she'd been there for him, but it was over.

So there.

During the second week of haying, Carly decided it was time to open her own checking account at the local Big Piney bank. If she wanted to buy something in town, she was sure the area merchants would prefer a local check rather than one from her San Francisco account. So, after feeding the men out in the field at noon, Carly and Amanda took the Blazer and headed for town.

She wasn't worried about getting lost. The area was simple to navigate. If she turned right at the end of the ranch road, she would end up in the Wyoming Mountains. If she turned left, Big Piney. Pretty simple.

Yet as Carly took in the vast openness of the sage-dotted plains around her, she couldn't help but compare this trip to the bank with the ones she made in San Francisco. There she'd had a four-block walk down sidewalks crowded with tourists, shoppers and businesspeople rushing in and out of buildings or dashing to catch a cab or cable car.

This drive, she decided, was infinitely better than the walk had ever been.

Everything went fine at the bank. Amanda stood next to Carly's chair while Carly filled out forms. People were polite, said her paperwork was in order. Until she endorsed the paychecks she'd been collecting from Tyler.

The woman behind the desk raised her brow in horror. "Good heavens. What is he paying you for?"

Carly raised a brow of her own. She supposed it was because Big Piney was a small town and most everyone knew everyone else's business. Still, her business with Tyler was no one else's business, for heaven's sake.

"Excuse me," the woman said. She rose from her chair and carried the Bar B checks behind the counter, where she showed them to another woman and a man.

The three huddled together over the checks and whispered. Occasionally one of them would look over at Carly with an odd expression, almost...disapproval.

Finally the woman waiting on Carly returned to her desk.

"Is there a problem?" Carly asked.

"None at all," the woman answered with a breezy manner. "You're the one Tyler hired to help little Amanda, aren't you? The one living out at the Bar B. And how are you doing, you sweet thing?" she asked Amanda.

Carly might have felt more comfortable had the woman's smile reached her eyes. In answer, she merely nodded.

"I had no idea things like that cost so much. Although I'm sure it's none of my business."

"I'm sure," Carly muttered.

The minute she had her new temporary checks in hand, Carly nudged Amanda out the door and fled for the safely of the ranch.

Twice she'd been to town now, and twice she'd been the subject of whispers, the recipient of questions, of suspicious, sometimes hostile looks. No more. She wouldn't go again unless forced.

When they returned to the ranch, Amanda lay down for a nap.

Carly decided to finish the filing in the office. She was looking for a misplaced receipt from the feed store, which, according to the records, should have been in the file, but wasn't. That's when she ran across the notebook.

It was an accident, really. If it hadn't had several pieces of paper sticking out of it, any one of which could have been the missing receipt, she probably would never have opened the notebook.

What she found there made her slightly sick to her stomach. It made her feel guilty. It made her whopping mad.

She didn't say anything to Tyler until Friday night when he went into the office to sign the checks she'd written. Since that night in the kitchen when he'd kissed her, she hadn't exactly been throwing herself in his path. Truthfully she'd been shying away from him.

Which was silly, on her part. Not once, by word, deed, or look, had Tyler hinted he even remembered kissing her.

A devastating thought, yet not surprising.

But this was something she was not willing to put off. She followed him into the office and watched him sort through the checks she'd written.

"You forgot one," he said.

"No, I didn't."

"Carly," he said with a smile, "you forgot to pay yourself."

She shook her head. "I'm not taking any more of your money."

Looking bewildered, he asked, "What the devil are you talking about?"

She counted slowly to ten. Twice. "You let me assume you had money to burn, that you wouldn't miss two thousand dollars a week."

He eyed her sideways. "What's this all about?"

"It's about a new pickup, an enclosed horse trailer, a new barn, a champion mare for your breeding program, a whole damned list of things you've been saving for for years."

Tyler's brow arched. "What's any of that got to do with your paycheck?"

"I told you from the beginning you were offering too much money," she said.

"You also made it clear that money was the only reason you agreed to come." He flipped open the checkbook and scrawled out her paycheck.

"I won't take it," she told him.

He tore the check loose and closed the book. "Yes, you will." He reached across the desk and placed the check in her palm.

"No," she said firmly, tossing the check back to him, "I won't."

"Dammit, Carly, just take it." He slapped it back on her side of the desk.

"I won't." She shot it back at him. "And if you try to give it back to me, I'll tear it up."

"Why are you doing this? You can't seriously expect me to let you work without pay."

"You've already paid me plenty for a six-month job. Those things on that list are obviously important to you, to the whole ranch."

"We've survived this long without them. My daughter is more important."

"Amanda isn't the issue. You know I'm not about to leave her. I'm here, and I'm staying until she's talking or until you throw me out. I feel like a leech, taking all that money from you."

"That's ridiculous. We agreed on the amount." With his eyes narrowed and his jaw flexing, he stood and leaned over to slam the check onto the desk before her with his palm. "Take it."

"I—" she tore the check in half "—will—" she stacked the pieces and tore *them* in half "—not."

Tyler's jaw bunched. "It's not up for discussion." He flipped open the checkbook and started writing again. "I'm going to pay you what we agreed on, and you're going to take it."

"You *need* that money, Tyler."

"Damn it, Carly, Prancer can make that much money in less than one season in stud fees alone. I'll make it up next spring. I promised this to you, and you're going to take it."

"What will I do with that much money?" she cried.

"What will you do without it?"

"I'll do just fine."

"Gonna go home and get your old job at Burger Barrel back? Just shut up and take the damned check, Carly." He held it out to her.

She stood and backed toward the door. "No." With that, she whirled. And ran smack into Arthur.

"What's all this yellin' about?" he asked.

Carly snarled at him. "Does he get all that stubborn, stiff-necked pride from you?" She didn't wait for Arthur to answer, but fled upstairs to her room and closed the door. Firmly.

"Doesn't want your money, huh?" Arthur stared at the empty doorway before facing Tyler. "Maybe I was wrong about that girl."

Tyler widened his eyes and cupped a hand to his ear.

"What was that? I must be hearing things. I could have sworn I heard you say you were—"

"Stuff it, kid."

Tyler chuckled, then sobered. "You're right, though. You were wrong about her."

"I'm glad. We need that new barn and pickup, and you've been pining after one of those fancy enclosed horse trailers for years. And if you don't get your hands on Magnificent Cutter soon, somebody else is gonna snap her up. That's one fine mare, I'm tellin' ya."

"Damn the damned mare."

"You mean you're still gonna pay Carly?"

Tyler leveled a look at his father. "I gave my word. Would you go back on your word?"

Arthur opened his mouth, then sighed and shut it. "No."

"There you have it."

"Well, hell, how you gonna pay her if she won't take the money?"

Tyler shrugged and rose from his chair. "She opened a checking account in town this week. I'll call the bank Monday and have them transfer the money directly to her." He stepped around his father and made for the door.

"Where you going?"

"I'm going to try to calm her down."

Arthur gave a rueful shake of his head. "That girl does have a temper on her, I'll say that much."

Tyler frowned. Yes, she had a temper. She could fire up for Amanda's sake. She could rip into him because she thought he was going to impoverish himself. Yet she'd let that witch in Union Square that day walk all over her.

On the other hand, she was the warmest, most giving woman he'd ever known. Just the memory of what she'd given him when he'd kissed her was enough to turn his knees to rubber.

Now she acted as though they'd never shared anything personal at all, that he hadn't needed, that she hadn't filled those needs.

He shook his head. He didn't understand.

And he didn't for the life of him understand what had just happened in his office, why she had been so angry.

By the time he made it upstairs, the door to Carly's room stood open. From the bathroom at the end of the hall, he heard the shower running.

Tyler checked on Amanda and found her sprawled across her bed sound asleep. He tugged the blanket from beneath one outflung leg and pulled it over her. With a brush of his finger across her silken cheek, he whispered, "This lady we found to help you, she's really something, isn't she? She's helping you, but I think she's driving me crazy. Sleep tight, sweetpea."

He dropped a kiss on Amanda's brow, then closed the door partway when he left. As he paused in the hall trying to decide what to do next, the bathroom door opened.

Carly froze in midstep, one hand on the doorknob, the other raised to fluff the back of her damp hair.

Chapter Eight

Tyler bit back an oath. Rather than angry, she looked startled. And so damned vulnerable. Her hair was damp, her face scrubbed clean. Her skin looked fresh and dewy and...delicious. Her mouth...oh, Lord, her mouth practically begged for his.

Her blue terry-cloth robe ended several inches above her knees, leaving those long, long legs bare to his gaze.

He felt his mouth dry out. By the time his gaze reached her feet, her toes were curled under. He wanted to smile, but couldn't.

He had no business getting near her when she looked like this. No business at all. Yet he couldn't walk away.

"Can we talk?" he asked.

She looked down at herself, then up at him. "Now?"

No, he thought. Not now, not here. He'd never be able to keep his hands to himself. "I'll buy you a cup of coffee downstairs."

She gave him a hesitant nod. "Let me get some clothes on."

Please, he thought fervently. "I'll meet you in the kitchen."

When he turned and started down the stairs, his heart was racing. He was being ridiculous, he knew. It wasn't as if she'd been naked, for crying out loud. He'd been around women wearing a lot less than that robe and hadn't had this kind of trouble with his pulse, or his breathing.

But then, those women hadn't been Carly.

Carly, who knew how to ease away his pain and give him something infinitely precious in return.

Carly, who he strongly suspected hadn't had a stitch on beneath that robe. One simple tug on the tie at her waist...

Down, boy.

By the time she cautiously entered the kitchen five minutes later, Tyler felt he had his unruly emotions and his equally unruly body under control. That she had on jeans and a sweatshirt along with those fuzzy house shoes with teeth and eyes helped. Sort of. Except the jeans were so tight...

"What did you want to talk about, as if I couldn't guess?"

Tyler cleared his throat and offered her a cup of coffee. "Let's sit down." He pulled out a chair from the kitchen table and offered her a seat.

Still eyeing him warily, she sat.

He took the chair across from her. To stall for time, since he really had no idea what to say, he sipped his coffee. He'd thought to somehow calm her anger, but she didn't seem angry any longer.

"What do you want?" she asked again.

He studied her shiny-clean face and gnawed on the inside of his jaw. "I guess I want to know why you were so mad earlier."

She grimaced and shook her head. "I'm not sure. I think it just all sort of hit me, you know?"

"No, I don't know. All of what hit you?"

This time she used the coffee to stall. Three sips before she finally set her cup down and looked at him. She held his gaze only a moment before looking back to study the steam rising from her cup. "I don't know. Everything. You understood what I was up against in San Francisco. The minute you saw that tow truck, you knew I didn't have any choice but to accept your offer. What you weren't aware of was, it was even worse than that. I'd lost my job at the Burger Barrel the night before."

Tyler winced. Damn, but her back had been against the wall. He hadn't known she'd lost the burger job.

"First there was James, and the accusations at work. I really think that if Walter Blalock hadn't been like a second father to me since I lost my real one, I'd probably be in jail right now."

"You mean if he'd had any real evidence, which he didn't," Tyler told her.

Carly ignored his interruption. "Instead of filing charges, all he did was fire me. Then I couldn't get another job, and when I finally did, I couldn't keep it. I was desperate for money. And there you were, dangling a hundred thousand dollars in my face like the proverbial carrot. Even when I finally gave in and agreed to your job, I felt guilty about accepting that much money. But I convinced myself that anyone who had that much cash to burn obviously wouldn't miss a measly hundred grand. Then you told me about having oil and gas wells, and that just reaffirmed my belief that you'd never miss the money." She shook her head and took another sip of coffee.

"I assume you're getting to the point, here."

"I'm working up to it. I think," she added with a wry smile. "Maybe if I hadn't gone to church with you that Sunday, and if I hadn't gone to the bank this week, I wouldn't have thought much about what my pay was costing you."

"What do church and the bank have to do with anything?"

"Are you kidding? Didn't you see the looks your friends and neighbors were giving me that Sunday? And your family, I might add. Then there were the whispers. Everyone acted like I was some kind of piranha, and I didn't understand why. And the bank—my word. It was just like being back at Blalock's, when everyone thought I'd stolen all that money."

"Carly," he said, totally bewildered. "What are you talking about? These people are my friends. They wouldn't—"

"Oh, yes, they would, and they did. They are. But to their credit, I think they're just trying to look out for you. I assume they think like your father, that I'm just out to take you for a ride. Except for the ones who obviously think you're paying me for something other than what you're really paying me for."

Tyler straightened in his chair. "I think...I hope you're only imagining all this."

She shrugged. "Maybe I am, but I doubt it. At any rate, it hurts, you know? And then I found the notebook and saw that you've been saving that money for years and years for things you want and need. I looked around at what I was doing to earn my pay, and it didn't seem like much. All of a sudden the money, my paycheck, seemed more like charity than earned wages. I guess I just...lost my head."

Tyler wrapped both hands around his coffee cup to keep from reaching for her. "And now that you're not angry, how do you feel about the money?"

She shook her head. "I'm not at all comfortable with having people think you're paying me to...to be here for you, rather than Amanda."

"Assuming you're right, and that's what people really think—which I don't believe for a minute—how is my not paying you going to make any difference, assuming anyone knows I'm not paying you? Won't they feel like they were

right all along? That you're...how did you put it? Here for
me, rather than Amanda? After all, you wouldn't be receiving a salary for keeping house or taking care of
Amanda. You'd just be living here. With me.'' The very
thought sent a shaft of heat through his blood.

Something flickered across Carly's eyes, but before he
could decipher it, she blinked and lowered her gaze. A dry
chuckle came from her throat. ''I hadn't looked at it that
way.''

When she didn't say anything else, Tyler asked, ''Would
you mind telling me exactly what happened at the bank?''

''Nothing, really. Just some disapproving looks and a
snide comment or two.''

It was Tyler's turn to shake his head. ''I don't get it.''

''I think,'' she said slowly, ''your friends are just looking
out for your best interests. I'm an outsider, and this is a
small town.''

''Why didn't you stick your tongue out at them?''

Carly blinked, then choked, then laughed outright. God,
how could he make her laugh when what she wanted to do
was cry?

His chair scraped across the floor and he came around
the table to her side. ''Come here,'' he said softly.

Before she realized his intent, he pulled her into his arms.
She stiffened. ''What are you doing?''

''Relax. I'm holding you.'' He wrapped both arms
around her and pulled her flush against his chest.

Carly shivered at his heat, at how solid he felt. Lord help
her, but she couldn't pull away. ''Tyler, we shouldn't be
doing this. We're supposed to be friends.''

''Hush. We are friends. Friends can offer a little comfort
to each other, can't they? Like you did for me not too long
ago?''

Carly swallowed. ''Is that what you're doing, offering
me comfort?''

''Aren't you comfortable?''

She heard the smile in his voice, but couldn't answer

him. Comfortable wasn't how she felt. She felt hot and tingly and shaky. She felt…scared. She felt…wonderful.

Comfort wasn't what she wanted, either. But when she asked herself what she did want, she was too afraid of the answer to even let the thought form.

"I know we're friends. But every now and then," Tyler said, raising her head with a finger beneath her chin, "I get the strongest urge to feel you against me. Sometimes, like right now, I just get tired of fighting it."

The heat in his eyes sent a shiver down her spine. She tried to pull away.

"No," he whispered. His head lowered until his lips were only a breath away from hers. "Stay. Please."

And then he kissed her. Softly, gently, with so much tenderness, her throat swelled. For a moment Carly thought about resisting. But only for a moment. Less than a fraction of a second.

She didn't want to resist. She closed her eyes and let her arms slip around his waist, let his mouth take full advantage of hers. It was a mistake, but she didn't care.

Tyler didn't think it was a mistake at all. He thought kissing her was the most right thing in the world. When his blood heated and pressure built in his loins, he relished the feeling. He deepened the kiss, wanting more. More of Carly.

Yet even as she responded to his mounting hunger, he felt the difference between this kiss and the last one they shared. Then, she had offered. This time, he was taking. And she was holding part of herself back.

Reluctantly he eased his mouth from hers. He didn't want to push her away or scare her off. Searching her face, he saw wariness and bewilderment in those big brown eyes.

She was going to say something. He could see her gathering her thoughts. Probably something like how they shouldn't have kissed, shouldn't do it again.

He didn't want to hear the words. He came up with some

of his own. "I'm sorry if people are making you feel uneasy about being here."

He read the confusion in her eyes. She hadn't expected him to resume their previous conversation.

Too bad. He wasn't going to give her the chance to say anything just yet. "But Carly, you don't have to take it. If I'd sensed anything at church that day, I would have told them all to take a flying leap. Just because I didn't say it doesn't mean you can't."

His distraction tactics worked. He could tell by the way she gnawed the inside of her jaw that she was once again centered on what he was saying.

"No one has the right to judge you," he told her. "Not here, and not in San Francisco. Why do you let people hurt you?"

She didn't answer, but then Tyler hadn't expected her to. He suspected she didn't realize what she was doing to herself, or why. To him, taking the undeserved criticism seemed a great deal like her inability—or refusal—to eat ice cream. Somewhere inside her, she thought she deserved to get sick if she ate it. And somewhere, buried just as deep, was the belief that she deserved to be hurt. By Mr. Junior Executive, by her best friend, by Tyler's own friends and family.

And it was wrong, dammit.

But that was something she was going to have to figure out on her own. Maybe then, maybe when she learned to stand up for herself, she could look him in the eye and admit she wanted him.

Until then, he vowed to keep her close and win her trust, if he could. Because he knew he never wanted to have to stand back and watch her walk out of his life.

She squirmed in his arms. It was only then that he realized he'd tightened his hold until he was practically crushing her.

"Sorry." He loosened his hold, and she slipped from his embrace, leaving him feeling empty and cold.

* * *

Carly took each stair faster than the one before, until by the time she reached the top she was running. She slipped into her room, quickly closed the door, then leaned back against it and listened to her heart pound in her ears.

She didn't want to like the feel of his arms around her, the solid warmth of his chest against her breasts.

She didn't want to like the feel of his lips against hers. And she didn't want to shiver at just the memory of his taste.

He didn't mean it. He didn't mean for her to read anything more into that kiss than what it had been—an offer of comfort and friendship. He'd even said so before he kissed her. And if he hadn't, the way he resumed their previous conversation while her head and heart were still reeling would have removed any remaining doubt.

Yet heaven help her, she knew if he tried to kiss her again, she would let him.

Stay away from me, Tyler. Please, please stay away from me.

He didn't stay away from her. The minute he walked into the kitchen the next morning for breakfast, she knew things were different between them. Back to the way they'd been before he agreed they should be just friends.

For one thing, every time she looked up, she found him watching her. Sometimes intently, sometimes with a smile. Sometimes he stared blatantly at her lips while running his tongue over his own. When he left with the others for the hay field, she breathed a sigh of relief.

Then she got Amanda up, fed her and started making lunch to carry out to the field. Where she would have to face Tyler again.

Did he know what it did to her to feel his arms around her, much less to taste his lips? Surely he must have noticed the way her heart had pounded against his chest. He couldn't help but have heard her ragged breathing.

The next time he touched her, she honestly didn't know

if she would be able to keep from...from what? Throwing herself at him?

Maybe. Yes, maybe. She wanted him to kiss her again, she admitted. She wanted to feel him, taste him. And she wanted more.

She wanted him to want her.

Lord, help me.

Tyler's behavior at lunch was a continuation of what he'd dealt her that morning. This time, though, it was worse. She couldn't flee to another room when his stares became too intent, and jumping up to retrieve something from the pickup soon became entirely too obvious.

So she sat on the scratchy old army blanket with Amanda and the men and prayed the clouds building in the west would hurry lunch along. Prayed it was only the scorching August heat rather than Tyler's gaze that had sweat beading on her forehead.

Even the men raised an eyebrow or two at the attention Tyler paid her. Arthur, although he'd been nicer to her lately, got that disapproving, speculative look in his eyes again. Willis blushed, but then the boy blushed over just about anything.

Tom watched Tyler and her and laughed out loud. Smitty, bless him, concentrated on tapping tobacco from his pouch onto a cigarette paper and pretended not to notice what was going on.

Neal was the one who made her uneasy. His gaze turned calculating. His smile, more like a leer, sent a tingle of apprehension down her back.

"Come on." Tyler tapped her thigh with the back of his hand. "Let's get you loaded up so you can get back to the house. If we get back to work quick, and if those clouds don't roll in and dump on us, we ought to have the last of the bales stacked by this evening."

"You sticking around this afternoon?" Arthur asked him.

"We're too close to being finished. I don't want to come back out here tomorrow. If I stay now, we might just get it done."

"Good enough," Arthur said.

Carly jumped to her feet, eager for an excuse to move from Tyler's side. She hadn't realized the haying process was drawing to a close. Lately it had seemed as if it would go on forever. But huge stacks of bales now marched across the fields, where before only waving grass had been.

All but the last two stacks, separated from each other by a half-mile stretch of stubbled field, were already fenced to keep out the moose, elk and deer that would soon come down from the mountains. Cattle and horses, too, had to be kept out. They would only be allowed what was given them, as the hay had to last all winter. In Wyoming, winter would be long.

Carly gathered the debris and empty food containers from lunch, and she and Amanda returned to the house. She heard the phone ringing before she had the door open.

"Bar B Ranch," she said into the receiver.

There was a pause, then a man's voice demanding, "Who is this?"

If there was one question a single woman living alone should never answer over the phone to a stranger, it was that one. Carly was single, and she normally lived alone, so her immediate silence was a reflex action. The question invariably came, she knew, from someone who'd dialed a wrong number and had been expecting a different voice. But since she'd answered the phone with the name of the ranch, the man should know already whether or not he had the right number. Her identity should have been irrelevant. His imperious tone didn't do anything to endear him to her, either. With narrowed eyes, she answered his question with one of her own. "Who wants to know?"

"Are you that woman Tyler hired to take care of Amanda?"

The way he said *that woman* made her grit her teeth. "Like I said, who wants to know?"

"Howard Tomlinson." He said it with great impatience, as though any dimwit should have known who he was. "Amanda's grandfather."

Carly wanted to like the man. For Amanda's sake, she really wanted to. But she never had liked being talked down to.

"Now," he said. "As I asked, who am I speaking with?"

That wasn't precisely what he had asked, but she supposed it was close enough. She identified herself. "And yes, I'm the one hired to look after Amanda."

"Let me talk to Tyler."

"I'm afraid he's not in right now."

"Oh, I know he's not usually in the house during the day. Just run out to the corral or the barn or wherever he is and get him."

"I'm sorry, but he's not close enough for me to get him. He's out in the farthest hay field."

"Oh," the man said. "Well, then, run on out there and have him come in and call me. Can you do that?"

Now his voice held a sneer. What was the man's problem? "Is this an emergency?"

"What? No. He called last week while I was out. I just want to talk to him. You get out there and tell him that."

Carly ground her teeth. What a jerk. "I'm afraid I can't," she told him. "The men are trying to get the last of the hay stacked before a storm hits. Tyler may not be back until dark. I'll be glad to take a message out to him, if it's important. I'm sure he'll call you back as soon as he gets in tonight."

"That won't do," he said. "I want to talk to him this afternoon. Now, are you going to go get him?"

Not, "I need to talk to him," but "I want to," Carly thought. What should she do? She knew if all the man wanted to do was visit, Tyler would gnash his teeth at being called in from the field. Yet it wasn't her place to decide what phone calls he should take.

Nor was it her place to run around the ranch delivering messages, either. She had the feeling that Mr. Tomlinson's insistence on her getting Tyler right then was more about control—Mr. Tomlinson's control of her—than any urgent need to speak with Tyler.

Still...

"Well if you have to think about it that hard," the man said, "never mind. Just have him call me when he gets in tonight. And you might want to remember, young woman, that you are a paid employee. I don't imagine he'll be too pleased about not getting my call."

Carly fought the urge to tell him what she thought. Still, Tyler had told her she shouldn't take whatever others decided to dish out to her, and he'd included his family in that suggestion.

"I'll be sure to give him your message, Mr. Tomlinson," she said. What she wanted to say, but didn't, was that she was hired to get Amanda to talk, not to run all over the countryside pulling Tyler away from his work for a phone call it took the old goat more than a week to place.

Besides, the men had been working so hard to finish that damned hay. Especially Tyler, who still managed to work with his horses each day. Today he'd chosen to preempt his training schedule to get the last of the hay stacked and fenced. He wanted to be finished with it. So did the others. To pull him away when they were so close... No. She couldn't do it. Not without a very good reason. So far, Mr. Tomlinson hadn't given her any reason at all, other than "he wanted." Well, his wants were going to have to wait.

The words burned in her throat, but she swallowed them. After hanging up the phone, she settled for sticking out her tongue.

A sound, a breath, a shuffle from behind had her whirling, a blush already heating her cheeks.

It was Amanda. And she was silently giggling.

Carly moaned. "You weren't supposed to see me do that."

Amanda's eyes filled with laughter.

"It wasn't very nice of me."

Amanda shook her head, and tried to stop grinning.

Carly chuckled. "But you know what? It sure felt good."

An hour before sunset, the dark clouds that had been gathering over the mountains all day broke loose and boiled across the sky. Carly stepped out the back door and felt the temperature dropping rapidly. The wind carried grit and the smell of rain.

Were the men finished?

The stories she'd heard at dinner during the past weeks, of lightning burning up fences, striking haystacks and barns and pickups, had her gnawing the inside of her jaw.

She held her blowing bangs back from her face with one hand and looked to the west, straining to see through the gathering darkness and the clouds of dust driven before the storm.

There. Something…yes. The pickup. They must have decided to leave the tractors in the field until tomorrow. Thank God. Those old relics would have been much slower to drive than the truck.

Were all the men there?

She strained and rose on her toes as the pickup came nearer. It looked like three in the cab, and more in the bed. As the truck pulled up to the barn, all six men piled out.

The first drops of rain, big and fat and heavy, hit the hard-packed earth with audible *splats*. Carly dashed back to the house.

The men weren't as fortunate. No sooner had the back storm door swung shut behind her, than the clouds opened up and cut loose. From the window over the sink, Carly watched first the willows along the creek, then the farthest corrals, then even the closest barn disappear into the solid torrent.

And the horses were still out in the pastures and corrals.

Soon it was so dark outside that all she could see in the window was her own reflection. It gave her back a wry grin. The men were undoubtedly drenched, or soon would be. Yet she had dashed for the house at the first drop of rain.

Running to get out of the rain—that was simply what people did. No one wanted to get caught out in a downpour. Yet, really, what would happen? A person would get wet. Just like in the shower, only obviously not as warm. Yet people—herself included—acted as though purposely allowing oneself to get wet in the rain was unthinkable.

And to have to work while wet, well, for heaven's sake. No one would choose a job requiring that.

She chuckled. One was not required to get soaked to the skin to balance a monthly statement or issue payroll checks in a department store. But Tyler and his father and men like them chose this way of life, knowing full well that working in the rain, or even sleet or snow, was merely one more fact of ranch life.

She put on a fresh pot of coffee, then headed upstairs to the linen closet for a stack of towels.

When Tyler and Arthur finally made it to the house, both were exhausted and soaked to the skin, but elated to have the haying behind them for another year. Arthur even went so far as to thank Carly for putting out the towels in the mudroom.

Carly waited until after dinner to tell Tyler that Howard Tomlinson had called.

To return the call, Tyler went in his office and closed the door.

A few minutes later, Carly and Amanda were just settling in on the couch to watch a Disney movie on one of the satellite channels when Tyler stuck his head out of the office. "Sweetpea, your grandfather and grandmother are on the phone. They'd like to talk to you. Wanna come in here?'' He held out his hand.

At the mention of her grandparents, Amanda tensed beside Carly. When Tyler held out his hand, she looked up at Carly, her big eyes beseeching.

"What is it?'' Carly asked softly. "Don't you want to talk to them?''

Amanda looked decidedly uncomfortable, more than a little upset, even guilty. She made no move to answer Carly's question, or to reach for Tyler's outstretched hand.

"It's okay, honey,'' Carly told her. "You don't have to talk to them if you don't want to.''

Her look of profound relief was mixed with gratitude, and again, that hint of guilt.

Carly patted the girl's leg, then crossed the room to Tyler. She entered the office and pulled him in after her, closing the door behind them.

"I don't think it's a good idea for her to talk to them just yet. She's been making good progress lately, but she's still emotionally fragile. She associates her grandparents with her mother, and with all the trauma of her mother's death. She's obviously not ready to deal head-on with that yet. To push her now, I think, would be a mistake.''

With a frown, Tyler rubbed the back of his neck. "I hadn't looked at it that way, but I think maybe you're right. In any case, she sure didn't look eager to come to the phone. Thanks, Carly. I'll tell Howard.''

Carly sighed. "He's not going to like it.''

"I don't care what he likes. Amanda comes first.''

Chapter Nine

"**W**hy don't I see that new mare you've been talking about?" Robert, the oldest of Tyler's brothers, asked.

Tyler propped one boot on the bottom rail of the corral fence and watched his two current competition horses, Bingo and Duster, grazing down near the creek. "I won't be getting the mare."

"What?" Joe, the youngest brother, looked stunned. "Hell, Ty, you've been trying to get your hands on Magnificent Cutter since the first time you saw her perform at the World Championship Quarter Horse Show down in Oklahoma City five years ago. Don't tell me you've changed your mind now that Johnson's finally decided to sell her."

The shrieks and laughter of his brothers' children as they raced around the corner of the house drew Tyler's gaze. Amanda should have been with them. Her childish laughter should right that minute be echoing through the barn with theirs as they chased after one of the barn cats.

Like the others, Amanda, too, should be sporting grass stains on the seat and knees of her jeans. She ought to have straw sticking out of her hair. A little manure stuck to the bottom of her boots wouldn't bother him any, either.

Except she wasn't wearing boots. Or jeans. She was, at that very moment, sitting demurely—silently—on the front porch with the adults, doing her best not to soil her pretty pink dress.

The last outdoor fling of the year before school, before winter—their traditional "End of Haying" family cookout—and Amanda wouldn't let herself cut loose enough to play with her cousins. Still, there was progress. Carly had convinced her to trade her patent leather shoes for sneakers. Maybe by the time school started...

The reminder of school starting tied Tyler's stomach in knots. Amanda... God, his baby would have to go to school this fall. *Next week!* Panic clutched him by the throat. She wasn't old enough. She couldn't be old enough! She was just a baby!

"Hey, big brother." Joe nudged Tyler's arm. "You still here?"

Tyler turned his gaze reluctantly back to his brothers. "Yeah, I'm here."

"So what gives with the mare?" Robert asked.

Tyler shook his head. "I'm using the money for something more important."

Robert crossed his arms and leveled a narrow-eyed stare at Tyler. "Yeah, we heard that woman was costing you an arm and a leg. But I don't hear Amanda talking yet. When are you gonna quit fooling around and get Amanda some real help?"

Tyler stiffened. "Carly is helping. The doctor in San Francisco thought he knew a therapist who was moving to Jackson. Turned out he moved to Jackson*ville,* instead. So for now, Carly's all we've got—and she's helping, dammit."

Robert pursed his lips. "She might be helping you, but what's she done for Amanda?"

"What the hell's that supposed to mean?"

"It just means," Joe said in a placating tone, "that we're worried about you, that's all."

"There's nothing for you to worry about."

"We beg to differ," Robert said.

"We? I suppose you've all gotten together and decided you know what's best for Amanda and me?"

"Take it easy," Joe said, responding to the harsh challenge in Tyler's voice.

"Quit tiptoeing around it," Robert told Joe. To Tyler, he said, "We think maybe you just want to help Amanda so much that you're not thinking straight."

Tyler swore to himself. He didn't need this conversation, didn't want it, but he knew from experience that his brothers would say what they thought, with or without his permission. Better here and now, away from the others, where Carly couldn't hear.

"All right, I'll bite. Just what is it that makes you think I'm not thinking straight?"

Tyler felt a hand on his back and stiffened. He jerked his head around, relieved—sort of—to find his sister, Sandy, rather than Carly. Not that Carly would have laid her hand on his back that way, but a man could dream.

"What they're trying to say, and obviously doing a poor job of it," Sandy said with a glare at Robert and Joe, "is that...well, dammit, Tyler, you've been alone a long time, and Carly's so cute, and she's not qualified to help Amanda, not really, and we're worried that—"

"We're worried that maybe Carly's better qualified to fill up your nights than she is to help Amanda," Robert said.

Tyler ground his teeth and clenched his fists. "It's been a long time since I felt the need to teach any of you some manners. I think maybe too long."

"Come off it, Ty," Joe said. "We're not blind. We see what happens every time you get around her."

Robert smirked. "Yeah. You act like a stallion sniffin' flank."

"Why, you—"

Sandy cried out and caught Tyler's arm in both hands before he could complete his swing.

Robert met him stare for stare. "Don't get me wrong. I'm not really blaming you—we're talkin' prime flank here."

"Robert," Sandy cried. "Damn you, just shut up."

"I just don't want to see big brother taken for a ride again by another city girl," Robert said harshly. "The ranch, not to mention Amanda, can't afford the price tag, even if he thinks he can."

"Ty?" Sandy tugged on Tyler's arm.

Tyler jerked free, his glare still centered on Robert.

"Ty, we just want you to be careful," Sandy said. "We don't want you to get hurt."

"And if you don't get rid of Carly," Joe said, "Amanda's gonna get hurt, you're gonna get hurt and Carly Baker's gonna sashay her cute little butt back to San Francisco pretty as you please with all your money and dreams in her pockets."

"I don't believe the three of you," Tyler cried. "Where do you get off telling me how to run my life? And what makes any of you so damn perfect you think you have the right to judge a woman you barely know? You're out of line," he said. "All of you. I won't listen to any more of this crap."

He stepped forward and jabbed a forefinger at Robert's chest. "And I damn sure better not hear one more word— not *one*—from any of you about Carly. She's good for Amanda. That's why she's here. If anything else comes of it, it's none of your damn business."

Before his rage broke free of his will, Tyler whirled and stomped off toward the creek. He needed privacy to get himself under control before facing anyone else. Before facing Carly.

He couldn't believe how easily he'd dismissed her concerns about the attitudes of his family and friends. He felt like kicking himself for not taking her seriously. Damn, if she had picked up on what his brothers and sister were thinking, if their thoughts had shown in their eyes, no wonder she was hurt. No wonder she'd been extra sensitive to the money he was paying her. At least she'd given in and started accepting her paychecks again.

But Tyler wasn't hurt by his family's interference. Bless those idiots, they thought they were looking out for him. No, he wasn't hurt. But he was damn good and pissed off. He wanted to hit something. Unfortunately, the only thing along the creek worth hitting was the occasional trunk of a willow tree. He hadn't lost quite that much sense yet.

So he walked. And swore. And fumed.

He didn't dare go back to the party until he'd cooled down.

Nearly half a dozen kids barreled around the side of the house, tumbling and giggling their way across the front yard. The two young cousins from Big Piney, and all of Tyler's nieces and nephews—except the two-year-old. All the children on the ranch. Except Amanda.

Carly watched as Amanda eyed the other kids at play. Was that a touch of wistfulness on the girl's face? Carly hoped so, she dearly did. If anything could get Amanda to trade those fancy dresses for more appropriate play clothes, it would be the other children. How long would Amanda be able to sit on the sidelines while they romped?

"Oh, Carly, those look delicious." Barb, Joe's wife, snatched a deviled egg from the platter Carly had carried out to the picnic table beneath the temporary awning erected in the front yard.

"Thanks." Carly smiled, but without real feeling. Barb's

words were the nicest anyone had said to her since the relatives had started arriving that morning.

"Oh, bits of bacon in the filling," Barb said. "My favorite way."

Carly set the platter on the table and brushed the back of her hand across her forehead. Everyone had been talking all morning about how glad they were that the temperature was so cool. While eighty-five was certainly cooler than it had been, it was still a heck of a lot hotter than Carly was used to.

She scanned the yard, noting Tyler's continued absence. He and his brothers had disappeared earlier to look at the horses. Robert and Joe were back now, giving Arthur advice on the perfect way to grill hamburgers, but Tyler hadn't returned with them.

"Have you seen Tyler?" she asked Barb.

Barb immediately looked away. "Oh," she said, her cheeks turning pink, "he's around somewhere." She left and darted across the grass toward the men at the grill.

From the corner of her eye, Carly saw Barb whisper something to Joe and Robert. The two men shot Carly a glance. Their sister, Sandy, jabbed them each in the arm, and they turned back toward the grill.

Carly had been fighting the return of her paranoia for the past hour, to no avail. The speculative looks, the covert whispers, smiles that didn't reach eyes—all of it was getting to her. And it was much worse when Tyler wasn't around.

Robert's voice drifted on the slight breeze. "...soaking his head in the creek, I hope."

"What did you say to him?" Barb asked.

Someone hissed something that sounded like a warning to keep quiet.

"Just...how we all feel about..."

Even with missing words, Carly thought she knew what they were talking about. They were talking about her. They'd said something to Tyler about her.

Easy for Tyler to say she didn't have to take it, even from his family. What was she supposed to do about it? Somehow, she didn't think sticking out her tongue would be appropriate. His solution, to kick someone in the shin, didn't sound much better.

Just then Tyler rounded the side of the house, his jaw set at a stubborn angle. He shot a narrow look at the group around the grill, then scanned the yard. When his gaze lit on Carly, the firm set of his mouth softened, as did his eyes.

He was at her side in seconds, stealing a deviled egg from the platter before her.

"What's going on?" she asked him.

"I'm starving."

"I mean with your family. Something's happened, hasn't it?"

Tyler studied the table, then reached for a stuffed celery stick. "I don't know what you're talking about."

When he finally raised his gaze, she gave him a sad smile. "Liar. I'm not totally stupid, you know. The tension in the air around here is worse than the heat."

Before he could answer, the contingent from the grill headed en masse for the table. Bearing a huge platter of juicy hamburgers, Arthur led the way.

Tyler shifted to Carly's side and put his arm around her shoulders.

She stiffened. "What do you think you're doing?"

The look he gave her dripped with feigned innocence. "I don't know what you're talking about."

By then the others had arrived at the table.

Carly saw their glares, felt their animosity and suddenly she'd had all she could deal with. "Well, I do," she told Tyler. "You said I didn't have to take this from anybody, and I don't have to take it from you, either."

"You've lost me," he said with a frown.

She jerked out of his embrace. "You're using me to

make them angry. I don't know why, but I won't have it, do you hear?''

One of the women gasped.

Her stomach in knots, Carly started up the yard toward the house.

"Where are you going?" Tyler called.

She whirled back to face him and his family. "I'm going to pack. You can take me to the airport at your earliest convenience."

"When hell freezes over," Tyler said harshly.

"Yeah, well, I'm sure one of them," she said with a wave toward his family, "will give me a ride out of here." She turned away again, so hurt, so angry, she didn't know how she managed to put one foot in front of the other.

"Carly," Tyler cried.

"Never thought you were a quitter."

Arthur's voice stopped her. Sheer fury spun her around. "Get off it, Arthur. You don't want me here any more than they do. You've been trying to get rid of me from the minute I got here."

The old man pursed his lips and narrowed his eyes. "So maybe I've changed my mind."

Carly couldn't help but notice the incredulous looks on the faces of his children. All his children.

"Don't get me wrong," Arthur went on, "I'm not sayin' I want to adopt you into the family just yet, but you've got a job to do here, and it ain't finished. Near as I can see, you're Amanda's only hope. You can't leave."

Carly closed her eyes against the painful truth. She couldn't leave Amanda. Not like this. She couldn't let the others ruin the progress Amanda had made.

But God, she didn't know how much more of this animosity she could take. She didn't know how much more of Tyler's games she would be able to handle. When she opened her eyes, Amanda stood before her with wide, pleading eyes and threaded her fingers through Carly's.

Carly felt the fight drain out of her. She looked at Arthur. "You're right, of course. I can't leave yet."

The man eyed her a long moment, then gave her a sharp nod. "As for us," he said, looking around at the rest of the family, "we all owe you an apology. It's not our way to be rude. I think we've all been a little crazy since you came. For that, we're sorry. Aren't we?" he barked at the others.

It was almost funny the way gazes darted to the ground and grown men shuffled and blushed, but Carly couldn't bring herself to laugh.

"Now," Arthur said with authority, "let's eat. This is supposed to be a celebration. We got the damned hay baled and stacked, didn't we? And we've got a new neighbor down the road to celebrate. Tim called this morning. Tammy had a baby girl last night."

The commotion stirred by the news took the focus off Carly, for which she was fervently grateful.

Tyler finished building his burger and filling his plate, then grabbed a beer from the ice chest and made his way to where Carly sat alone on the grass beneath the shade of the cottonwood.

"Mind if I join you?" he asked quietly.

Without looking up, she muttered, "Suit yourself."

He dropped down beside her and balanced his paper plate on one knee. He spent an inordinate amount of time nestling his beer can into the grass until the can stood perfectly straight, then he picked up his hamburger and stared at it.

If he put so much as one bite of food in his mouth, he knew he'd choke. He was still furious. So furious, his stomach was in knots. The only trouble was, now he was equally as pissed off at himself as he was the others. He couldn't believe he'd hurt Carly the way he had. With a sharp curse, he dropped the burger back onto the plate. "God, Carly, I'm sorry. I...I'm sorry."

She gave a harsh laugh. "Whoever said being right was

supposed to make you feel good? I was right, wasn't I? You were using me to make them mad.''

She still wasn't looking at him, and he didn't trust himself to look at her. He let out a gust of breath. "More or less. But not the way you think. My brothers...said some things—''

"I can imagine.''

"No, you can't.'' He gave a short laugh. "They think you're leading me on.''

At her sharp gasp of denial, he raised a hand. "I know, I know. That's about as far from the truth as it can get. They also think I'm falling for you.''

"That's ridiculous.''

"No, it's not, but that's another subject entirely.''

He chanced a glance at her and caught her staring at him openmouthed. He looked away quickly. "Anyway, they had no right to say anything. Whatever's going on between you and me is none of their business.''

"There's nothing going on between you and me.''

He met her gaze then and held it. No more fooling around. No more tiptoeing. "Don't kid yourself, honey. It's here, and it's not going away.''

She shivered. He held his breath, waiting.

"You're wrong,'' she told him.

Tyler let out his breath. She'd said exactly what he'd expected. Not what he'd wanted, but she was fighting him, denying whatever it was that happened when they were together. It was natural for her to tell him he was wrong. "I'm not, and you know it.''

Amanda sat on the porch swing and watched her father and Carly. Poor Carly, she was so sad. Amanda knew what it was like to be sad.

Before long her daddy carried his plate to the trash can and stopped to talk to Cousin Bev.

The other kids were through eating already and had started a game of tag on the lawn. They looked like they were having so much fun, Amanda felt all alone and left out.

Just like Carly.

Amanda knew what she was going to do about feeling sad and left out. She was going to eat the biggest bowl of homemade ice cream her grandad would give her. Ice cream was so good, it always made her feel better. She figured it could fix just about anything.

Then she remembered—Carly didn't eat ice cream.

Why would anyone not eat something that tasted so good and was such fun to eat? Ice cream made people happy. If anybody needed ice cream today, it was Carly.

Amanda carried her paper plate to the trash, then stood in line behind Uncle Joe for the ice cream Grandad was dishing out of the ice-cream freezer at the end of the porch.

"There you go, little darlin'," Grandad told her after heaping two big scoops into a bowl for her.

Amanda smiled her thanks, then stood at the steps.

Maybe Carly would change her mind about eating ice cream today. Surely she didn't *want* to feel all sad and alone, did she?

Amanda walked to the big tree where Carly sat and offered her friend the bowl.

"Thank you, sweetie, but no. Remember? I told you I don't eat ice cream."

Amanda frowned and walked back to resume her seat on the swing. She let out a big sigh. She knew why Carly wouldn't eat the ice cream. It was because of that story she'd told her about her daddy.

It wasn't that Carly *couldn't* eat it, like Amanda couldn't talk, but that Carly *wouldn't* eat it, like Amanda wouldn't wear anything but the pretty dresses her mother had liked so much.

Amanda frowned again, thinking hard. Carly's ice cream and Amanda's dresses weren't things God was doing to them. God was only keeping Amanda from talking. And she deserved that, she knew.

But the dresses were her own doing.

Just like not eating ice cream was Carly's own doing.

Didn't Carly know how much fun she was missing by not eating the very best thing in the whole wide world?

A squeal from the yard drew Amanda's attention.

Oh, goody, she thought, grinning. One of her cousins must have smuggled in a squirt gun. Sissy had it now and was chasing her brother, Bobby.

Amanda remembered playing with squirt guns, back before Mother had taken her to Chicago, when Amanda had been little. Squirt guns were almost as much fun as ice cream. They were even fun when somebody else was doing the squirting, as long as you were the one getting squirted.

She looked down at her pink ruffled dress. No, she couldn't play squirt guns with her cousins. She would ruin her dress. The dress she wore because of her mother.

Was that why her daddy and Carly kept trying to get her to wear jeans? So she could play and have fun?

Was that what she was doing, wearing dresses so she *couldn't* have fun? Just like Carly wouldn't eat ice cream because she used to like it so much?

It looked to Amanda like she and Carly were both being silly. Maybe...

Tyler sat next to Bev, his cousin Frank's wife, on the picnic bench under the awning and watched Amanda watch the other kids play. He saw her offer her ice cream to Carly, knowing as she did so that Carly would refuse.

Then Amanda had returned to the swing and seemed to ponder some weighty matter. Tyler ached for whatever was running through her mind. She kept looking from the kids to her ice cream to Carly. A look of...he could only call it determination, crossed her face. Then she got up and started over to him.

When she arrived, she solemnly set her bowl of ice cream on the table before him.

"Are you giving this to me?"

She gave him an arch look, as if to say, "You've got to be kidding."

"You want me to just hold it for you?"

She nodded, then turned and walked into the house.

"What's she up to?" Bev asked.

"I don't have the slightest idea," he said. But she was up to something. He glanced toward the cottonwood and found Carly staring thoughtfully at the door where Amanda had disappeared.

Tyler stayed at the picnic table and waited for his daughter to come back outside. Just when he was about to give up and go after her, the front door opened, and out she came.

Tyler's chest tightened. Gone was the pretty party dress, the full, fluffy petticoats. In their place, Amanda wore spanking new blue jeans, a red checkered shirt and the cowboy boots he had about decided she would outgrow before ever wearing.

"Look at that," Bev whispered in awe.

Tyler blinked to clear his vision. "Yeah. Did you ever see anything so beautiful in your life?"

The several conversations among the adults on the porch trailed off into silence as one by one, the family realized what they were seeing.

Tyler shot a glance at Carly and saw her fighting tears. She, better than anyone, must know how hard this move had to have been for Amanda. He wondered what had made Amanda finally give in. Someday, when she could talk again, he would ask her.

Amanda must have noticed the way everyone was staring at her, for she ducked her head and wouldn't look at anybody on her way back to Tyler. She stopped next to him and slowly raised her gaze.

His heart pounding with excitement, Tyler said, "Hi, there. I like the new duds."

She smiled at him shyly.

"I don't suppose it was too easy, giving up the pretty dress."

She shook her head slowly as her eyes watered.

"I'm proud of you, sweetpea."

She sniffed, then her gaze darted across the yard to Carly before coming back to him. Except her gaze didn't come back to him. It rested on her bowl of ice cream. She picked it up and looked at him, all trace of shyness gone from her face. In its place he again saw determination.

She looked back at Carly, at the ice cream, then at him. *Oh, good God.* A slow grin widened his mouth. He gave Amanda a nod. "You're gonna make her do it, aren't you?"

Amanda nodded back solemnly.

"Well, go to it. She owes it to you now."

With no other look or sign, Amanda took the bowl of ice cream and walked directly to Carly. But instead of sitting down beside her, Amanda took her by the hand and tugged her up off the grass.

"What's going on?" Bev whispered.

"Just watch," Tyler answered, his heart thudding like crazy.

Amanda led Carly past the end of the lawn onto the dirt driveway, then she sat down, right in the dust, and pulled on Carly's hand until Carly sat beside her.

Tyler nearly choked on emotion. His baby, his sweet, sweet baby, was deliberately getting dirty for the first time in probably two years. And she was doing it to please him, to please Carly.

"What—"

Tyler hushed his father, who'd come to stand beside him. "She's going to make Carly eat ice cream."

"So?"

"So, Carly's father had a heart attack and died going to the store to buy her ice cream. She hasn't touched the stuff since she was nine years old."

"Amanda knows this?"

"She does."

A long silence, then, "Why, the little dickens."

"By putting on those jeans, she gave up a big piece of her mother. Now she expects Carly to let go of her father."

Arthur grunted.

Out on the driveway, Amanda had tears on her cheeks. So did Carly. "Oh, baby, I'm so proud of you," Carly said.

Then carefully, deliberately, Amanda scooped ice cream onto her spoon and held it out toward Carly.

Carly stared wide-eyed at the girl, the ice cream. "Oh, I get it." Even from halfway up the yard, Tyler heard the quiver in her voice. "If you can do it, I can, right?"

Amanda nodded once. Firmly.

Carly took a deep breath and closed her eyes briefly. "All right. Here goes nothing." She put her hand over Amanda's on the spoon handle and raised the ice cream to her lips. Tyler could see the battle plainly on her face and in the way her hands shook. She didn't want to eat it.

But in the next instant, she closed her lips over the spoon and pulled the ice cream into her mouth.

Tyler held his breath, waiting for her to swallow, waiting for her to get sick. He could tell by the look on her face after she finally managed to swallow that she, too, was waiting.

She closed her eyes and held her face up toward the sky. Then, slowly, she grinned. She opened her eyes, looked at Amanda and laughed out loud.

Tyler let out his breath. By the time he got his feet under him and made it out to the driveway, the two were laughing and crying and hugging and feeding each other ice cream. When he knelt beside them, a painful lump rose in his throat.

He couldn't talk. All he could do was put his arms around them both and pull them close to his chest. He kissed Amanda's nose, then turned to Carly.

Her eyes were bright with tears and joy. Her lips were moist from ice cream. He couldn't help himself. He kissed her. It was brief and hard, and oh, so sweet, tasting of vanilla and tears. "God, I'm so proud of you two," he said in a choked voice. "You okay?" he asked them both.

They each nodded and laughed and cried. Carly seemed not to even realize he'd just kissed her on the mouth in front of his entire family. She was too caught up in the excitement of the moment.

Then he remembered what she'd said had happened the last time she'd eaten ice cream. "Is it going to stay down?"

"You bet," she told him. "And it's wonderful. Delicious. The best thing I've ever tasted in my life."

She leaned down and hugged Amanda. "Thank you," she told the girl. "You were much braver than I was."

"I think you're both incredible," Tyler said. "Now, who's gonna give me a bite of that ice cream?"

Chapter Ten

"**Y**ou keep on like that," Tyler said that night, "and
we'll have to widen the doors around here."

Carly gave him a big smile. "I believe the appropriate
response to that comment is, 'Blow it out your ear, Barnett.'"

He tossed his head back and laughed.

It was good to see him so happy. His laugh was music
to her ears. Her own laughter felt pretty damned wonderful,
too, she decided.

"Pretty cocky, huh?" he asked.

"Yeah." With a grin—a cocky one—she dished up another spoonful of homemade vanilla ice cream. "I guess I
am."

She felt another round of laughter bubbling up inside her
and let it loose. All sorts of things had been building up
inside her since that afternoon. Good things. Warm and
tingly things. Laughter, pride—not only in herself, but in

Amanda, too, for the giant step each of them had taken that day—gratitude to Amanda for forcing her past her old guilt.

The best of the feelings, however, was the lightness of spirit, the sheer freedom Carly felt at shedding the last of her guilt. She could almost see her father smiling, saying, *It's about time, kiddo.*

Tyler smiled at her. "You look…happy."

She laughed again. "I feel like I swallowed a Fourth of July sparkler."

He chuckled and leaned a hip against the cabinet next to the sink. "What does that feel like?"

Carly pulled the ice cream off the spoon and into her mouth, closing her eyes to savor the cold sweetness. "It feels all tingly and bubbly inside. Kind of fizzy. Like all these sparkling-bright little bursts of light and energy are going off inside me. I feel…euphoric. Invincible."

She looked it, too. Tyler shuddered with the need to pull her close and touch the sheer vibrant energy shimmering from her skin. She *looked* like she'd swallowed a sparkler. The air around her fairly crackled. He'd never seen her more alive, more sure of herself. More beautiful, with the light of pleasure in her dark eyes.

She looked…turned on.

All because of the ice cream.

Deep inside, he ached. Selfish though it was, he wanted to be the reason for her sudden euphoria.

Someday, he vowed, would he be.

He didn't have the heart to tell her that what she was experiencing was pure adrenaline mixed with relief at putting the past behind her. The feelings would fade in time, become less volatile. But before they faded, he wanted to touch her. He wanted to feel all that energy radiating from her in waves. Wanted to taste it. Let it vibrate through him.

"Did Amanda make it to bed okay?" she asked.

"Yeah," he said. "But I think we've created a monster. Two, in fact."

"What monsters?"

"You and your ice cream, and a certain young lady who is, at this very moment, upstairs asleep. In her jeans."

Carly grinned. "She wouldn't take them off?"

He shook his head.

"Don't worry, she will. They're not *that* comfortable." Her spoon clanked against the bowl as she scraped the last of the ice cream—the melted dregs—and finished it off. Then she scooted her chair back from the table and walked to the sink beside him to rinse the bowl. She reached to open the dishwasher, but Tyler stood in the way. "Move your buns, buster."

"Oh, ho. You really are feeling your oats, aren't you?"

"What I'm feeling," she said with a grin and a toss of her head, "is my ice cream."

"You've got some on your chin."

"Where?" She looked down as though she'd be able to see her own chin.

"Here, let me." With a hand on her shoulder to keep her from backing away, Tyler leaned down. He heard her breath catch, felt her stiffen, but didn't let either stop him. With the tip of his tongue, he swiped at the smear on her chin.

"I think..." Her voice, all breathy and hesitant, trailed off.

Unable to deny himself another taste, he nibbled again at her chin. "Don't think."

"I think...maybe...there's more."

He raised his head enough to look into her eyes. "More what?"

She swallowed. Her lips parted. "Ice cream."

Tyler was afraid to move, afraid to even breathe. If she was saying what he thought she was saying, he didn't dare do anything to break the spell. "Where?" he whispered.

She reached up with one hand and pointed to the corner of her mouth. "Here."

Heat flashed through his veins. She was inviting him to kiss her. Could a woman get high on ice cream? A man could damn sure get high on a woman. On the look in her eyes, the taste of her skin.

With the tip of his tongue, he touched the corner of her mouth and felt her shiver. She clasped his shoulders, her fingers digging into him. It was all the sign he needed.

But still he moved slowly, a slight swipe of his tongue along her full lower lip. Sweet. She tasted sweet and creamy. Her lip quivered beneath his touch.

He took another taste, this one from her upper lip, before covering her mouth one exquisite bit at a time with his. "Mmm, cold," he murmured.

"I think my tongue is numb," she whispered against his lips.

"Can't have that," he answered between short kisses. "Let's warm it." To keep from pushing too hard too fast, he started slow, nuzzling her lips with his, barely darting his tongue between them before withdrawing.

For Carly, it was too slow. He was torturing her. She felt wild and free and eager. She wanted his kiss, wanted it desperately. With a moan of frustration, she leaned against his chest, wrapped her arms around his neck and opened her lips to him.

His answering moan was music to her ears. His big, hard hands spread across her back. His thighs nudged hers. His breath brushed her cheek. And finally, at last, his mouth took hers fully, firmly, with no more teasing.

The contrast of the warmth of his mouth against the cold of hers intrigued her. She met his stroking tongue with hers until he'd warmed not only her tongue, but all of her.

She savored the taste of him, hot and dark and just a little dangerous. She could feel urgency building in him, the need for more, just as it built in her.

Yes, yes, she wanted to cry. Being in his arms, holding him, kissing him…it all felt so right. There was no one around to know or care. He wasn't trying to prove a point or make someone angry. He was kissing her simply because he wanted to. She felt that much in her heart. And oh, how she wanted the kiss to never stop.

In his arms, she could forget the terrible mess her life was in, the uncertainty of her future at home, the way Tyler's friends and family treated her. She could forget everything, as long as he kissed her.

And he was most assuredly kissing her, more thoroughly than she'd ever been kissed in her life. Her heart set up a tremendous pounding, and his answered. Her breath came in short, swift gasps, vying with his for the shortest, the swiftest.

Heat and yearning built inside her until she felt her breasts swell against his chest, felt her nipples tighten with anticipation. Moist warmth pooled and centered down low in her body.

Then his hands began to move across her back. One slid up to cup the back of her head, where his fingers massaged her scalp and toyed with her hair. His other hand moved down to press her hips flush against his, to show her that she wasn't the only one feeling the heat down low. Then that hand, that hard, treacherous hand, caressed its way up her side until his thumb brushed the full outer curve of her breast.

Something inside her melted. It may have been her bones. All of them.

Then his fingers curved around her breast, molding, shaping, lifting. She couldn't stifle the moan, nor the gasp a moment later when his thumb brushed across her nipple.

He answered with a low growl vibrating from his chest.

God, but his touch was exquisite, torturous, glorious. She'd always thought her breasts were too small, but if he could make her feel this way by just touching them through her clothes, she didn't care anymore. He stroked the tip of her breast again and again, making her moan each time, making her want more. Making her desperate.

She felt his arousal grow harder against her abdomen, and a corresponding ache bloomed deep inside her. Instinctively, knowing the yawning emptiness was something only he could fill, she moved against him.

Like a snap, he tore his mouth from hers and moved his hand from her breast to her back, leaving her aching for the return of his touch. She cried out in protest.

"I know," he whispered harshly, his breath rasping in her ear. "Oh, God, honey, I know." His hands clutched at her, held her tight against him.

When he lifted his head, she opened her eyes. He looked as stunned as she felt. His voice, when it came, was soft and low and filled with what sounded to her dazed mind like wonder. "Wow," he said.

She swallowed, searching his blue-green eyes, dark now with heat and arousal. The intensity she saw there, along with her own riotous emotions, made her shiver. Yeah, she thought. Wow.

What had he done to her, that she could lose all sense that way? Never had she given so much of herself to a man before. Not even when things had gone much farther than they had tonight. Not even when she and James had gone all the way. She'd never felt such an aching need to be filled with a man's hardness. And the need was for this man—Tyler Barnett—no other.

She swallowed again. "I...it's late."

Was that a flash of hurt in his eyes? No, it couldn't have been.

Afraid he might try to kiss her again, afraid she would let him, Carly pulled herself from his arms and fled.

Tyler spent a tortured night reliving every second of that kiss. He hadn't had to coax her this time. He'd barely made the first move. The next advance had been hers.

In his arms she'd felt the way she had the rare other times he'd held her—perfect. Right. As though she belonged there against him.

"She does, dammit," he whispered into the darkness of his bedroom. "She does belong with me."

He'd thought, for a few brief moments while they'd kissed, that she had finally realized the same thing. But when her eyes had cleared and her senses leveled, he'd seen the panic.

No, she didn't understand yet.

She would, he vowed. He would make her. Somehow.

But during the next few days she did her level best to keep him at arm's length. She was damned successful at it, too. Not once was he able to see her alone, and it was killing him. He wanted to hold her again, feel her breast in his hand, her lips on his. He needed her warmth, her sweetness.

Tomorrow he would need those things even more, yet he knew she wouldn't give them. Tomorrow was going to be one of the worst days of his life. For tomorrow, he was going to have to let, even urge, his baby, his Amanda, take her first step toward growing up. He was going to have to take her...oh, God—to *school.*

A shudder tore through him at the mere thought. She was too little, too vulnerable, still had too many problems. She was his *baby,* for crying out loud. How could his baby be old enough for school?

But she was. God, help him, she was. And it was shredding him to pieces. He wanted to keep her home with him forever and refuse to let her grow up. He wanted to bury his face against her soft curls and hold on to her forever.

Knowing he couldn't, he thought he would have settled for having Carly put her arms around him and assure him he would live through the experience.

Hell, he was ten times more upset about the coming day than Amanda was. Amanda's confidence, too, was Carly's doing.

In a panic, Tyler had called Dr. Sanders in San Francisco, trying to get the man to tell him Amanda was still too troubled to deal with the trauma of school.

To give the man credit, Dr. Sanders had done his best not to laugh out loud.

Carly had done too good a job. Amanda, bless her, was actually looking forward to school, especially knowing three of her cousins would be there, two of whom were going for the first time, as she was. Carly had convinced Amanda that school would be a great adventure.

For Tyler, it would be agonizing torture.

"You have to come with me," he told Carly in a moment of weakness the morning of the Big Day.

"I can't, Tyler."

"Of course you can. You don't expect me to do this alone, do you?"

She gave him a halfhearted smile. "I don't think it's wise for me to go. There's enough talk and speculation about me already. I don't want any of that to rub off on Amanda. I don't want her exposed to the talk. She'll be much better off if I stay here."

Tyler tried to change her mind. They argued. He cursed and cajoled and threatened, but she wouldn't give in. He nearly tried whining, but he figured he'd already come closer to that than was comfortable, and it wouldn't have budged her anyway.

Carly was upstairs changing the beds when she heard Tyler return from taking Amanda to her first day of school. She finished stuffing the dirty sheets down the laundry chute that led straight to the table next to the washer, then she went downstairs to start the first load.

She stopped short at the kitchen doorway. She hadn't heard him come in the house. She'd expected him to be outside working. She knew the haying had put his training schedule behind, and that he was trying to get three two-year-old colts ready for sale.

But instead of working his horses, there he sat at the kitchen table, shoulders slumped, gaze transfixed on the cup of coffee he held between his hands.

Sympathy swamped her. But not being a parent herself,

her feelings were tinged with amusement. "She didn't die, you know."

He jerked his head around. A deep scowl marked his face.

"She only went to school. She's still your little girl."

He gave an irritated grunt. "Some big help you are."

Carly took pity on him then. She moved to stand behind his chair and started rubbing his shoulders through the soft cotton of his shirt. "I'm sorry. I know this is hard on you."

He sighed and rolled his head back. His eyes were closed. He looked tired. As tired as he'd looked during those weeks of haying. "Leaving her at school was damn near as hard as watching her go when Deborah took her away."

Carly slipped her arms over his shoulders and down his chest, pulling his head back against her. "You're not going to lose her this time. Not for years and years." She rested her cheek against the top of his head. "She'll be home this afternoon."

He sighed and settled his head against her. "Are you making fun of me?"

"I wouldn't," she said sincerely. "Not about this."

He raised his head and straightened, then pulled her around in front of him. "I'm glad." With his hands at her waist, he lifted her and sat her on the table.

"What are you doing?"

His hands slipped from her waist and cupped her hips. "I'm satisfying a need."

Her mouth went dry. "A need?"

His thumbs worked their way into the creases at the tops of her thighs. "You know by now I want you."

She started to protest, but his hands squeezed her, halting her words.

"You know," he insisted. "Sometimes, like the other night, the want turns into a craving, a need so hard I ache with it."

From the look in his eyes, she knew he was talking about

the last time they'd kissed. Maybe the time before that, too. The mere reminder had the power to shake her.

"Then there are times like now," he said, laying his head on her lap, "when I just need you to touch me."

Carly sat frozen as a soft wave of emotion flooded her. His words...did he have any idea what his words meant to her? She couldn't remember anyone ever really needing her. Even if he didn't mean it, the very idea that he might need her sent a sweet shaft of pain through her chest.

"Just touch me, Carly."

The weight of his head on her thighs was heaven. The need she saw on his face, heard in his voice, made her eyes sting. Slowly, afraid he might disappear if she moved too fast, she brought her hands to his back and rested them there.

The heavy sigh that left his lips sounded like relief and was balm to her soul. He nuzzled the side of his face against her legs and wrapped his arms around her hips.

In that moment, Carly Baker fell in love.

Oh, Tyler.

Could he really need her? Or would any soft touch soothe him on this day when he felt low?

She didn't know, didn't care. For now she would savor his need and pretend it was just for her.

They stayed that way a long time, with his head on her lap, her hands stroking his back, his neck, his hair. The house was peacefully quiet, only the hum from the refrigerator filling the silence. From outside came an occasional cackle from one of the hens, a snort from a horse. Now and then, the sound of voices—Tom's maybe, and Smitty's—drifted up from one of the far corrals.

Tyler didn't move. She wondered if he'd fallen asleep. His hot breath seared through the denim of her jeans and scorched her left thigh. She wanted to lean down and kiss him but was afraid of breaking whatever spell held him against her.

Tyler savored the contact. She couldn't know how much

it meant to him that she would accept him this way, give him the comfort he needed. She couldn't begin to understand what it meant to him to walk into his home and find her there, warm and welcoming even when she didn't mean to be.

But he had those two-year-olds to work. Tom was good with horses; Smitty was, too. But Tyler always put his horses through their paces himself before judging their readiness for sale. It was past time he did just that.

With great reluctance, he lifted his head from the cradle of Carly's lap. He was almost afraid to look into her eyes. Had his moment of weakness brought pity? Disdain? Deborah would have—

But Carly wasn't Deborah. Carly's eyes, when he met them, were open and warm and soft, deep brown. Soothing.

Without letting go of her hips, he stood and pressed a kiss to her cheek. "Thank you," he whispered.

As his hands slipped away from her and he turned to go, Carly shivered with the yearning to call him back.

Tyler needed to take his mind off Amanda, off Carly. Off his eagerness to turn around and march back into the house and haul Carly upstairs to the nearest bed. If he would even make it that far. Hell, that damned old kitchen table was starting to look good to him.

He couldn't work the colts when he was this distracted. He had no business even being around the younger horses when his thoughts were focused elsewhere. But there was one thing guaranteed to sidetrack him, get his concentration back.

"Tom," he called out. "You 'bout through working Striker?"

"Just finishing."

"When you get him back in his stall, you and Smitty go herd those calves into the big corral."

Tom stuck his head out the barn door, a wide grin on his dark face. "No kiddin'? You gonna do some cuttin'?"

"Thought I would."

"Bingo or Duster?"

"Duster, I think. I'll save Bingo for this afternoon."

"Hot damn. Hey, Smitty! Saddle up. We got cattle to herd."

"No kiddin'?"

Tyler gave a dry chuckle. He knew better than to let their sudden excitement over the prospect of his working Duster go to his head. It wasn't his riding they looked forward to, but Duster's cutting. And Duster was something to watch. Every bit as good as his multichampion sire.

Tyler strode through the barn and out into the back corral. Duster snapped his head up and perked his ears.

"Hey there, big fella."

In response, the blood bay stallion, one of Tyler's two current competition horses, tossed his head up with a shake.

"Been a while since you went eyeball-to-eyeball with an ornery calf. Think you're up to it?"

The horse snorted and pawed the ground.

"Well, come on then. Let's do some work."

Carly was folding laundry, thinking of Tyler, and missing Amanda when she heard the commotion. Not that there wasn't always something noisy going on outside, but this was different. She'd never heard the cattle so close to the house before, never heard such excitement in the men's voices. Those small things were enough incentive to have her dropping Arthur's underwear on the laundry table and rushing to the window over the sink to see what was going on.

In the big corral just west of the stallion barn, Tyler sat astride a horse. Sun gleamed off the animal's sleek bronze hide. Ears, muzzle, mane, tail and lower legs were shiny black.

In the east corral, Tom and Smitty were herding in about a dozen bawling, wild-eyed young cattle. Willis manned the corral gate and prodded the cattle on through. Neal and

Arthur were headed over from one of the sheds to see what was going on.

"Stir 'em up, boys," she heard Tyler call. "Duster likes 'em feisty."

Tom shouted something back that Carly couldn't make out.

Curious, Carly made her way outside. By the time she arrived at the corral fence, Willis had closed the gate, shutting the cattle inside, and had come around to join her. A minute later, Arthur and Neal stood beside her, too.

"What's going on?" she asked.

Neal sidled up to her. "You ever see a cutting horse in action?"

"Not that I remember."

"Then you must not have," Willis said. Then, as if realizing he'd actually spoken to her, he blushed. "It's, uh, not something you'd ever forget. Not one of Ty's horses, anyway."

This must be a big deal, indeed, to get painfully shy Willis to say that many words at once to her. Carly pursed her lips and turned to watch Tyler ride out of the other corral and into the one before her with Tom and Smitty, who'd ridden their horses in with the cattle.

"Don't worry about a thing, darling," Neal said beside her. "I'll explain it to you."

Was it her imagination, or had Neal moved closer? She felt…crowded.

"Tyler's gonna ride Duster into the herd and cut out one calf, separate it from the others. Then it'll be Duster's job to keep the calf from rejoining the herd. Tyler's job is to move with the horse, keep his weight centered so's not to throw Duster off balance. He might give a nudge now and then with his legs, but he can't use the reins once Duster starts working."

Carly wasn't mistaken. As interested as she was in what Neal was saying, she couldn't help but realize he had moved closer. So close that when he gestured, his arm brushed her shoulder.

"Ty's real good at it. One of the best in the world. Me, though," Neal said, leaning down to her ear, "I used to do the real dangerous stuff. I was a bull rider."

Carly twitched at the feel of his hot moist breath on her ear. Scooting a step away, she ran up against Willis and apologized for bumping into him.

Willis blushed. "Tom and Smitty are in there to keep the cattle from getting away," he offered. "Duster's supposed to keep the calf from going back to the herd, but it's not much of a contest if the calf just wanders off from the horse instead of trying to get past him."

"Never seen a cutting horse, huh?" Arthur said with a disgusted drawl.

Carly stiffened. "And just where, on Nob Hill in the middle of San Francisco, would I see a cutting horse?"

"You ever get down to the Cow Palace?"

"A few times, but not for a rodeo."

Arthur snorted. "Cutting ain't done at a rodeo. It's a show event."

"Now, boss," Neal said placatingly. "Don't go pickin' on the city girl just 'cause she doesn't know about horses. I'd be glad to teach her all she wants to know."

Neal's slick voice sent prickles of disgust down her arms. She'd bet that in a former life, he sold snake oil from the back of a wagon.

"Don't waste your time," Arthur told Neal. "She's not staying long enough to learn much of anything."

"She also has ears, a voice and feelings," Carly said tightly. "And she doesn't appreciate being talked about as though she were a fence post."

Arthur gave another snort, then propped one boot on the bottom rail of the corral fence.

Neal may have said something else, but Carly tuned him out and watched Tyler cut one red, white-faced cow away from the others. The cow—or was it a calf? Carly wondered—gave a low bawl and started to go around the horse to rejoin the other cattle.

Then the action started.

For every move the cow made, the horse countered. They shuffled and two-stepped along an imaginary line, an elegant *pas de deux* of two superbly graceful athletes, as though some great choreographer had planned each step.

Muscles—bovine, equine and those oh, so human muscles along Tyler's thighs and shoulders—bunched and stretched as the horse and cow stared each other down, matched each other move for move. It was as though the horse could read the cow's mind and move with it, rather than merely react to its moves.

The cow was plainly agitated. The stallion, however, was a study in arrogant aggression yet playful concentration and grace. Carly had never seen such moves from a horse. One moment Duster would lean back on his haunches, scant inches away from sitting in the dirt, front legs out in front of him, one hoof dancing back and forth as if daring the cow to move.

Then the cow would dodge, and Duster was right there, step for step, dancing, prancing, crossing one foreleg over the other to keep nose to nose with the cow.

When the cow stopped, splayed its legs and stared, the horse matched it by crouching down like a cat ready to spring, or a puppy, forelegs almost flat on the ground, rear end in the air, ready for play. Duster swung his head back and forth, so low to the ground that his mane brushed the dirt.

"Hot damn, look at him," Arthur said in a low, excited voice. "That horse is every bit as good as his sire."

Carly knew from talk around the dinner table that Prancer, Tyler's multichampion stud, was Duster's sire. Most of the trophies in the house bore Prancer's name, but Duster, along with Bingo, had been bringing in his fair share during the past couple of years.

Trying to decide which way to go, the cow swung its

head back and forth. Duster shifted gracefully from side to side, head swinging, weight changing from one hoof to the other in time with the cow's movements. Power. Precision. Keen intelligence in every motion the horse made.

And Tyler, anticipating Duster's every move. He had to keep his weight centered over the horse's shoulders so as not to throw the animal off balance during a quick maneuver.

Tyler made it look easy, as if he were only a passenger. One hand held the reins—loosely, Carly thought—down against the horse's neck. The other hand rested on the saddle horn.

The cow suddenly made a mad dash toward the far side of the corral. Duster and Tyler shifted as one, running parallel, the stallion keeping his head even with that of the cow every step of the way. At the fence, the cow decided she'd had enough and turned away from the horse and the herd.

Then Tyler started over, cutting another cow, this one a young black steer. Carly watched in awe as Tyler and Duster danced with one cow after another, step for step, rush for rush. Tyler's concentration was total. He never took his eyes off the cow before them. Neither did the horse. They were a team. A hell of a team.

One by one the cattle gave up, Duster never letting a single one get past him. When the last one turned away, Tyler patted the horse's sweaty neck and looked directly at Carly, as though he'd known exactly where she had been the entire time.

Sweat ran in rivulets down the sides of his face. The front and back of his shirt clung damply to the fluid muscles beneath. When his gaze met hers, intent, hot, piercing, Carly's breath caught.

Then Neal's voice rumbled low in her ear. "You spreadin' that around, sweet thing, or is it all for the boss?"

Carly flinched at the crude suggestion.

Tyler swung down from Duster's back and led the stallion toward her.

"It's all right if you wanna share," Neal said, low enough to keep his voice from carrying. "Ty won't mind, you know."

Revulsion had her stomach rolling over. She shoved abruptly away from the corral fence and fled to the safety of the house, ignoring Tyler's voice calling her name.

Chapter Eleven

Tyler followed Carly into the house, determined to know why she'd ignored his call. When she told him she hadn't heard him, but that she thought she'd heard the phone ring, he let the matter drop. He was in too good a mood over Duster's performance to go looking for trouble.

His good mood lasted until he stepped out of the shower a short time later and Carly reminded him of the time. "Shouldn't you be going to pick up Amanda from school?" she added.

The reminder that Amanda *was* in school shocked him. He might never get used to the idea. Then, chagrined, he confessed, "She didn't want me to pick her up. Made me promise she could ride the school bus home."

Carly winced in sympathy. "I don't have to ask how you felt about that."

"Like I've had the rug yanked out from under me. But she agreed to let me meet the bus at the end of our road." Checking his watch a final time, he went to do just that.

When his baby girl stepped off the school bus, she was all grins and flashing eyes. There was a new confidence in her step, in the set of her shoulders. School, it seemed, agreed with Amanda Barnett.

"Ah, hell." Tyler slumped against the open back door. "It's only been a week since she started school. I'm gonna die of old age before she turns seven."

From behind him in the mudroom, Carly chuckled as the taillights of Cousin Frank's station wagon disappeared down the driveway in the twilight. "You didn't have to let her go spend the night with Frank and Bev and their girls. What's the matter? Are you after a little sympathy again?"

With a narrow-eyed stare, Tyler turned into the house and closed the back door firmly behind him. "Are you teasing me?"

Swallowing a laugh, Carly backed through the mudroom into the kitchen, one hand out in front of her to ward him off. "I wouldn't."

"You shouldn't," he said, his voice growing deeper with every word. "This is not a good time to tease me."

He was serious, she realized with a start. Very serious. "What do you mean?"

"I mean," he said, stepping into the kitchen after her, "that it's Saturday night, the hands have all gone to town and won't be back till tomorrow evening. Amanda's gone to spend the night with her cousins. And Dad's kicking up his heels at the Watering Hole and won't be back for hours."

Carly swallowed and took another step back, her playfulness forgotten under his steady gaze. "Meaning?"

"Meaning—" he matched her step for step "—that for the first time since we met, you and I are totally, completely, one hundred percent...alone. And I, for one, am very, very glad."

The intensity of his gaze, the blue-green heat shimmering there, turned her knees weak. Dear God, he was going to kiss her. The minute he got his hands on her, he would take her mouth with his, and she would let him.

Suddenly she knew deep inside that tonight it wouldn't stop with a kiss. She didn't want it to.

Amanda was getting better every day, growing more open, laughing and happy. It was only a matter of time until she let go of her guilt and got her voice back. Then Carly's job would be done. She would have no more excuse to stay on the Bar B. It would be back to San Francisco for her.

The very idea of leaving this sage-covered plain for Nob Hill, leaving Tyler and Amanda, and God help her, even cranky ol' Arthur, left a yawning gap of emptiness inside her she feared would never heal.

She wanted this night, wanted Tyler. She would take and give all she could. Build up memories to see her through the loneliness lying in wait for her just around the corner of her life. If only she had the nerve.

"Alone?" she whispered.

Tyler tried to read her expression but couldn't, and it scared him.

Amanda was getting better every day. She was happier, more playful than she'd been since the divorce. With the help of her cousins and Carly, she had weathered her first week of school like a little pro. The new light in her eyes glowed with a self-confidence she hadn't shown in months. It seemed as though any day now, the rest of her guilt, whatever its cause, would slip away and she would start talking.

The kicker was, when Amanda talked, Carly would leave. She would hightail it out of Wyoming so fast it would take a week for her dust to settle.

Tyler clenched a fist at his side. Why should getting the most important thing in his life, the one thing he'd prayed for for months—Amanda's recovery—cost him the one woman he wanted to get closer to, the woman he thought he might be falling in love with?

He wouldn't accept it, dammit. Amanda would get well, he knew. The time was coming. But he wouldn't accept that it had to cost him Carly.

Him, hell. Who was he kidding? Amanda herself was so damned attached to Carly she was bound to suffer when Carly left.

Okay, then. There was no sense in Tyler and Amanda both getting their teeth kicked in. Carly would just have to stay, at least for a while. He would just have to see to it.

But first he had to get a rein on his emotions. He had to calm down. "Yeah, alone," he finally answered. "Just you and me." He had to take that look of caution out of her eyes. He improvised. "But the sympathy can wait. What I'd really like is your company while I check on the stock. How about it?"

Carly didn't know what she'd been expecting... No, that wasn't true. She knew exactly what she'd expected, and it hadn't been an offer for an evening stroll through a couple of aromatic barns. Swallowing her disappointment, she offered him a smile. "I'd like that."

His answering smile warmed her. "Better get a jacket," he warned. "The temperature's already dropping."

When she stepped out the back door with him a few minutes later, she hoped he didn't notice that her cheeks were flushed from rushing. After all, she didn't want him to think she was so eager to be with him that she'd taken the stairs two at a time, then stopped to brush her hair before flying back down.

With the exception of the bookkeeping and the brief outdoor tour he'd given her on her first day at the ranch, Tyler had never offered to share details of his work with her. He'd never invited her to watch him work, nor asked for her company.

She didn't count that she'd taken over feeding the chickens and gathering the eggs. That, as Arthur so politely pointed out, was, after all, merely women's work, not ranching.

Carly had picked up a lot of information and some actual knowledge of the ranch workings, however, from over-hearing the men's conversations around the table. But it wasn't the same as if Tyler had actually shared those things with her.

She took in a deep breath of the clean air already chilled now that the sun was down. The slight breeze carried a hint of sagebrush, dust and hay. God, but it smelled good.

The outdoor utility lights were already on, casting streaks of light and shadows across the dark buildings.

"What do you have to do?" she asked as they crossed the bare ground toward the stallion barn. "Can I help?"

He gave her a curious look. With one hand he straightened his hat; the other hand stayed in the pocket of his denim jacket. "I always got the impression you'd rather not have anything to do with the outdoor aspects of ranch life."

Carly gaped at him in the gathering darkness. "Where'd you get an idea like that?"

He pulled open the barn door and shrugged. "I don't know. I guess from the fact that except for a trip to the chicken yard now and then, you rarely ever stick your head out of the house."

His tone was light, but Carly thought she detected an underlying tension in his words. She stood in the open doorway and blinked against the sudden brightness in the barn as Tyler flipped on the overhead lights. He stared at her with a mixture of curiosity and caution.

"I was never invited," she explained. "I didn't want to get in anyone's way."

The caution in his eyes faded as a slow smile spread across his face. "Ah, hell." He swung an arm around her shoulders and started down the aisle between the long rows of stalls. "No bigger than you are, you couldn't get in the way if you tried."

As they strolled the aisle, Tyler eyed each horse they passed. Occasionally he stopped to scratch behind an inquisitive set of ears here, along a muzzle there, his voice soft and low, almost crooning. Carly wondered if he would use that same tone on a woman while making love.

Oh, good grief. Where the devil had that thought come from?

But then, she knew where. It came straight from her own lonely fantasies, from her heart.

She stepped away from his loose, one-armed embrace and kept her gaze carefully averted lest he read more than he should on her face.

By the time they finished their tour of the first barn and made it to the second, Carly realized that this nightly "checking the stock" was, for Tyler, more of a ritual than an actual chore. All the work had been done before the other men left for town. Still, Tyler came, because he genuinely loved horses and cared about each animal he was responsible for. That caring came through in his eyes, his voice, the gentle way he stroked a glossy neck, patted a muscle-bound hip or shoulder, combed through a mane with his fingers.

By the time Carly and Tyler left the last barn and headed back toward the house, the night was cold. Carly shivered in her lightweight jacket.

Without a word, Tyler slipped his arm around her again and pulled her so close to his side that their hips bumped. She welcomed his thoughtfulness and his heat.

The moon was a huge rosy disk in the eastern sky. From out in the pasture, a calf bawled, and the breeze carried the far-off howl of a coyote. The quiet night sounds soothed something inside Carly, even as they tugged at her heartstrings. Before long she'd be back in San Francisco listening to traffic and sirens and the voices of her neighbors through the walls of her apartment.

Tyler pulled open the back door and dropped his arm from her shoulders so she could enter the mudroom. There they both took off their jackets and hung them on pegs.

"You're quiet tonight," he said as he followed her into the kitchen, then on into the living room.

She turned on the table lamp beside the sofa. "I could say the same for you. You had a lot more to say to your horses than you did to me."

"Did I?" He shook his head, more at himself than at her. "Sorry. I guess I had things on my mind."

The way his gaze roamed over her made her knees tremble. There it was again, that look she thought she'd only imagined earlier. The look that stirred her blood. "Anything in particular?"

His gaze lingered on her lips. "As a matter of fact," he said softly, "I was thinking how much I'd like to kiss you."

Something hot and sweet shot through her and stole her breath.

He stuffed his hands into the front pockets of his jeans, suddenly not looking at all like a man who was getting ready to kiss her. Not looking like a man who was even thinking about it, as he now stared at the toes of his boots, his jaw flexing.

"So why don't you?" she asked, her voice sounding faint and trembly in the quiet house.

Tyler's head shot up. His gaze pierced hers, then he closed his eyes and took a slow, deep breath. "Because we're alone." He opened his eyes again and looked at her. "Which will make it all too easy for me to push you for more than I think you're ready to give."

Sweat broke out on her palms. "More?"

"More than a kiss, Carly. I don't want to stop with just a kiss. Not tonight."

Intense heat flared in his eyes, along with the promise of making her feel that heat for herself. "Oh."

"Yeah." He turned his back and stared out the front window into the darkness. "Oh."

Carly licked her parched lips and felt a trembling deep inside. "Tyler?"

Tyler stiffened. He should have kept his mouth shut. He didn't want to face her now. Just thinking about what he wanted from her made him hard. But something in her voice compelled him to turn around.

The look in her eyes shook him. He read a dozen things in those brown depths. Longing and heat, mixed with the certain knowledge of what he wanted. Desolation and loneliness so deep it hurt him just to see it.

"Kiss me," she whispered.

A hot shiver slid down his spine. In what felt like slow motion, he pulled his hands from his pockets. Despite the knowledge in her eyes, he felt driven to ask, "Do you know what you're saying?"

Her throat worked on a swallow. "We both know I won't be here much longer. Amanda's getting better. This... tonight might be...our only chance."

They stood there, with six feet of pine floor and Navajo rug between them, each acknowledging the truth of her words, while Tyler's mind screamed in protest. This couldn't be their only chance, their only night together. God help him, it couldn't.

"I don't think," he said as he closed the distance between them, "that one night is going to be enough."

At her soft sigh, he cupped her face in unsteady hands and let his hunger loose. He hauled her against him and took her mouth with all the intensity of a starving man suddenly presented with a feast. And she was a feast. A banquet of sweetness and warmth to fill the yawning emptiness inside him.

When her tongue met his eagerly, it touched off a chain reaction of sparks that ignited into shattering explosions down his arms, his legs, his back. His loins.

God, how could just a kiss...ah, but then with Carly, it was never just a kiss. It was a mating of mouths and a melding of bodies and souls that stirred a yearning deep down inside him to possess her fully, to make her his, to stake his claim. To brand her.

Her response, as it always did, drove him wild. He slid one hand down to her hips and pulled her closer, tighter, but it wasn't enough. He wanted her so damned bad, not being able to get close enough was killing him.

Then he felt her hands at the front of his shirt, trembling fingers tugging at the snaps. His knees went weak. He nudged his hips against hers.

Her tiny whimper of want accompanied the answering thrust of her hips and made him groan into her hot, sweet mouth.

The first snap of his shirt gave, then the second. She didn't bother with more, but slipped her cool fingers inside to touch him. The exquisite feel of her skin sliding against his made him want more. More skin, hers and his, naked, touching, heating, soothing.

The third snap gave of its own accord.

Tyler tore his mouth free and gasped for breath. Never had a woman pushed him so far so fast. "Come here." He swung her up in his arms and carried her upstairs.

He wanted her in his bed, but some dark corner of his mind warned him that if she didn't stay, if she left him, he would never be able to escape the memory of her there. The room, the very bed, would become, for him, a torture chamber. Self-preservation led him down the dark hall and into her room. He told himself she would be more comfortable there.

Bright moonlight poured through the open curtains, spreading patches of light and shadow across the room. Tyler nudged the door closed behind him and carried Carly to the bedside.

His lips ached for the feel of hers. After all, he hadn't kissed her in at least twenty seconds. That was more than enough time for a calf to bolt, a horse to stumble, a man to die of need. "You make me crazy," he whispered as he took her lips with his.

He let her legs slip from his grasp, and as she stood before him and pressed her body to his, he moaned. Sizzling heat shot through his veins like wildfire. By the time he came up for air his chest was heaving.

She pulled away from him. He stifled a cry of protest. An instant later she turned on the bedside lamp. "If this is our only night together, I don't want to miss any part of it," she told him, voicing his own thoughts.

She looked and sounded calm. Too damned composed for his peace of mind. He wanted her hands to shake as violently as his. He wanted her skin to tingle with the need for his touch, her lungs to ache for air, the blood in her veins to turn molten.

He wanted her to feel as desperate as he did.

With deliberate slowness, he pulled her back into his arms.

Ah, the lady wasn't quite so calm as she appeared. Her pulse fluttered rapidly in the hollow of her throat as if it were a trapped butterfly trying to escape. Her heart thundered against his chest. She met his kiss eagerly, her hands curving around his neck. Her fingers threaded into his hair and sent heat racing down his arms.

He needed to touch her, feel her skin, taste it.

Carly shuddered as his mouth left hers to blaze a trail of kisses along her jaw and down her neck. His hands found their way under the back of her sweater. Where he touched, she burned. Hard calluses gently scraped her flesh, leaving a path of fire in their wake. Her breasts swelled in response, aching to feel that rough skin against them.

No man had ever made her feel so shivery, so needy. So greedy. She wanted her hands on his flesh so badly she fumbled with the remaining snaps on his shirt before finally baring his chest.

His skin was smooth and taut and warm, the muscles beneath, hard and quivering under her touch. She shoved the shirt over his shoulders and out of her way.

Under her eager fingers, Tyler felt his restraint slipping. Impatiently he yanked his shirt down his arms and flung it aside.

She stood back and ate him with her eyes, her hot gaze every bit as arousing as her touch. He closed his eyes and fought for control. Then her fingers brushed across his nipples. He jerked and sucked in a sharp breath as the circles of flesh beneath her touch drew exquisitely tight. The flesh behind the zipper of his jeans grew hotter, heavier, harder. Achingly hard.

With a low growl, he reached beneath her sweater again and unhooked her bra. "Turnabout," he whispered against her lips, "is fair play." In one motion, he drew the sweater and bra over her head and tossed them aside. They landed somewhere near his shirt. She tried to lean into his chest, but he held her back. "Let me look at you. God, Carly, you're beautiful."

She hung her head and hunched her shoulders forward. "I wish..." She motioned toward her breasts. "I wish I was bigger."

"I don't." He trailed his fingers down the outer curves of her small, perfect breasts and was gratified by the quickening of her breath. With the backs of his fingers, he brushed both nipples and watched them peak. "You're perfect." He pulled her to him slowly, until their bare chests mated. "So damned perfect."

She tilted her head to meet his gaze. "I want to be," she whispered with a stroke of one slender finger along his jaw, "for you." With both hands, she pulled his head down to hers and kissed him.

He was lost. He wanted to whisper her name, to describe all the emotions that were flooding him, but he wouldn't—couldn't—take his mouth from the sudden sweet possessiveness of hers.

Carly's head spun as he swept her into his arms and lowered them both to the bed. She felt him shove off his boots, heard them hit the braided rug beside the bed with a dull thud.

The empty, aching void inside her grew and grew, begging to be filled by him, with him. Only him.

He covered her with his hands, his body, his mouth. One hand worked its way between them and inched down her stomach to the snap on her jeans. Carly sucked in her breath.

Tyler raised his head. The light from the lamp turned one side of his face golden. His usually blue-green eyes were so dark a blue they looked almost black.

One finger delved beneath her waistband and slid slowly back and forth. With a slight tug on the snap, he whispered, "All right?"

The roughness in his voice turned her body moist between her thighs. His finger moved again, and her stomach fluttered. "Yes," she managed to say. "Yes."

Tyler watched the undulation of her stomach muscles beneath his hand and felt an answering movement in his own body. God, she was so responsive. He popped open the snap, pulled down the zipper and slipped his hand inside, feeling his way beneath elastic and lace, over springy curls, to cup the dark dampness that seared him with its heat.

Carly arched against his hand with a cry that echoed along his nerve endings.

The waiting was killing him, but he wouldn't rush, not now, not yet. He pressed an openmouthed kiss to her shoulder, then worked his way down to her breast. When he settled over the distended tip she cried out again. The nipple pearled against his tongue, driving him crazy, making him harder.

He couldn't wait, not any longer. He shoved and tugged until the rest of their clothes were gone and she was there, gloriously, totally naked in his arms. Her lips moved. He thought maybe she whispered his name, but all he could hear was his own labored breathing and the rush of blood in his ears.

She moved beneath him, shifting until he lay right where he belonged, cradled between her firm, smooth thighs.

Her hands roamed over him frantically, driving him nearer and nearer the edge of sanity.

"Touch me." God, he was begging, and he didn't care. Not when she complied so sweetly, her fingers gliding around his hip to brush against the part of him that pleaded to be buried inside her.

This time it was he who arched and cried out, squeezing his eyes shut to hold in the mind-numbing pleasure of those soft delicate fingers wrapped around him. "Yes, oh yes," he breathed.

Carly shivered at the sheer power that filled her with his reaction, and at his own power, the essence of which she held in her hand. He was smooth and sleek, as soft as velvet and as hard as steel. And she wanted him, ached for him to fill the emptiness that threatened to destroy her.

Then he was there, surging into her, filling her, driving her far beyond anything she'd ever known. Emotions she'd never experienced swelled until she thought surely she would burst with them. Ecstasy, desperation, passion. *Love*.

He set a slow, steady rhythm. All on their own, her hips matched his as he tortured her exquisitely with long, lingering strokes. Her name fell like a prayer, or maybe a blessing, from his lips as he pressed them to hers.

Then the fire and heat took over, and thought fled. Again and again he filled her, harder, faster, taking her higher than she'd ever flown, until the sensations deep inside her exploded in a rainbow of colors.

An instant later, he followed her over the edge with a sharp cry and one final, shattering thrust.

Long after his breath and senses returned, Tyler was still buried deep inside her. He never wanted to leave. But he was so big and she was so small, he worried about crushing her. He rose onto his elbows. "Am I too heavy?"

Her arms, which had slid from around him only moments ago in what he expected was sheer exhaustion, curled around his back and clutched him tightly. "No. Don't leave."

It was the word *leave* that did it. The very reminder that she would leave him one day soon had him lowering himself again to take her lips with a fierceness for which he should not have had the energy, much less the inclination.

He could ask her to stay. The thought had crossed his mind more than once. She must care for him, must have some pretty damn deep feelings for him, or she would never have given herself the way she had tonight, so wholeheartedly, so gloriously.

But the words lodged in his throat and wouldn't budge. *Coward,* his mind accused.

Yes, that's what he was, all right. A rank coward. She was young and beautiful and vibrant. She was used to life on Nob Hill. With the money he was paying her, plus the promised bonus when Amanda recovered her speech, Carly would have more choices for her future than she would know what to do with. Who was he to assume she would want to confine herself to an isolated ranch halfway between sagebrush and nowhere, with no one around but a bunch of uncouth cowboys and their horses?

In that regard he was comparing her to Deborah and knew he wasn't being fair. Yet he couldn't stop himself. Even if Carly thought she might be able to adjust, how long would it be before the isolation, the short summers and long, harsh winters, wore her down?

Don't leave, she'd said. Yet it was she who would leave him. The very idea made him desperate to hold on to her as tight as he could for as long as she'd stay.

Before he realized what was happening, he was hard again and thrusting into her over and over with a desperation that scared him with its intensity. And she was meeting him thrust for thrust, heartbeat for heartbeat, ragged breath for ragged, lung-crushing breath. The little sounds she made in her throat, the way she rocked her hips against his, had him fighting for control. He didn't want to go off without her. Please, God, not without her.

Then it was happening. She was clutching him with her thighs, her arms, her tight inner muscles, and crying out his name. He let go of his control and gave her everything he had, everything he was, knowing even as he emptied himself into her that it, *he*, wouldn't be enough to hold her.

The next thing he became aware of, before he'd even caught his breath, was the slamming of a pickup door outside Carly's bedroom window. He swore; she stiffened.

"Your father."

Tyler rose above her and watched in the lamplight as her expression closed off and she emotionally withdrew from him. Even her skin, still slick with sweat and pressed so intimately against his, seemed to cool too fast. He swallowed. "Do you want me to leave?"

Outside, footsteps crunched on gravel.

She turned her face away from the light, away from him. "I think it would be best."

No, he cried softly. Not best. Nothing could be "best" if it meant leaving her arms.

But because she asked, he would do it.

He gave her one last kiss, keeping it as gentle as he could when what he wanted to do was kiss her harder than ever and stay right where he was, still buried deep inside her. Slowly, one reluctant, aching inch at a time, he withdrew from her, gritting his teeth against the need to thrust forward again, rather than pull out.

Downstairs, the back door creaked open.

"Could you...hurry?" she asked, her voice strained, her face still averted.

"Yeah, right," he said, stung by her withdrawal. He rose from the bed and grabbed his clothes and boots from the floor. At the door, he gave her one last look. "I love you, too," he bit out.

Chapter Twelve

Tyler spent a long night kicking himself for the way he'd left Carly. She'd had every right to get uptight over his dad coming home; *he'd* had no right to get sarcastic about it. No right to hurt her that way.

"Your insecurities are showing, bud."

His harsh whisper filled the darkness in his room. Terrific. Now she had him talking to himself.

The next morning he realized he might as well talk to himself, because she sure wasn't going to let him talk to her. She frustrated his every attempt at apologizing, by the simple method of sticking so close to his dad's side during breakfast, Tyler would have sworn the two were joined at the hip.

No. Don't think about her hips.

With a frustrated oath, Tyler slammed his hat on his head and left the house. This was shaping up to be the perfect day to repair the gate Prancer had kicked apart yesterday. Tyler was definitely in the mood to pound nails.

Mostly he was still angry with himself. What he felt regarding Carly's behavior wasn't anger, it was fear. Fear that she was withdrawing from him completely. After the way she gave herself to him the night before, he wouldn't be able to stand the cruel reality of never feeling her sweet warmth again.

By the time the sun was halfway across the sky, Tyler had repaired the corral gate plus four stalls in the stallion barn. He was shoeing his second horse of the day when a shadow loomed beside him.

"You headin' in for lunch?" his dad asked.

Eat lunch with Carly and his dad? A repeat of breakfast, with her refusing to meet his gaze? Not very damn likely. "Go on without me. I'll get something later."

Worn boots shuffled in the dirt beside him.

Finally Tyler looked up. "Something besides lunch on your mind?"

Arthur worked a toothpick from one corner of his mouth to the other without benefit of hands. "Funny. I was just getting ready to ask you the same thing."

Tyler bent over the hoof he held clamped between his knees. "Meaning?"

"Oh, I guess I was just wondering if there was anything you wanted to tell me. About last night maybe."

Tyler felt his cheeks sting. Dammit all to hell and back in a little red wagon. He couldn't remember the last time his dad had made him blush. This time, however, embarrassment was only partly responsible. Most of the flush was due to anger.

"Oh," he said imitating his dad's drawl, "I don't know. I can't recall anything I did last night that could even remotely be considered any of your business."

Tyler heard a snort. He wasn't exactly sure if it had come from Mooser, who'd never cared for having his hooves picked at and hammered on, or if the sound had come from Arthur.

"Guess that pretty much answers my question," the old man grumbled.

"If you say so," Tyler muttered back.

"Let's be blunt."

Carly nearly strangled on a mouthful of macaroni and cheese. She'd never liked conversations that started with words like those. Most especially when they came from a man like Arthur Barnett, too shrewd for her peace of mind, and not particularly happy with her presence in his home.

She didn't need this. Her nerves were shot, her stomach was churning and she kept playing over and over in her mind the way she'd panicked last night at the thought of Arthur finding Tyler in her bed. The way she'd turned away from Tyler. His parting shot as he'd left.

He had tried to talk to her at breakfast, but she'd avoided him. She didn't have much experience with mornings after. Certainly not mornings after a night like she'd spent in his arms. And not after the way they had parted.

She finished swallowing, then carefully placed her fork on the edge of her plate before looking up to meet Arthur's piercing gaze. She was tired of his snide comments, tired of him telling her she had to stay one minute, then making her feel like a pariah the next. So, he wanted to be blunt, did he?

"Go ahead," she told him. "You usually are."

His eyes widened in surprise. "Well, so the kitten has claws, huh? Fine. That's good. Because I want to know what you're planning."

"About what?"

"You know about what."

"Arthur, I would never presume to even guess what runs through your mind. I'm afraid you're going to have to spell it out."

"All right. I want to know how long you're planning on staying here."

"I wish you'd make up your mind. I almost left two

weeks ago the day of the picnic, but you stopped me. Now you ask how long I'm staying like you can't wait to see the last of me. What do you want from me?'' she cried, her composure slipping.

He took a sip of coffee without relinquishing the hold his steady gaze had on her. "I want my granddaughter to be able to talk, and I want my son left alone."

For an instant, Carly wondered frantically if Tyler could have put Arthur up to this. Then she dismissed the idea as absurd. Tyler fought his own battles. If he wanted nothing more to do with her, he would tell her. That, she feared, was what he'd been trying to tell her all morning. But he would abhor his father's interference.

She steadied herself with a deep breath. "In answer to your question, my agreement with Tyler was that I stay six months, or until Amanda regains her speech, whichever comes first. That's what he's paying me for.''

"Is it?''

At his cutting remark, sickness churned in her stomach. "Now I know why he offered me so much money to come here. He must have known I'd be subjected to this kind of abuse.''

She scooted her chair back across the floor, stood and threw down her napkin. "Excuse me, but I believe I've lost my appetite." At the door to the living room she stopped and glared at him over her shoulder. "Be glad I care too much about Amanda to leave before my job is done. As much as Tyler is paying me, it's not nearly enough to put up with you.''

Like a coward, Carly hid in her room until she heard Arthur leave the house. She waited another ten minutes for good measure, then started down the stairs. Halfway down, she heard the pickup roar to life, followed by the sound of tires crunching gravel.

She dashed to the back door in time to see Arthur driving off toward town. She nearly slumped in relief. For a moment she'd feared Tyler had gone to pick up Amanda and left Carly alone with his father.

Instead Arthur had gone, leaving her alone on the ranch with his son. The rest of the men wouldn't be back from wherever they'd spent the night until late that evening. Nothing to be relieved about, after all, she realized.

But Tyler was busy somewhere outside, so she felt relatively safe. She set aside a plate of food for him should he want it later, and was halfway through loading the lunch dishes into the dishwasher when the back door creaked open.

Her nerves screamed in protest. She wasn't ready to face Tyler yet. She didn't have any idea what to say to the man who had turned her world inside out with a kiss, the man she wanted to make love with again so badly she ached.

He crossed the room, spurs jingling, boots thudding on the floor, until he stood just on the other side of the open dishwasher door. "Are you shutting me out?"

Slowly and with great effort, Carly forced herself to meet Tyler's gaze. His expression was hard and closed, his eyes fierce. So much pride, she thought. And she'd shoved it in his face last night, all because of the sound of a pickup door slamming.

With the toe of his boot he nudged the dishwasher door closed and moved closer, placing his hands on her shoulders. "I won't let you shut me out," he told her. "Not after last night, Carly. I can't."

Carly squeezed her eyes in relief. He didn't hate her for the way she'd turned him away. "I'm sorry," she whispered, emotion making her voice break. "I didn't mean to act that way last night. I heard your dad coming and I got scared. I...got stupid. I didn't mean..."

"Hush." His hands flexed on her shoulders. "No more."

"I didn't mean to send you away like that."

"I didn't mean to leave you the way I did, either. I...ah, damn." He pulled her to his chest and claimed her lips. "I'll never get enough of you. Never."

He was sweaty and gritty and his clothes smelled like horse. Carly didn't care. She wrapped her arms around him and held on, letting herself sink into his kiss.

He trailed his mouth along her jaw and down her throat. She arched her neck, offering herself to him. "Your dad," she said with a gasp as he nipped slightly with his teeth. "Where...when—"

His lips fastened to her throat, Tyler cupped one breast in his palm and gently squeezed. "He went to town to get Amanda." He nudged his hips against hers, letting her feel how ready he was to take things well beyond a kiss. "It'll take him at least an hour."

His free hand swept up beneath the back of her T-shirt, sending shivers along her spine. "Then we have time to...go upstairs?"

When he raised his head, his eyes were practically glowing. "How shy are you?" he asked with a sudden grin.

His thumb flicking across her nipple made her gasp. "Less and less shy by the minute."

"Good." He kissed her eyelids, then traveled down one cheek to her mouth. "Because I don't think I can make it up the stairs in the shape you've got me in."

Before she knew what he was about, he lifted her and sat her on the counter, then nudged his way between her thighs until he nestled close and snug, his hardness against the softness that craved him.

Once more, his mouth left hers and trailed down her throat. This time he didn't stop there. With a boldness that made every nerve ending in her body tingle, he kissed his way to her breast. Through T-shirt and bra, he took the tip in his mouth.

Carly groaned at the exquisite tugging that stretched from his lips through her nipple, straight down some invisible wire to her very core. She wrapped her legs around his hips and pulled him closer, wringing a moan from deep in his chest that set her blood on fire.

Frantic to feel more of him, she yanked his shirttail free

of his jeans and ran her hands underneath, up the smooth hardness of his sleek back. His skin was hot and damp beneath her eager fingers.

With a hand to her hips, Tyler pulled her even closer and ground himself against her. Carly felt her world start to slip. The sensation, the throbbing heat, built to an almost unbearable level. She threw her head back and gasped for breath. "Tyler, I—"

"Well, my dear, it looks as though we're interrupting."

Carly jerked. Shocked and embarrassed to her soul, she opened her eyes and felt the blood drain from her face.

Tyler flinched at the intrusion. He felt Carly try to squirm free of his hold, but his brain was too fogged with heat to let go quickly. He'd be damned for all eternity if he'd jerk away as though caught doing something indecent in his own frigging kitchen. It took every last drop of his control to raise his mouth from Carly's breast. Even then, all he could do was turn his head and rest it on her shoulder while he gasped for breath and stared at his former in-laws standing in the doorway.

In his arms, Carly trembled violently. The four-letter word that left his lips was graphic and one he didn't normally use in mixed company, but for Tyler, in that moment, nothing else would do. It rang sharp and clear across the room.

"Yes," Howard Tomlinson said with raised brows. "It seems the two of you were about to do just that."

Tyler turned his face into Carly's neck, trying to keep from screaming in outraged frustration and fury. "God, Carly, I'm sorry. Some people obviously don't have the manners God gave a goat."

"Carly?" came Earline's cool, hard voice. "*This* is the woman you hired to take care of our granddaughter? Just what else, might I ask, are you paying her for?"

"And speaking of our granddaughter," Howard said coldly, "I do hope she isn't often exposed to this type of public display of animalistic mating."

Tyler ground his teeth and took a slow, deep breath. With measured care, he raised his head from Carly's shoulder and moved out of the warm cradle of her thighs. The untimely interruption should have cooled his ardor. Instead he was still so hard he could barely stand up straight.

One look at Carly's face told him she'd never been so mortified in her life. Her lips were red and puffy, and the wet spot from his mouth on the front of her T-shirt told its own tale. He ached for the pain of humiliation in her eyes. For a second, he squeezed his eyes shut, trying to hold back the rage that threatened to choke him. When he reached up to brush an errant strand of golden chestnut hair from her soft cheek, his hand shook. "In case you haven't guessed," he told her with wry tenderness, "this is Howard and Earline Tomlinson, Amanda's grandparents."

Carly felt a bubble of hysteria rise to her throat. What the hell was she supposed to say, "Nice to meet you"? Oh, God, oh, God. One instant she'd been anticipating running her hand down inside the front of Tyler's jeans, and...and the next...oh, *God*.

Tyler stepped away, depriving her of his warmth, his protective presence, and turned to face the couple at the door. The sheer fury in his eyes shook her. She'd never seen a person so absolutely livid.

If nothing else, the very softness of his voice, the precise way he pronounced each word, the careful way he drew in his breath should have told the world he was ready to rip someone apart with his teeth when he said to the Tomlinsons, "We'll accept your apology now."

While his voice made Carly shiver, both Tomlinsons appeared immune.

"*My* apology?" Howard Tomlinson obviously thought the words were meant for him alone.

"For barging into my home unannounced, *uninvited*. And for your viciously rude crack about Carly."

"I do notice," Tomlinson said, "that you haven't bothered to answer the question."

Tyler's fists clenched at his sides. "Crap like that doesn't deserve an answer. What are you doing here?"

The tall, thin man in the obviously custom-made European suit raised his chin, looking for all the world like a disdainful king peering down upon his lowly subjects. A full head of silver hair over a long narrow face with predatory eyes only added to the illusion. "We came to see our granddaughter. Where is she?"

A muscle along Tyler's jaw bunched; his nostrils flared. "She spent the night in town with her cousins. Dad's gone to pick her up. You probably passed him on the road."

Earline Tomlinson, in her winter white wool slacks and sweater, her neck undoubtedly straining to hold up the heavy weight of a full half-dozen gold chains, stepped forward with a stiff spine. "You let a child with her obvious emotional problems spend the night away from home?"

Eyes narrowed, Tyler advanced on her. "Where the hell was all this concern about her emotional problems a few months ago, when you insisted on taking her to some damned ear, nose and throat specialist instead of getting her the counseling she needed, *Grandma?*"

Carly could tell by the way he said that last word that he'd done it to irritate Mrs. Tomlinson. She could tell by the way the woman's mouth pinched that he'd hit his mark. The woman was generally referred to as Amanda's grandmother, not grandma. To Earline Tomlinson, Carly was sure there was a distinct difference between the two.

Shivering against the hostility in the air, Carly forced herself to slide off the counter and stand on the floor. The movement drew all eyes to her. She stiffened and took a moment to let her knees steady.

All she wanted to do was flee. As fast as her legs could carry her. But she couldn't leave Tyler to face the animosity of his in-laws alone. She moved to stand beside him. His arm came around her waist and gave much-needed support. She felt the tension humming through him.

Mrs. Tomlinson's hair was the exact same shining shade

of silver as her husband's. She turned that immaculately groomed head toward Carly with slow deliberation. "This does not concern you. You may go."

Against her side, Tyler stiffened. "Don't—"

"If it concerns Amanda," Carly interrupted, "it does concern me."

"Not if we have anything to say about it," Mr. Tomlinson said, his voice low and threatening.

"You don't," Tyler answered bluntly.

"Please." Carly licked her lips nervously, her hands shaking, her knees threatening to. "This isn't getting us anywhere. Would you like to go in the living room and have a seat? I was about to make coffee."

"No, my dear, that is most definitely *not* what you were about to do." Mrs. Tomlinson's voice dripped with sarcasm.

"One more insult, just one more," Tyler said between clenched teeth, "and I'll be asking you to leave."

"We're going nowhere without seeing our granddaughter."

"Amanda has made incredible progress in the past few weeks," Carly offered. Damn, she wished her voice would quit quivering. "I'm not sure her seeing you just now is a very good idea."

Mr. Tomlinson turned his disdainful gaze on Tyler. "If you do not wish me to insult her, kindly instruct your...*employee* to remain silent."

With a low growl, Tyler surged forward.

Carly grabbed his arm with both hands. "Tyler, no."

Tyler trembled with impotent rage. Never had his lack of sophistication bothered him until that moment. Short of resorting to name-calling, the only method of dealing with the present situation that came to mind was to punch the living daylights out of the bastard before him.

Carly's tug on his arm stopped him. Even then, he gave the idea serious thought, but the sound of the old pickup rattling over the rutted road toward the house held him

back. That, and the sure knowledge that Carly would probably find some way to blame herself for the situation. Hell,
she was probably already doing that. Seething with fury,
he kept his gaze locked on Howard.

Outside, tires ground to a halt, a pickup door slammed,
footsteps crunched across the ground. "Don't recognize the
car," came Arthur's voice. "Let's go in and see who's
here. You want me to carry that? Okay, kiddo, suit yourself."

As the back door in the mudroom flew open, the Tomlinsons stepped aside and turned toward the kitchen doorway.

Amanda was the first to enter, with Arthur right behind
her.

"Hey, sweetpea," Tyler called, hoping his voice
sounded welcoming.

Watching the blood drain from his daughter's face as she
recognized her grandparents was like getting kicked in the
gut by an angry stallion. Carly had been right. Amanda
wasn't ready for this.

"Well, now." Arthur's gaze darted swiftly around the
room, assessing the situation. "Isn't this a surprise?" he
said carefully, slowly.

Another pot on the fire, Tyler thought. His dad had never
cared for the Tomlinsons, and that was putting it mildly.

Earline bent down beside her husband and held out her
arms to Amanda. "Hello, dear. Come, let me give you a
hug."

Slowly, reluctantly, Amanda lowered her backpack to the
floor and stepped obediently into her grandmother's embrace, her gaze flying to Tyler then Carly, then back to
Tyler, her eyes filled with distress. God, he should have
found a way to spare her this.

"Hello, darling," Howard said.

Amanda offered her grandfather a shaky smile that
quickly faltered.

Seeing her distress and confusion, Tyler took a deep

breath and strove for normalcy. He forced a grin. "Come here, you." He swooped Amanda up in his arms and gave her a squeeze. "Let me get you all dirty and smelly. You're much too clean after a night in town. Did you have fun?"

She gave him a slight nod and shy smile. God, Amanda hadn't been shy about a single thing since she'd stopped wearing those frilly dresses.

He planted a big kiss on her cheek. "Missed you, sweet-pea." Looking toward his father, he asked, "How'd you get back so fast? You just left."

Arthur shrugged. "Met Bev on the road to town. Little Emily came down with a cold, and Bev thought she'd better get Amanda away from her before she caught it."

Tyler peered at Amanda. "You gonna catch Emily's cold?"

Amanda gave him a smile and shook her head.

"Good." He gave her another kiss.

She hugged his neck sweetly, then he let her slide down his leg. She turned and practically threw herself at Carly.

"Amanda?" Earline called softly.

Carly knelt and gave Amanda a noisy hug, keeping the girl from turning toward her grandmother. "Why don't you run up to your room and take care of that stuff?" Carly nodded toward Amanda's backpack. "Have you had lunch?"

Amanda nodded, relief flooding her face. She cast a swift look at her grandparents. As she glanced away, her eyes held a haunted look.

"Okay, then," Carly told her. "When you come back down, you can have those last two cookies I saved for you. Now, scoot," she added.

The minute Amanda hit the stairs, Carly turned toward the Tomlinsons and met their twin glares. Wanting to shield her from their wrath, Tyler started to step between her and them, but Carly cut him off.

"Tyler told you over the phone that Amanda wasn't

comfortable with hearing from you just yet," she said firmly.

The fire of battle lighting her eyes made Tyler's chest swell with pride.

"As I explained, it's not you that's the problem," Carly told them. "She loves you both. But she's still suffering guilt over whatever she did that she thinks was so terrible. It centers around her mother, and she associates the two of you closely with her, and obviously with her own guilt. I really don't think your visit just now is a good idea."

Howard took a menacing step toward Carly that had Tyler moving to stand beside her. "And as I told Tyler, you obviously have no idea what you're talking about. You're nothing more than a child yourself, unqualified to be giving out unwanted advice. I should have you arrested for practicing medicine without a license."

"That's it," Tyler shouted. "No more. You'll leave now."

"Wait, Tyler," Carly said, her voice soft yet firm. She kept her gaze on Howard and raised her chin a notch. "First off, Mr. Tomlinson, I'm thirty years old. The only person I'll put up with calling me a child is my own mother. Second, if I were unqualified to help Amanda, one of the country's foremost child psychologists would not have recommended me for the job."

For the first time since Tyler had met her, Carly was sticking up for herself. Not for Amanda, not for him, but for herself. Bittersweet emotion filled him that she had need to do so in his own home.

"I've worked with other children in the past. I've faced problems in my own life similar to what Amanda is going through, so I understand better than most what she's feeling. I believe in a few more weeks, when she's emotionally stronger, she'll want very much to see you. When her voice returns, she'll want to talk with you on the phone. But right now the absolute last thing on earth she needs is to be reminded of her supposed guilt, which is what your presence is doing. Second only to that, she cannot, *must not* be subjected to the hostility in this room.''

Tyler wanted to applaud, he wanted to shout, he wanted to kiss her right then and there. He had to give Howard credit, the man was making every effort to control himself. The struggle on his face was obvious. Just when Tyler thought the old goat had managed to reel in his sharp tongue, Howard opened his damned big mouth again.

''The books I've read on the subject—''

''Books?'' Carly cried. ''Bravo! Give the man a cigar. He's read books. We're not talking about books, Mr. Tomlinson, we're talking about a lost little girl who needs every break she can get to deal with having her entire world torn apart by a tragic accident for which she somehow manages to blame herself.''

''What you're saying is, you haven't studied from books.''

''Of course I have. But I've also lived the anguish, the pain, the guilt myself, and I've learned to deal with it. I've helped several other children deal with it.''

''We're not talking about other children,'' Howard said, his voice rising. He took another threatening step toward Carly. ''We're talking about *my grandchild.*''

Just as Tyler once again prepared to step between the two, Amanda flew into the room and shoved against her grandfather's legs until he staggered backward. Then she shoved again, backing him up even farther.

Gone was all trace of the shy, uncertain child. No guilt marked her expression as she glared at the man. Mouth pursed in obvious anger, she planted her tiny fists against her waist and turned a look on Carly, then Tyler.

Her eyes questioned him hotly, then she did something he didn't understand at all. She lifted one foot from the floor and swung it back and forth.

''I don't understand, sweetpea.''

Brow furrowed, she looked at Carly.

"What is it, honey?" Carly asked. "What are you trying to say?"

Frustrated, Amanda stomped to Tyler's side and pointed toward his foot, then lifted her own again and swung it back and forth.

Beside him, Carly gave a sudden squeak. Tyler watched as her eyes widened. She looked like she was strangling on, of all improbable things, laughter.

"Amanda," she said, choking, "I don't think—"

Amanda cut her off by stamping her foot. Good God, she actually stamped her foot. Tyler couldn't remember the last time his daughter had felt enough self-confidence to get angry, let alone show it.

With a determined glare, Amanda tugged on the crease of his jeans until he lifted his foot for her, then she jerked until he made the same swinging motion she had shown him. Next she dropped his foot, stomped across the room to Howard, and knelt beside his legs. With a sharp nod, she slapped her hand against the man's shin.

"This is ridiculous," Howard said. "The child is obviously so confused she doesn't know what she's doing."

Amanda glared up her grandfather's long, lean length. Then she looked at Tyler again and started a new set of motions. She curled her lips down in an exaggerated frown, then brought her fists to her eyes to indicate crying. She pointed to Carly, repeated the crying gesture, then pointed to herself and repeated it again.

Then she pointed to Tyler, then his boot, and slapped her grandfather's leg once more.

In a horrified, hilarious flash, Tyler understood. "Oh, God." His sudden hoot of laughter earned him another squeak from Carly, a grin and eager nod from Amanda, and shocked, furious glares from Howard and Earline. Arthur, from where he leaned against the door to the mudroom with his arms folded across his chest, watched the entire scene with narrowed eyes and pursed lips.

Tyler finally managed to control his laughter. "You're

absolutely right," he told his daughter. "He deserves that
and more for being mean to Carly. But I think Carly was
right," he added with an uncontrollable grin and a shake
of his head. "It's really not nice to kick people in the
shins."

Carly folded her lips in on each other, mashing them flat
to hold in her laughter.

From the doorway, Arthur choked and cleared his throat.

Howard and Earline gasped in unified shock.

Amanda gave her father the most disgusted, perturbed
frown he'd ever seen on a child.

"However..." He held out his hand. When she took it,
he swung her up in his arms. "I think Carly's alternate
suggestion the last time the topic came under discussion
was highly appropriate."

Can we? Can we? Amanda mouthed eagerly.

"You bet we can, sweetpea. On three?"

She giggled silently and nodded.

Carly slapped a hand over her mouth while her eyes
bulged.

Tyler shifted Amanda in his arms until the two of them
faced her grandparents. "Ready?"

With narrowed eyes, Amanda gave a sharp nod.

"Okay. One...two...three."

Tyler and Amanda turned toward her grandparents and
simultaneously stuck out their tongues.

Chapter Thirteen

"Good God," Howard cried.

"Yes." Tyler laughed as Amanda sidled down his leg and took hold of his hand. "God is good, Amanda Barnett's the greatest thing since sliced bread, Carly Baker's a wonderful woman, and all is right with the world."

"Howard." Earline placed a perfectly manicured hand dramatically across her breast as if for protection—or to show off her rings. "I do believe they've all gone mad in this house."

"And I believe," Tyler said, sobering, "there have been more than enough insults flying in this house today to last a lifetime. If the two of you would care to get a room in town for the night, maybe we can get together tomorrow with a little more civility than we're all currently capable of."

Earline blinked. "Howard, he's throwing us out."

"How perceptive of you," Tyler drawled.

"You," Howard said fiercely, jabbing a finger in Tyler's

direction, "have not heard the end of this. Not by half. I'll not have my granddaughter brought up in such a disgusting atmosphere."

"Well, now, I don't think you have anything to say about how *my daughter* is raised."

"We'll see about that," Tomlinson said, ushering Earline out the door. "We'll just see about that."

"Okay, okay, so maybe we shouldn't have done it," Tyler admitted over supper.

"No comment." Carly kept her gaze locked firmly on the mound of mashed potatoes before her, not daring to look up. If she looked up, she knew she'd break out laughing again.

"We really shouldn't have done it. You know that, don't you, sweetpea?" he asked Amanda.

From the corner of her eye, Carly saw Amanda give a sober acknowledgment.

Then she heard the grin in Tyler's voice. "Felt good, though, didn't it?"

The grin Amanda had been fighting finally broke free.

Carly allowed herself to look up and chuckle with the others. Even Arthur was laughing.

"Unfortunately," Carly said, "all it accomplished was to hurt their feelings and make them angry. They came because they were concerned about Amanda and wanted to see how she was doing."

"That doesn't excuse the way they just walked in—"

Cheeks stinging over what the Tomlinsons had walked in on, Carly averted her gaze from Tyler's.

"—nor the way they acted after that."

"Ol' Howard was a mite overbearing," Arthur offered.

Carly knew, or hoped fervently, that Arthur had no idea what she and Tyler had been doing when the Tomlinsons had surprised them. Still, she couldn't quite look him in the eye.

"Overbearing?" Tyler claimed with a snort. "He was an out-and-out—"

Carly interrupted with a loud clearing of her throat and a sharp glance from Tyler to Amanda.

"Anyway," Tyler said, looking at Amanda, "if they come back, are we gonna try to be nice to them? They do love you, sweetpea."

Amanda frowned at her plate.

"No need to decide right now," he offered. "Just think about it. If you don't want to visit with them just yet, you don't have to."

Relieved gratitude crossed the child's face as she looked up at her father.

"As long as we all agree that it's not nice to stick our tongues out at people, and we really shouldn't do it anymore. Right?" Tyler asked.

Amanda pursed her lips and glanced around the room as if suddenly deaf.

"Amanda."

She heaved a sigh, then nodded.

"All right, then," Tyler said.

They spent the rest of the meal talking about Amanda's overnight stay in town with her cousins, and about her school. Carly was thrilled with the way Amanda had adjusted in class. Her teacher, it seemed, was wonderfully patient and supportive when dealing with Amanda's inability to speak.

Tyler had heard from his cousin, Frank, who'd heard from his seven-year-old, Emily, that one boy at recess had made fun of Amanda and called her a dummy. Not only had Amanda doubled up her fists and threatened to punch the much larger boy—Tyler wondered where she'd learned that little bit of self-defense—but all four of her cousins, including Bobby, who usually had no use for *girls,* had stood up for her.

Little Emily had told Frank that Cousin Amanda would

have no more trouble at school. She had her own personal set of six- and seven-year-old bodyguards.

Tyler, too, seemed to be getting used to the idea of his baby going to school. He'd surprised Carly when he'd given permission for Amanda to spend the previous night with Emily and Laurie.

Sudden memories of how last night had progressed on the ranch had the dishes clattering in Carly's hands as she carried them to the sink. Before she could drop them, she hurriedly set them on the counter. On the exact spot where she'd sat earlier that day and held Tyler's head to her breast.

That reminder was enough to make her knees weak.

Two hours after dinner, with Amanda upstairs taking a bath and Arthur in the living room reading a farm-and-ranch equipment catalog, Tyler cornered Carly in the laundry room. She was folding towels at the table next to the dryer when his arms came around her from behind without warning.

Carly had been thinking of him so much, she wasn't even surprised. She simply sighed and leaned back against his chest.

He tightened his arms around her just beneath her breasts and pulled her close, then settled his chin on the top of her head. "I was so damned proud of you today," he told her. "You defied that ol' bastard better than anyone I've ever seen."

"I'm afraid all I did was cause more problems."

"No, you didn't. You, better than anyone, know what's best for Amanda. I'm just sorry they didn't have the courtesy to call before they came barging out here."

Despite the sudden heat in her cheeks, Carly managed a wry chuckle. "Yeah, me, too."

"Speaking of barging..." Tyler turned her around and lifted her onto the table, then nudged his way between her knees. "Where were we when we were so rudely interrupted?"

Carly slid her arms around his waist and laid her head against his shoulder. "We were about to do something unspeakable on the kitchen counter."

He nestled his hips firmly into the V of her thighs. "Something unspeakably fantastic, you mean. God," he said hoarsely while hugging her tight. "I'd have given anything to keep you from having to face them today. I'm so sorry about what happened."

"No more sorry than I am. We lost our chance."

With a hand to the small of her back to hold her steady, he nudged his hips against her and groaned. "Lost, hell. We were robbed. Cheated. God, I want you."

She could feel the truth of his words in the tightness of his grip, the pounding of his heart beneath her cheek, the hardness of the ridge of flesh pressed so intimately, so erotically against the very heat of her. She barely heard her own whimper of need over the roaring of blood rushing in her ears as she flexed her hips against him. "We can't," she whispered with a moan. "We can't."

"I know. I know, honey." And he did know. The rushed secrecy of trying to make love while his daughter and father were only a few feet away wasn't what he wanted for Carly, nor for himself. But that didn't keep him from kissing her.

Her lips parted softly, instantly for him. The kiss was long and hard and desperate, then he tore his mouth from hers. "I'm sorry. I didn't mean to take us this far when we can't finish. I...wanted, needed to feel you against me. I didn't mean—"

"It's all right," she whispered.

"It's not all right. You're trembling." He pulled back far enough to look into her eyes. The stark need he saw in those deep brown depths, darker now with arousal, made his chest tighten. Last night he'd been so intent on the rest of her, he hadn't noticed how dark her eyes turned when she wanted him. The urge to look into them at the precise moment she came gripped him and wouldn't let go.

He slid his hand between her thighs and cupped her, feeling her moist heat even through her jeans. She let out another one of those tiny whimpers that drove him straight toward the edge. His lungs threatened to collapse.

Fingers flexing against her, he said, "Just because we can't do it right now doesn't mean I have to leave you like this. Come here, honey." He replaced his hand with his hips and pressed himself tightly against her again. "Move against me. Take what you need."

"No." With a groan of protest, she jerked her hips away and raised her head, her eyes nearly black with need. "Not without you."

"It's all right," he soothed, while inside his blood seethed. He reached for her again. "Let me."

She shook her head. "No, Tyler. Not without you. It should happen together, for both of us, with you buried deep inside me. I don't want it any other way."

Her words, such sweet, sweet words, nearly cost him his control.

Upstairs, Amanda pulled the plug on the bathtub. Water, and Tyler and Carly's moment, gurgled and chugged down the drain.

Carly watched Tyler close his eyes and fight the fire raging between them. The skin across his cheeks stretched tight. His lips, still moist from hers, firmed and pulled into a grim line.

She ran shaking fingers along his beard-roughened jaw. "Another time, perhaps?"

His lids rose halfway, leaving his eyes glowing through fierce, narrow slits. "You can count on it."

During the next days, Carly and Tyler were never alone long enough to consider making love, but it was always on both their minds. Tyler showed it in the way he grabbed her every chance he got and kissed her breath away. Carly showed it in the way she clung to him and kissed him back.

Except for Monday afternoon when Tyler drove to town to talk to the Tomlinsons, only to find them gone, he was always nearby. He seemed to be everywhere, waiting for the opportunity to pull Carly around a corner, behind a door, anywhere away from prying eyes long enough to torment them both and keep the fire blazing hot and high.

And Carly was becoming less and less shy about putting herself in his path. On her way to the chicken house early one afternoon, she stood outside the gate and waited until Tyler, working with a colt in one of the corrals, looked up and saw her. She gave him a long, slow grin, then crossed through the fenced chicken yard and into the henhouse.

Before she'd gathered half a dozen eggs from the nest boxes into her wire basket, his long shadow stretched through the open door.

With a gleam in his eyes, he kicked the door shut behind him, took the basket from her hand and placed it on the floor, then pulled her into his arms. Carly reveled in the fierce hunger of his kiss. It spoke directly to her own starving need for his touch, his scent, his taste.

By the time he left a few moments later, his chest laboring as hard as hers to draw in air, neither of them had spoken a word. They didn't need words. Not now. They only needed each other.

With trembling hands, Carly picked up her basket and bent to reach another egg in the bottom row of nest boxes.

The long shadow loomed again in the doorway. With a smile, Carly straightened and turned. "Back for more already?"

But it wasn't Tyler. It was Neal Walters, with a predatory look in his eyes that made the hair on the back of Carly's neck stand on end.

He sauntered forward. "Can a man stand in line for some of what you're passing out, or are you saving it all for the boss?"

Carly's first instinct was to flee. Short of that, she longed to turn her back and hope he'd leave. But no, she was supposed to stand up for herself. Tyler had told her more than once that she didn't have to let anyone hurt her or walk on her feelings.

Standing up to the Tomlinsons had been heady stuff. She still wasn't very good at facing down Arthur, unless it had to do with Amanda, but Neal Walters was a different matter. He was a hired hand, not her boss's father or her charge's grandfather. He'd been making snide, lewd comments for weeks and she was getting damned sick and tired of it.

She stooped and picked up the egg she'd been after, then stood. Neal took the brief opportunity and stepped farther into the small building. When she turned back around he was practically on top of her.

"Back off, Neal. I'm not interested."

He grinned and stepped closer. "You don't mean that."

Carly glanced down at the egg in her hand. With no further thought, she dropped it down the open collar of Neal's shirt.

Neal's eyes widened in shock, and an odd, strangling sound came from the back of his throat. The egg slid down inside his shirt until it stopped by his belt.

Carly gave him an exaggerated smile and batted her lashes. "Don't mean it?" When her fist connected, the egg gave a satisfying *crunch.* "Why, of course I mean it."

Neal let out a cry and staggered back, glancing down in shocked disgust at the spot where his shirt was turning wet and gooey from the inside out. After a long moment, he raised his sickly, chagrined expression to her. "I, uh, think I get the message."

"Any problem in here?" In the doorway, just behind Neal, stood Tyler, legs spread, fists clenched at his sides, his fierce gaze boring a hole in the back of Neal's head.

"Nope." With a smug grin, Carly stepped around Neal and out the door. "No problem at all."

* * *

The following Tuesday, the bubble of teasing anticipation in which Carly and Tyler had been living burst under a cold blast of reality in the form of a process server who arrived during lunch.

Curious, Tyler took the papers meant for him and sat back down at the table to glance over them. Instant rage roared in his gut like wildfire on the open plains. "Son of a bitch."

Arthur set his coffee cup down sharply. "What is it?"

"Son of a *bitch*." Tyler stood so fast his chair fell over. "Damn them. Damn them to hell."

Carly watched, stunned, as Tyler stomped out of the room, practically breathing fire with every step. A moment later a sharp oath rang out. The office door slammed so hard the kitchen window over the kitchen sink rattled.

The men hurriedly finished gulping down lunch and fled outdoors, sensing they didn't want to be around to find out what had caused the eruption.

"Arthur?" Carly said hesitantly. "What in the world could be wrong?"

"I don't know," he answered grimly. "But I intend to find out."

Carly swiftly cleaned up the dishes, then went to pace the living room, instinct telling her that Tyler's initial reaction to the papers was only the beginning.

When the office door flew open a moment later and banged against the wall, Carly flinched.

Tyler stalked out, fire shooting from his eyes. Arthur followed swiftly. Tyler stopped before her, chest heaving, jaw flexing. "I have to go into Jackson Hole. I, damn, I want you with me, but I don't want Amanda coming home to an empty house."

"I'll stay," Arthur offered gruffly.

Tyler jerked his gaze to his father. "Will you?"

Arthur gave a sharp nod.

"Thanks." Tyler grabbed Carly by the arm. "Let's go."

"What's happened? Where are we going?"

They were in the pickup and all the way to the highway before Tyler spoke again. He hadn't even given her time to grab her purse.

"We're going to see my attorney in Jackson Hole. Howard and Earline are suing for custody of Amanda."

Shocked, all Carly could do was stare at him with her mouth open for a long moment. "Good God." Then, like a dawning light, she understood. Her palms broke out in sweat and her lunch rose to her throat. Without asking, she knew. This was because of her.

Chapter Fourteen

"Tell me they don't stand a chance," Tyler demanded.

His attorney, a short wiry man in his early forties named
Bill Hendricks, gave Tyler back a steady look. "I'm not
going to lie to you. Legally, morally, they don't have a leg
to stand on. But you and I both know that doesn't stop men
like Howard Tomlinson."

"What do you mean?" Carly had been silent as long as
she could. The grim looks the two men shared were scaring
the daylights out of her. "If he doesn't have a legal leg to
stand on, why can't you stop him?"

Hendricks glanced at Tyler. "She doesn't know about
him, does she?"

Tyler gave a weary sigh. "No."

"Know what? Tell me," Carly demanded.

The attorney looked to Tyler for permission. After Tyler's resigned nod, Hendricks tossed his pen onto the desk
and leaned back in his chair. "First of all, Howard Tomlinson's got more money than Wyoming's got sagebrush.

If that isn't enough, he's a former United States senator *and* a former ambassador to the United Nations. He's got a reputation for ruthlessness and probably has every corruptible judge in the state of Illinois in his back pocket.''

With each of his words, the knots in Carly's stomach twisted tighter. ''What grounds is he stating?''

''He's claiming Tyler is an unfit father.''

''What?'' Carly bolted from her chair. ''That's the most outrageous thing I've ever heard! There is no better, more loving father in the world than Tyler.''

The two men shared another look. Carly swallowed heavily and dropped back to her seat. ''This is about me, isn't it? He thinks, among other things, that I'm not qualified to help Amanda, and he's using that to get to Tyler.''

Hendricks kept his gaze on Tyler, who refused to look at her.

''One of you want to tell me what these 'other things' are?'' Hendricks asked. ''Aside from his belief that Carly's not qualified to counsel Amanda, is there something else going on?''

''No,'' Tyler said curtly.

''Yes,'' came Carly's soft reply.

Hendricks arched a brow.

''Carly, don't,'' Tyler warned.

''He needs to know exactly what happened.'' With her breath coming in shallow pants, her gaze lowered to her twisting fingers, and her cheeks flaming, Carly haltingly told the attorney about the Tomlinsons' surprise visit. All of it.

Hendricks listened silently while Tyler closed his eyes and flexed his jaw.

When she finished, Carly buried her face in her hands. After a long moment of gathering her nerve, she raised her head. ''Will it make a difference to the case if I leave?''

''No!'' Tyler cried, his eyes wide and stunned.

Hendricks passed Carly a brief look of apology, then turned to Tyler. ''You're not paying me to agree with you,

you're paying me to tell you the truth. And the truth is, yes. It would severely undermine Tomlinson's claims."

Carly squeezed her eyes shut against the pain. "Well. I guess that settles that."

"It settles nothing," Tyler told her fiercely, his eyes fever-bright. "Marry me. That will settle it."

Carly reeled as though he'd slapped her. "No!"

Tyler flinched at her sharp cry. "Well, I guess that settles that," he mimicked, his voice cracking slightly. "You didn't even have to think about it, did you?"

"Think about it?" she cried, bewildered, and hurt—*crushed*. "What is there to think about? Everybody, and I mean everybody I've come in contact with since I came here—including your own father—thinks I'm after your money. My marrying you would only confirm that. What good will that do in court?"

"When the hell are you going to stop worrying about what everyone else thinks?"

"When are you going to start?" she retorted. "What chance will you have in court when Tomlinson tells them about Blalock's? He'll find out, you know he will, and he'll use it against you. I have to leave, Tyler. I won't let you lose Amanda because of me."

Tyler pushed himself from his chair and crossed to stare out the window. His raw curse filled the air.

Carly tried to swallow past the lump of pain in her throat, but couldn't. Moisture trickled down her cheeks from the effort. "Tyler, I know you'd do anything to keep Amanda with you, but you're not thinking straight. Marrying me is not the answer. My leaving will help you more than anything."

After forcing an explanation about Blalock's and the embezzlement, Hendricks stated he would contact the Tomlinsons' attorney, then get in touch with Tyler. From there, they would proceed.

The one thing Hendricks hadn't done, Tyler kept remembering starkly all the way home, was to tell Carly she was wrong. That her leaving would *not* help his case. Nor had he sided with Tyler that her marrying him would be a better choice. The man had remained ominously silent. As silent as the long drive home.

The pickup's headlights cut a swath across sagebrush and barbed wire as Tyler turned off the dirt highway onto the ranch road. His hands ached. He hadn't relaxed his white-knuckled grip on the steering wheel for a single minute of the past two hours.

The fury in him over the Tomlinsons' lawsuit had him hot one minute, icy cold the next. And if he were honest with himself, he was not only more angry than he'd ever been in his life, but he was scared. Terrified at the mere thought of losing Amanda. It couldn't happen. He refused to believe they could take her away from him.

Then there was the pain, and another type of anger, this directed in equal shares at both Carly and himself. She was determined to leave. Nothing he'd said so far had swayed her. Maybe because he'd blown it big-time.

He rounded a low rise and stomped the brake pedal to the floor. "Dammit." He threw the truck into Park and slammed his fist against the steering wheel. "I didn't say it right, and I know my timing sucks, but my proposal was real, Carly. I want us to get married." His words were the first spoken by either of them since leaving Jackson Hole, and he said them to the windshield, afraid to look at her where she sat hugging the door.

"You know we can't," she answered softly.

"I don't know any such thing."

"You need to be making peace with the Tomlinsons, placating them somehow, not flinging me in their faces."

"Placating them?" he cried, finally facing her. "They barge in uninvited, insult you, upset Amanda, threaten me, and I'm supposed to *placate* them?"

"Yes!" She leaned toward him, spine straight, shoulders stiff, face ghostly pale in the green glow from the dash lights. "Apologize, grovel, do whatever you have to do to get them to back off. What's more important, your pride, or your daughter?"

"You know the answer to that, dammit. Amanda's a thousand times more important. But what the hell kind of father will I be to her if I can't look myself in the mirror? I can't *grovel,* as you put it. In the first place, it wouldn't do a damned bit of good. Tomlinson would eat it up and rub my face in it. In the second, I'd never be able to hold my head up again."

She sat back and faced the windshield. "So your pride is more important."

"The hell it is! I'm just not able to throw myself on the ground and let everybody that comes along walk all over me the way you do. I'll never give Amanda up. I'll fight them in every court in the country till the day I die. But I'll do it with my head up."

"That's your choice, but you'll get much better results without me in the picture."

"Dammit, Carly, I don't want you to leave." Tyler wasn't accustomed to panic, but he felt it now, wrapping its claws around his throat, squeezing off his breath. "Don't walk out on me now. Not now."

She wrapped her arms around her stomach. "I have to, don't you see?" Her voice cracked with emotion.

"No." He reached across the cab and pulled her to him. "All I see is how much I need you," he told her fiercely.

There was no gentleness in his kiss. He was too desperate, too close to the edge for that. Urgency clawed at him, making his heart pound, his hands shake. "God, don't leave me, Carly."

She tore her mouth free and held his face in both hands. "Think," she cried. "Think, Tyler. How long would you be able to stand the sideways looks and snide comments from your friends and family if you married me? How long before the taunts reached Amanda's ears?"

"I don't care. It won't happen. Everyone will see how

much you love me. And you do, I know you do, or you would never have let me get close to you. I don't care what anybody else thinks.''

"But you would," she cried. "You'd get angry and defensive, and before long you'd despise me for costing you your friends, for coming between you and your family."

"You're wrong," he swore fiercely, feeling her slip away.

"I'm not." A quiet sob broke from her throat and pierced his heart. "You know I'm not."

He would change her mind. He had to. He would burn away her doubts and insecurities. She hadn't denied she loved him. He knew she couldn't. "I love you," he told her in a voice strained with emotion. "I won't let you go."

He pulled her hard against his chest, and Carly gasped. His mouth covered hers. No teasing nips—there had rarely been such things between them when they kissed, but this time was different, even harder, more desperate than ever.

He fumbled with her jeans, and in a heated frenzy, she helped him tug them and a shoe off to free one leg. Frantic for the feel of him filling the aching void inside her, Carly reached for his belt. Her fingers shook so hard he had to help her.

Without apology—she didn't need one; she was as desperate as he—he lifted her astride his hips and buried himself in her depths with one powerful thrust that took her breath away.

What happened between them, there on the dusty seat of the old pickup, was wild and hot and fierce. He grasped her hips and helped her move against him, faster and harder, thrusting to meet her, and it had very little to do with lust.

This stormy passion had nothing to do with mating or recreational sex or even making love. What held them in its grip so fiercely was sheer need. Raw, primitive desperation. The need to hold on to each other as long as possible, knowing the end of their time together was near. The need

to shut out the world, make the darkness go away. The need
to stave off until the last possible moment the stark loneliness that both knew if Carly had her way, would soon
envelop them each in separate prisons of bleak isolation
and never let them go.

Carly felt the exquisite tension grip her and build until
she cried out in the violent throes of fulfillment.

.Tyler pushed himself against her, as deeply inside her as
he could go, and triumphed in the feel of her shattering
release. In watching her, the way she threw her head back,
arching her slender neck. In hearing his name on her lips
like a prayer, a curse. Feeling her fingers dig into his shoulders; her thighs, one still covered in denim, squeeze against
his; her inner convulsions. He even relished the tears on
her cheeks, because they told him how much she cared.

From every direction she assaulted his senses. With a
groan, he held back his own deliverance. It couldn't end
yet, not so soon.

Carly slumped against him, her throat raw from gasping
for air, sweat trickling between her breasts. It was a long
moment before she realized what the tension in his arms
meant. He was still hard and full within her.

She raised her head. "You didn't—"

"I will." He reached over and turned off the ignition
and killed the lights. Then his arms worked their way beneath her blouse and pulled it up until her breasts were
bared. "Now," he added, as if it were an afterthought.

He moved inside her, slow and strong, making her breath
shudder.

"And so will you," he swore. "Again."

Her head drooped to his shoulder. "I don't think I can."

His hands splayed across her ribs. "You will," he
vowed, and pushed her away from his chest to take one
nipple in his mouth.

With a moan of sheer ecstasy, Carly clenched her thighs
around his and thought, yes. She would. Again.

Tyler purposely tormented her, suckling on her nipples

until she was practically weeping, rotating his hips until she trembled. He would show her body what her mind refused to acknowledge—that they were right for each other; they belonged together.

The air in the cab chilled, but their skin slicked with sweat. The only sounds were those of harsh breathing and the occasional groan of profound pleasure.

"Tyler, please. Now. I need you now."

He flicked his tongue across her nipple. "Then tell me."

"Tell you what?" she managed to say.

His thumb tormented the other bud. "Tell me you love me. Say it."

"Tyler, don't."

Grinding his teeth against the urge to pound into her, he withdrew almost completely. "Say it."

She reached for his hips, trying to force him back home, but he held back. "Damn you."

"Say it!"

"I love you!"

With a low growl of triumph, he filled her, pushed into her until she took all of him.

"I love you," she said again. "I love you."

Then it was on him, and he couldn't stop. With one final thrust, he reared off the seat and she stiffened in his arms. Her scream and his sharp cry burst from the enclosed cab and echoed across the empty plains.

Tyler told himself the dampness on his cheeks was sweat.

Amanda knew something was wrong. Grandad was trying not to show it, but she knew. He was acting like she had the time she was little and one of the barn cats had had kittens. One by one, the kitties had all gone to new homes. When it came time to give the last one away, Amanda had carried it with her everywhere, trying to hold on to it as long as she could before it left for its new home.

That's just how Grandad was acting with her. Like she was the last kitten. He wouldn't let her out of his sight.

Now it was almost bedtime and Daddy and Carly still weren't home. All Grandad would say was that they'd had to go to Jackson Hole, but they would be home soon.

He'd told her that before supper. They still weren't home yet, and as far as Amanda was concerned, it was way past soon.

Then, finally, she heard the old pickup outside. *They're back.* Whatever was wrong and had Grandad worried, Daddy and Carly would fix it. They could fix anything.

But when they came in, her daddy hugged her and hung on to her just the way Grandad had. If that weren't enough to scare her, Carly's eyes were red and puffy. She'd been crying.

Oh, how Amanda wished she could talk, so she could make them tell her what was wrong! *God? Are you up there?* Amanda waited, but there was no answer. *If you're gonna give me back my voice, now would be a good time, God.* Again she waited. She worked her voice, tried to speak. Nothing happened. God wasn't listening.

"It's late, sweetpea," her daddy told her. "You've got school tomorrow. Run on up and get ready for bed. I'll be along in a minute."

Just like a grown-up. Never tell her what was wrong, just scoot her off to bed. But Amanda went anyway, knowing she didn't have any way to argue.

She took the fastest bath on record, got her toothbrush wet in case anyone checked, then put on her nightgown and snuck to the top of the stairs. Maybe she could find out what was happening if they didn't know she was listening.

There was a lot of cussing going on down there. Then Grandad's voice boomed. "The hell you are. Amanda still needs you."

Amanda wrapped her fists around the stair railing and leaned forward as far as she could.

"I can't help Amanda anymore," Carly yelled. "I can

only hurt her, and Tyler, and I won't. Do you hear me? I won't let them use me as an excuse to take Amanda away from her father.''

Amanda's hands turned icy cold. What did Carly mean?

"So you're gonna cut and run, is that it?"

"I'm leaving in the morning."

"If you think I'm going to help you—" Daddy started to say.

Carly interrupted him. "If one of you won't give me a ride to the airport in Jackson Hole, I'll get there on my own. Hell, with what you've been paying me, I can call a damned cab. Either way, I'm going."

"Go, then, damn you," Amanda heard her daddy cry.

At the top of the stairs, Amanda pushed herself to her feet. Carly was leaving? Going away? No, no, she couldn't leave!

It's my fault, because I can't talk.

That had to be it. Carly had come to help her talk, and it wasn't working. Oh, why, why was this happening? Mother had left because Amanda wouldn't shut up, now Carly was leaving because she wouldn't talk.

Amanda had never had the chance to make things right with her mother, to realize she should have done what her mother told her. But Carly was still here. Maybe it wasn't too late to fix things this time.

With tears clouding her vision, Amanda raced barefoot down the stairs. What if it didn't work? What if she couldn't do it?

I have to try, I have to.

She ran into the kitchen where the grown-ups stood next to the table, still talking. Amanda couldn't hear them for her own harsh breathing and the thundering of her heart in her ears. She threw herself at Carly and wrapped her arms around her legs.

Startled, Carly hugged the child close, feeling a pain deep inside with the knowledge that this would be their last night together. For Amanda's sake she forced a calmness into her voice that she didn't feel. "What are you doing down here, honey? We thought you were in bed."

When Amanda looked up, Carly saw the tears and misery on the girl's face. She knelt and took the child in her arms. "Oh, honey, what is it? What's wrong?"

Tyler came and knelt beside them. "Sweetpea, why the tears?"

Amanda turned her gaze on him and he nearly wept at the pain in her eyes. She must have overheard them and knew Carly was leaving. She moved her lips and worked her throat, but as usual, only a breath of air came out.

If Amanda could have made a sound just then, it probably would have been a scream of sheer frustration. She had to be able to do this! She *had* to.

She looked up at Carly, begging her silently to change her mind. *Don't go, Carly, please don't go away.*

She could tell by the look on Carly's face that her efforts weren't good enough. Carly didn't understand.

Don't go. Don't go. Don't go.

Not good enough! She had to try harder! Angry and scared, Amanda swiped the sleeve of her nightgown across her nose, then looked up at Carly again. She took a deep breath, parted her lips and placed her tongue against the roof of her mouth. "Don't...go."

Chapter Fifteen

The room fell into an instant hush.

Kneeling on the floor beside Amanda and Carly, Tyler held his breath until his chest burned. Was he hearing things? Dear God, had Amanda really spoken?

He watched her stare up at Carly and caught the instant that realization dawned across her young face. Her eyes widened. Her arms jerked. She swallowed and for a moment, looked lost and frightened.

"Baby?" he whispered, hoping, praying, reaching out a hand that trembled violently. "Sweetpea?"

Amanda turned her wide-eyed gaze on him and swallowed. "Daddy?" came her soft, tentative voice.

Never in his life had he heard a more beautiful sound. No music could have rang sweeter, no birdsong more pure. "You did it, sweetpea." He opened his arms, and she came tumbling against his chest.

"Daddy, Daddy," came that pure, sweet sound again.

Now it was Tyler who could not speak. His heart was

too full of the miracle still ringing in his ears. *Thank God, thank God.*

Blindly, because his vision had suddenly fogged over as if he was wearing glasses and had walked through steam, he reached for Carly and felt her take his hand.

His chest tightened until he feared his lungs would burst with sheer emotion. At his shoulder, he felt his father's hand. With his eyes squeezed shut, Tyler rubbed his face against Amanda's hair and finally managed to speak, although shakily. "Oh, baby, you did it. I'm so proud of you."

"I can talk!" came Amanda's excited cry as the knowledge finally sank in. "Daddy, Grandad, Carly, I can talk!"

"'Course you can," came Arthur's voice, husky with emotion. "We knew you could do it, sugarplum."

Amanda squirmed in Tyler's arms, making him realize he was practically strangling her. He loosened his hold.

She turned and faced the woman kneeling at his side. "Carly?"

Tears streaming unashamedly down her face, Carly gave Amanda a wobbly smile that nearly broke Tyler's heart. "You are the smartest, bravest, strongest girl in the world, Amanda Barnett, and I'm so proud of you."

Amanda met her gaze at eye level and swallowed again. "Does that mean you won't go away now?"

Tyler stiffened, holding his breath for her answer.

Carly hung her head and sniffed. "Oh, honey, how I wish I could stay. I love you, you know. Very much. But I have to go."

"Daddy," Amanda wailed, turning to him. "Don't let her go. Tell her she has to stay."

He couldn't look at Carly. If he did—hell, he was already on his knees. Next thing, he'd be begging. And that, he'd already done in the car. He couldn't do it again. Still, when her name fell from his lips, it sounded an awful lot like a plea to him.

Carly put her hand on Amanda's shoulder. "Honey, I can't stay."

"Is it...because somebody wants to take me away from Daddy?"

Carly stiffened, her gaze flying to Tyler's.

"I heard you say it," Amanda said softly. "But who would want to take me away from Daddy?"

"Sweetpea," Tyler started.

"It's Grandmother and Grandfather Tomlinson, isn't it?"

Suddenly weary beyond belief, Tyler slid from his knees to his rear and sat on the floor cross-legged. So much for keeping secrets in this house.

"I don't want to live with them," Amanda cried. "I want to stay here with you and Carly and Grandad."

The three adults looked at each other, bewildered by the turn of events, unsure what to do next, how to explain.

"Honey," Carly said into the stillness. "Your grandparents aren't doing this to be mean or to hurt you. They...they love you very much."

"Remember that litter of kittens we had in the barn when you were little?" Tyler asked. "Remember how you hung on to that last one? Then that boy from town came out and took it away, and you cried and cried?"

Amanda sniffed. "I remember."

"He didn't take the kitty away to hurt your feelings or to make the kitty unhappy. He took it because he wanted it for himself, because he thought he could take care of it and give it a better home than that drafty old barn."

"But I don't live in a drafty old barn, I live in the house! I don't need a better home. I don't want to live in Chicago."

"We know that, honey," Carly offered, smoothing a hand down Amanda's hair. "That's why I have to go away. As long as I'm here, they think you'll be better off with them. If I go back to San Francisco, maybe they won't try to take you away."

Amanda opened her mouth to protest, then closed it, bewildered by things no six-year-old should even know about, let alone have to come to terms with.

Tyler silently called his former in-laws every filthy name he could think of for putting them all through this.

Amanda sniffed again. "You'll come back, won't you?" she asked Carly.

Tyler held his breath, waiting for her answer.

Her voice shook when she said, "I can't, honey. If I come back, they might try to take you away again."

"But why?" Amanda wailed. "Don't they like you? Don't they know how nice you are?"

Carly shook her head. "I'm afraid I wasn't very nice to them when they were here."

Amanda's eyes widened. "Is it...because I stuck my tongue out at them?"

"Oh, Amanda." Carly hugged her close and rubbed her hand up the girl's back. "No, honey, no. That they don't like me has nothing to do with you. Nothing at all, I promise. They made up their minds about me long before that."

Sniffing, Amanda stood back and wiped her eyes on the sleeve of her nightgown. "Wh-when do you have to leave?"

Her heart breaking, Carly whispered, "In the morning."

Amanda stared at her a long moment, her face creased with dismay. "Can I...can I come see you sometime... maybe?"

Her stomach in knots, her throat filled with a huge lump, Carly looked at Tyler. His gaze was fixed stonily on the back of his daughter's head.

"I..." Carly tried to swallow, but her throat wouldn't work. "I'd like that very much." Then, before she could lose her courage, she gave Amanda a hug and a kiss, told her how much she loved her, and made her way slowly upstairs to her room. She had thought to run, but her feet seemed weighted down.

Odd how painless everything suddenly seemed. Leaving

Amanda and Tyler in the kitchen didn't hurt the way she'd feared it would. Nothing hurt anymore, because she couldn't feel anything. She saw her hand grip the banister, but could not feel the smooth wood beneath her palm. She couldn't feel her clothes against her skin, nor the shoes on her feet.

And when she looked at her reflection in the mirror of the dresser in her room, she dimly realized she couldn't even feel the tears streaking down her cheeks.

The numbness lasted through her encounter the next morning with Tyler, who handed her a check for the remainder of the hundred thousand dollars he'd promised her.

"Now you've got money of your own. You more than earned it," he'd told her. "No one can accuse you of being after mine."

She didn't want the money, wished she had the energy to tear up the check. Instead she tucked it into her purse without looking at it. She knew what he'd meant—now that she had money, her excuse for leaving was no longer valid. He must be blind, she decided idly, not to see what the animosity of his friends and family—animosity that would not go away just because she now had money of her own—would do to the relationship he claimed he wanted.

The numbness hung on even when Arthur drove her to the airport in Jackson Hole that same morning. It was curious that he made no snide comments about the trouble her presence had caused Tyler, but she didn't expend any great effort wondering at his uncharacteristic silence.

On the flight home Carly felt nothing but the dull vibrations of the airplane that carried her farther and farther from those desolate sage-covered plains and hills, closer and closer toward...nothing.

While waiting for her downstairs neighbor's sister to vacate the Nob Hill apartment, Carly stayed two weeks with her mother in Vallejo. She spent most of her time staring out the window of the den into the backyard, ignoring her mother's and stepfather's probing questions and worried glances.

It was nearly a month after moving back into her own apartment before the paralyzing numbness lifted. Feeling it go, Carly frantically clutched at it, trying to hold on, but the dullness slipped away. In its place came the sharpest, most crippling pain of her life.

Not a moment went by that she didn't picture Amanda's tear-streaked face begging her to stay. Amanda stepping from the house in blue jeans for the first time; feeding Carly ice cream from her spoon; sticking her tongue out at her grandparents.

Every vision brought a new pain, a new awareness of all Carly had once had and lost. Amanda. The ranch. The stark beauty of mile after mile of gray-green sagebrush blending slowly into the darkness of mountains and pines.

And Tyler. She didn't want to think of Tyler at all. She couldn't bear to remember the way his blue-green eyes crinkled at the corners when he smiled; the way he'd teased her about where milk and eggs came from; the many times he'd cornered her for a stolen kiss in the kitchen, the henhouse, the laundry room; the heat from his touch, the taste of his lips, the feel of his solid weight pressing her into the mattress. The way he filled her body, her heart, her very life, with his presence. The way he dominated it by his absence.

No. She couldn't think about Tyler.

But neither could she stop.

All she had left of him was his money. Damn him for leaving her with even that reminder, when all she wanted to do was put the last few months out of her head.

Yet all that money sitting in her bank account fairly screamed at her, reminding her every day of Tyler, Amanda, Wyoming. Well, hell, she could get rid of the money, couldn't she? Maybe then the memories would let her be and this agony in her chest would ease.

But no giving huge amounts of cash away to charity, not

for Carly. She'd given her friendship to Becky, her loyalty to James, her heart to Amanda and her body and soul to Tyler. With determination, she vowed she would give nothing else away.

She would spend the damned money. On herself. She had never been selfish in her life. It was about time she learned how.

She was going to buy whatever she wanted, no matter how frivolous, no matter how expensive. She had almost the entire hundred thousand left, and it was, figuratively speaking, burning a hole in her pocket.

Carly Baker was going shopping.

It wasn't working.

She'd gone to buy new curtains—not exactly frivolous or extravagant, but it was a start—and came home with a desert landscape painting dotted with sagebrush. Trying again the next day, she grimly set out for a slinky, expensive cocktail dress in hopes of lifting her spirits. She came home, instead, with two new pairs of jeans.

She rode the cable cars so long one day that the conductors started giving her odd looks. She supposed it was a sign of her improved state of mind that she even noticed.

At Fisherman's Wharf she treated herself to crab salad, but couldn't make herself leave the area without a balloon animal. She had tried for an orange giraffe and ended up with a blue monkey.

But today, sitting in her driveway with the engine running, she realized her plan was never going to work. She had decided that a person with as much money as she had was just plain stupid to drive an old, dilapidated car that threatened to quit on her every other day. So what had she done? Had she bought the sleek little sports car she'd been after? Oh, no, not Carly Baker. Not her.

With a heavy sigh, she looked around the interior of her new crew cab dually pickup and shook her head. What the hell was she going to do with a pickup in San Francisco?

Not an ordinary pickup, either, but one with luxurious lumbar captain's chairs, a full back seat, four doors, a long bed, double rear wheels, and for heaven's sake, a trailer hitch. And so much chrome, she was sure that when the sun struck it just right, she'd be able to signal clear to Mars and back.

Carly had been home two months and Thanksgiving was only a few days away when she saw the announcement in the paper that Becky and James were to be married next week.

Funny, but the thought of Becky marrying James didn't even hurt anymore. It saddened her to think that James was probably using Becky as he'd used her, but it didn't hurt. If he really did love Becky, she hoped the two would be happy together.

Carly paused in the process of folding away the newspaper.

What if James *was* using Becky to climb the corporate ladder? What better way to skip most of the rungs than to marry the boss's daughter, the woman who stood to inherit total control of Blalock's and all its assets?

Becky's not that gullible.

No? Carly would have sworn that *she* wasn't that easily taken in, either. And despite their years of friendship, Becky had believed Carly guilty of embezzling funds. Which proved that people will believe what they want to believe.

Why? Carly wondered for probably the millionth time. Why would Becky believe something so horrible?

She tensed, remembering Tyler asking her if she'd told anyone about James having her password.

No, she hadn't told anyone. It would have been too embarrassing, and no one would have believed her. She had opted to let them think she was a thief, so they wouldn't know she was a gullible fool.

Was it fair to keep quiet, no matter what anyone thought

of her story? Didn't she owe it to Becky and Walter to tell them the truth and let them decide?

God, how stupid she'd been. She couldn't let Becky marry James without at least trying to show her what kind of man he was. If Becky still chose to marry him, well, that would be her problem. At least Carly would know she'd told the truth. She would be taking a stand and openly admitting her mistake in believing in James's lies. Afterward, no matter what anyone thought, she would be able to hold her head up. It would beat the hell out of slinking around with her tail tucked between her legs.

Fearing Walter Blalock would not give her an appointment if she requested one, Carly donned her favorite pin-striped power suit and breezed past his secretary. "Don't bother," she said with forced cheeriness as a startled Marge reached for the phone. "I'll announce myself."

Once inside Walter's office, Carly let her smile drop. She was over the first hurdle—she'd made it in.

Walter Blalock, the man who had been like a second father to her most of her life, looked up, startled. For a brief instant, the old warmth and friendship was there. Then, in a flash of memory, the light in his eyes dimmed.

Panic threatened, but Carly fought it down. She'd come this far. This was something she had to do, for herself, for Becky. "I'd like to talk to you, Mr. Blalock." She had never called him Walter at work.

He leaned back in his chair and frowned. "Is this about what I think it is?"

Carly swallowed. "If you mean the missing money, yes. There's something I need to tell you, but Becky and James need to hear it, too, and I only want to have to say it once. I'd appreciate it if you would call them in."

The man stared at her hard for several moments, and Carly had to fight the urge to wipe her palms on her skirt. She dropped her gaze, knowing he assumed she was there to confess. Not that she had to feign her nervousness, but if he knew the real reason for her presence, he probably wouldn't even listen.

While he tried to decide whether or not to honor her request, Carly lowered herself onto one of the two chairs before his desk. The one angled so she could see the door.

Finally, lips pursed as if he'd sucked a lemon, he called Marge and told her to have James and Becky come to his office at once.

Carly breathed a surreptitious sigh of relief. Second hurdle cleared.

An uneasy silence filled the room for the several minutes it took James and Becky to arrive. Carly heard their voices in the outer office, so had a moment to compose herself.

When they entered, they stopped short, stunned to see her.

"Come in and close the door," Mr. Blalock told the couple.

Becky, her face pinched tight, was the first to speak. "Well, well, what do we have here?"

Mr. Blalock shot his daughter a terse look. "Carly has something she'd like to tell us. I, for one, would like to hear what she has to say."

"And high time, too," Becky muttered. "What prompted you to decide to spill the beans after all this time? Guilty conscience?"

Carly fought back a shiver at the animosity in her best friend's—*former* best friend's voice. "Actually," she said, "it was the announcement of your wedding that made me decide to finally come. There are things you need to know, and I thought it best to tell you before you and James were married."

Becky sank to the other chair before her father's desk.

James stood behind her and glared at Carly. He knew why she was there. He had to. "I don't think you've come here to tell the truth," he claimed. "I think you're here to tell more lies, make more excuses."

Carly met his gaze and raised her chin. "What lies have I told, James? What excuses have I given?"

"Good point," Mr. Blalock said. "You never said a word, except that you didn't take the money. You never offered any excuses at all."

"Because there aren't any." Becky gave her a look of icy disdain. "Not real ones."

James opened his mouth to add his two cents' worth, but Carly raised her hand to stop him. "Excuse me. You've all had your say ten times over. You let me know from the beginning what you thought of me, and you were quite clear about it. I didn't come here to listen to all that again. I came here to have my say, to answer all the accusations you've thrown at me."

"Be my guest." Mr. Blalock folded his arms across his chest. "Tell us, Carly. And I'd appreciate the truth. In view of our past relationship, I think you owe me that much."

Carly stared at her hands a moment, feeling how cold they were. Then she looked up at her former boss. "That's why I'm here. Because I do owe you the truth." She paused to gather her courage. "This is hard. It's...embarrassing."

"I'm sure it is," Becky offered with the first note of civility Carly had heard from her since the audit results months ago.

Carly gave her a sad smile. "As hard as it is for me to say, I have a feeling it's going to be even more difficult for you to hear."

Becky cocked her head, curious.

"I hope you'll remember all the years we were best friends, Beck, and understand that that's why I've got to say what I came here for. Because of that friendship."

"The friendship you betrayed?"

Carly shook her head. "I never betrayed you, except by my silence."

"Then quit dancing around the subject and get on with this confession." So much for Becky's civility. "I have a thousand last-minute wedding details to see to."

Carly winced, then steadied herself with a deep breath. "You and James announced your engagement the day before the audit uncovered the missing money."

"What does that have to do with anything?" James demanded.

Carly ignored him and spoke to Becky. "The two of you had obviously been seeing each other for quite some time, for you to decide you were ready for marriage. Yet no one in the office knew anything about it."

"This is useless," Becky told her father. "She's not going to confess to anything."

"Oh, but I am," Carly said. "That's why I brought up your relationship with James. During all those weeks or months the two of you secretly dated before you announced your engagement, did he ever tell you why he couldn't see you on Tuesdays, Thursdays and Sundays?"

"Of course he did." Becky frowned. She straightened in the chair and gave Carly a sharp look. "How did you know about that, anyway?"

"Because for nearly a year prior to the audit, James was with me every Tuesday, Thursday and Sunday night."

Becky blanched. "You're lying."

"Of course she is," James claimed. "You know me better than that, Beck."

"No, I don't think she does, James," Carly said. "I don't think any of us ever knew you."

"You realize I don't believe you," Becky told her.

"Naturally. He's very convincing, I know." Carly spared James a glance, then looked at Becky. "But you might want to ask yourself how I knew he never saw you those three nights each week, when at the time, I didn't know he was seeing you at all. What was his excuse for all the secrecy, by the way? With me, he claimed it would look bad at work. I expect it was something similar with you."

"My God, Carly," James said fiercely. "Becky and I are getting married next week. You were her best friend most of her life. How can you come here like this and try to destroy our future? No one's going to believe you, so why not give it up?''

Carly studied the man she'd once thought she loved. "I see why I fell for you now. You are very, very good, aren't you? Very persuasive."

"She's lying, Becky. Don't listen to her."

"Why would I make up something like this?" Carly asked. "It only makes me look like a gullible fool, which I'll admit I was. I didn't have to come here and say any of this, but I wanted Becky to know before she married you just what kind of man you are."

Walter Blalock's quiet voice broke in. "Just where were you those three nights every week, James?"

"Don't be silly, Daddy. He volunteers with several inner-city youth groups."

Mr. Blalock narrowed his eyes on James. "Which ones?"

James ground his teeth. "The Y, Big Brothers and Future Business Leaders of America."

"You can prove that, of course. That you were there every week?"

"Are you saying you don't believe me?" James's eyes widened.

Mr. Blalock shrugged. "Just curious. I'm also curious as to why Carly has chosen to carry this little tale. This has nothing to do with the missing money."

"Oh, but it does," Carly said.

Becky stiffened, outraged. "Surely you're not suggesting James had something to do with that."

"I'm not suggesting anything at all. I just came to tell the truth. And the truth is, James and I dated—secretly—for almost a year before the audit, apparently while he was also seeing you. During that time, he used to tease me by trying to guess my password on the computer system here at work." She gave a self-deprecating shrug. "It got to be such a long-running joke between us…I finally just told him."

"Oh, for heaven's sake," Becky cried. "Even if you were telling the truth—which I don't believe for a minute—what does it prove? Even I know your computer password. All the passwords are written down on a list in the controller's office."

"True, but last year when we upgraded the system I had mine changed. No one knew my new one except me, James's predecessor, Mr. Carson, who'd been our controller for twenty years, and James."

"Why are you doing this?" James cried. "No one was going to prosecute you. You don't have a thing to gain by accusing me, except some perceived revenge. And I'm telling you both," he said to Becky and Mr. Blalock, "this is all in her head. Everything she's said so far has been a lie. I never dated her, and she damn sure never gave me her password."

"Carly?" Mr. Blalock asked quietly.

"The only so-called proof you have that I took that money is the use of my password. Well, I'm telling you I did not take the money. You can believe me, or not. But as I've said, two other people also had my password. You have no more reason to suspect me than you do them. Frankly, after all the years we've known each other, I've never understood why you all were so eager to believe I'd betray your trust and friendship that way." She shook her head and rose from the chair. "But you do believe it, or I'd still be working here."

"That's what this is all about," Becky cried. "You're trying to throw the blame on James so you can get your old job back."

Carly gave a harsh bark of laughter. "Are you kidding? Work for people who call me a thief? Why in the world would I want to do that?"

"Because you're desperate. You don't have a job, I'd have heard if you did," Becky said. "You couldn't have had that much saved up. You must be just about dead broke by now, and Daddy won't give you a recommendation, so you aren't about to get hired by a reputable company. You couldn't even keep your job at Burger Barrel, for heaven's sake.''

''Yes, and we both know how I lost that job, don't we? I never thanked you for that. If it hadn't been for your interference, I might have been able to hang on quite a while. As it was, I was forced to take a job out of state for a few months.''

She paused, and for the first time was glad Tyler had practically forced all that money on her. The sudden realization that she had no need to accept whatever job came along just to support herself, the feeling of freedom and independence the money gave her, was heady.

With a smile, she said, ''That job paid obscenely well. If I'm careful, I won't have to work for anyone for a long, long time. No, I'm not after a job. I just came to tell the truth. Now, if you go ahead and marry James, I won't have to suffer a guilty conscience over letting you get into something unawares. And if more money turns up missing around here, I can honestly tell myself, 'Hey, they had all the facts. If they chose to ignore them, what can I do?'''

Becky leaped from her chair toward Carly. ''Why, you dirty little—''

''Oh, and Beck? I'd have him sign a prenuptial agreement if I were you. Just in case I'm telling the truth.''

Chapter Sixteen

In one respect, the confrontation at Blalock's lifted Carly's spirits. She'd done what she should have done months ago. That chapter of her life, as far as she was concerned, was over. Closed. Done.

But what came next? What was she supposed to do with herself in San Francisco, when she spent her days and nights longing for Wyoming and a pair of blue-green eyes? She still missed Tyler so much she ached with it.

She wanted to go back. She wanted to be part of his life, part of Amanda's. She wanted to love him and be loved by him. But how could she jeopardize his right to raise his daughter?

Marry me. That will settle it.

The memory of those words made her eyes sting. She had tried to tell herself he'd only meant them as a desperate step to retain custody of Amanda. Give her a new mother, and the court might look more favorably on letting him keep her.

But she knew Tyler better than that. If he hadn't wanted to marry her, he would never have brought it up. He loved her, she knew he did. No man could look at a woman the way he'd looked at her and not be in love.

And she loved him. God, how she loved him. Everything about him, from the way he set her blood on fire to the way he made her laugh. His skill with horses, his sharp business sense, his gentle tenderness with Amanda.

If it weren't for what everyone thought of her...

When the hell are you going to stop worrying about what everyone else thinks?

Her hands started trembling. She couldn't believe she was actually considering what was running through her mind. To go back to Wyoming without so much as an invitation would be incredibly presumptuous. What if he didn't want her anymore? What if the attorney still thought Tyler's chances for retaining custody of Amanda were better if Carly was out of the picture?

What if...dear God, what if he'd already lost Amanda?

The questions tormented Carly for days. Traffic on the streets pulled at her nerves. She looked for mountains on the horizon and saw only buildings. She searched the crowds on the sidewalks for a tall, dark-haired cowboy, but never found him.

A restlessness like she'd never known pushed her and allowed no ease. Even the article in the paper on James's arrest didn't soothe her. Nor did the personal visit from Walter and Becky two days later, both looking subdued and chagrined, Becky a little pale and red-eyed.

"We went back over the audit and discovered that most of the money was transferred to the dummy account that week you were out with the flu," Becky had told her. "Oh, Carly, can you ever forgive us?"

Carly had no trouble forgiving them, because regardless of her own recent lectures, she still felt that if she'd told the truth, the matter could have been cleared up immediately.

And if that had happened, she wouldn't have ended up out of work and desperate, volunteering her time at the clinic. She would never have met Tyler and Amanda.

In that respect, she ought to thank Becky and Walter for accusing her!

"We have a lot to make up to you, Carly," Walter had said softly. "We'd like you to come back to work for us."

Carly smiled sadly at the memory. She hadn't even been tempted by his offer. She had absolutely no desire for the job she'd once loved, or for any job in San Francisco, for that matter.

She knew now what she wanted to do. She wanted to go back to Tyler.

Yet, still, she hesitated. For what, she didn't know. For a means to make up for the way she'd left him? He must think she had no faith in his ability to fight the Tomlinsons. She had as much as come out and said so with her declaration that the only way to beat them was for her to leave. As though she and she alone had the power to control the outcome of the custody suit.

"Oh, God, I've done it again," she wailed as the thought dawned. Would she never learn?

She wasn't a damned bit smarter or more mature than Amanda, who somehow, Carly knew, blamed herself for her mother's death. Carly couldn't claim her own thought processes were any more logical.

Why did she think that all responsibility rested on her shoulders? Was she that much of an egotist, to believe she was responsible for everything? Oh, she knew the Tomlinsons hadn't trusted her ability to help Amanda, but they could simply have tried to talk to Tyler about it reasonably. Their antagonism was their doing, not hers.

At the age of nine, Carly had been convinced her love of ice cream had killed her father. Now here she was again, thirty years old, still thinking that the universe and everything in it revolved around her.

She could try to reason with the Tomlinsons. If that

didn't work, if they wouldn't back off, she'd get Dr. Sanders to help prove what a wonderful father Tyler was, how much better off Amanda was on the ranch with him.

Still, there was one little voice in the back of her mind that kept her from packing her bags and racing north to Wyoming. *What if he doesn't want me anymore?*

It could be true. She hadn't heard a single word from him in the two months she'd been gone.

"I won't doubt him until I have reason," she told herself firmly. His stubborn pride wouldn't let him call if he wanted to. She'd been emphatic about not having anything more to do with him. What man would come back for more after that?

The item that pushed her in the direction she wanted to go came in the form of a soft-spoken message on her answering machine. When she came back from the market, the light was flashing.

Carly put away the milk and lettuce, then played back the message.

"Oh. I guess you're not home."

Carly teared instantly and grabbed for the machine and the precious sound of Amanda's voice.

"I just called to say I miss you." A sob broke up the next few words. "...love you...Chicago...here...come..." *Beep.*

Carly's heart raced. What had Amanda meant about Chicago? Hands shaking, she fumbled in her purse for Tyler's phone number. To hell with pride and uncertainties. She had to know what was happening! As she grappled with her address book, the machine beeped again.

"It's me."

At the deep timbre of Tyler's voice on the tape, Carly's knees went out from under her. She ended up on the floor in front of her desk.

"No need to call back."

Pain knifed through her chest at his harsh tone.

"I, uh, overheard Amanda leaving you a message, and thought I'd better—" *Beep.*

Carly squeezed her eyes shut and rocked back and forth, praying for another message.

Beep. "If you're there, pick up the damned phone, Carly. I hate these stupid machines. A man can't get five words out before he gets cut off. What I was trying to tell you—" *Beep.*

No matter how much it hurt, even his anger sounded good to her.

Beep. "I'm getting pissed, here. The Tomlinsons have dropped their suit. That's what Amanda was trying to tell you. We went to visit them, and she, well, she told them if she had to live with them, she'd run away. They decided to back off. You left for nothing, Carly," he said, his voice softening. "You should have stayed." *Beep.*

With tears streaking down her face, Carly fell back on the floor. Laughter, just a little unsteady at first, then gaining strength, sounded odd in her apartment. She didn't remember the last time she'd laughed. She let it come, feeling its healing power strengthen her.

You should have stayed.

"I'll show you *should have stayed*, Tyler Barnett. Let's just hope you don't live to regret those words."

Within a matter of days, Carly moved mountains. She sublet her apartment again, bought the heaviest, most durable overcoat she could find, plus a tall pair of rubber, fur-lined boots, and a gorgeous new Navajo rug to replace the worn one beside Tyler's bed. She packed everything she thought she would want into the wide back seat of her shiny new pickup, and made one other important purchase before leaving town.

On her way to Wyoming she made a stop in Salt Lake City, and midafternoon on the fourth day after receiving Amanda's and Tyler's messages, she eased the pickup to a stop behind the main house of the Bar B Ranch near Big Piney in Sublette County, Wyoming.

Eagerly she feasted on the sight of the ranch. The driveway was more rutted than it had been. They must have had some rain.

Not rain, but snow, she realized. Small clumps of it still clung tenaciously at the bases of scrub and sagebrush out on the plains and hills. Along the creek, the willows stood stark and bare.

Suddenly Tyler appeared on the driveway, looking heart-stoppingly wonderful to her starved gaze.

At the sound of tires crunching on the driveway, Tyler had stepped from the stallion barn into the raw November wind. The long, fancy crew cab pulling the brand-new, fully enclosed, gooseneck horse trailer drew a low whistle from his lips. The rig was exactly what he'd been coveting for over a year.

Hell, he'd just have to save some more. Next year, he'd have his rig, by damn.

Sunlight glared off the windshield, making it impossible to see inside the pickup. Wondering who the visitor was, he tugged on his hat and headed closer.

The driver's door opened.

Still twenty feet away, Tyler froze in his tracks. Certain he was hallucinating, that this was just another one of those hundreds of daydreams he'd been having lately, he blinked to clear his vision. But she didn't vanish. He whispered her name, hardly able to believe she was really there.

Carly.

With her hands tucked into the pockets of a fur-lined parka and her long, jean-clad legs disappearing into tall, practical boots, Carly stepped around the front of the pickup and stopped a good ten feet from him. "Am I too late?"

Her soft voice sent rivers of fire racing through his veins. He swallowed once, twice. "Too late for what?"

She locked her gaze on his. "For you. For us."

Tyler tilted his head back and squeezed his eyes shut, afraid to believe, praying this was real.

"Tyler?"

He opened his eyes, but his vision suddenly blurred. He blinked. "Do you mean it?"

"Yes."

"For how long?"

"Forever, if you'll have me."

His knees turned to water. If he didn't get control of his emotions, he'd be fawning at her feet in seconds. He cleared his throat and forced himself to look away from her eyes. His gaze lit on the rig she'd driven. "What's all that?"

Challenge lit her eyes as she raised her chin and pulled her hands from her pockets to plant them on those hips of hers that drove him wild. "That," she said with a nod, "is my dowry."

Tyler choked back a sudden bark of laughter. God, look at her. She was getting mad. He'd never loved a woman so much in his life as he did right then. "Dowry, huh?"

"Every girl ought to have one, don't you think?"

A loud thud came from inside the trailer. "What've you got in there, a bull moose?"

"Don't be insulting." Fire and laughter mixed in her eyes. "That's a present for you. But only if you marry me."

His heart skipped at least one beat before kicking into double time. So she wanted to tease, did she? Well, two could play that game. He folded his arms across his chest. "I don't know. I'd have to see this gift before I made up my mind."

"You're gonna pay for this, buster," she muttered just loud enough for him to hear.

"Promises, promises."

"You can count on it." She spun on her heel and marched to the back of the trailer. "You might want to turn me down now, because you're not going to be able to in a minute.''

"This, I gotta see.'' He followed and waited while she opened the back of the trailer.

With a dramatic flourish and a sharp gleam in her eye that promised reprisal, she motioned toward... *Damnation.* "Resist *that,* cowboy.''

With his hands braced on each side of the open trailer door, Tyler stared inside at the back end of a buckskin mare, his eyes bulging. "Is that...no. I can't...Maggie?''

At the sound of her name, the mare twitched her ears and nickered softly.

"Magnificent Cutter,'' Carly offered from just behind his shoulder. "Signed, sealed, delivered and registered to one Tyler Barnett. According to her former owner, she's in top form, ready, willing and able to take on the competition at the National Cutting Horse Association Futurity in Fort Worth next month. He's already paid her entry fee.''

Tyler rubbed a hand across his mouth to keep from laughing out loud. He cocked one eye at Carly. "I don't know. I have to marry you to get her?''

"Tyler,'' she said, her voice low and threatening.

He turned back to look into the trailer. "But then, I suppose she is too tempting for a man to resist. You sure do know the way to a man's heart, honey.''

"Tyler,'' came Carly's low growl again.

Suddenly Tyler lost all desire to tease. Looking at the horse without seeing it, he gripped the sides of the door tighter and spoke to Carly in a choked voice. "I love you.''

Her reply was quiet but firm, without hesitation, tinged with relief, threaded with emotion. "I love you, too.''

"Then come here.'' He whirled and pulled her into his arms. Her lips were cold from the harsh wind. They tasted like heaven and tears. "Don't cry, baby, please don't cry.''

"I have to, or burst.'' She kissed him again with trembling lips. "I missed you so much.''

"I thought I was dying without you. Don't ever leave me again."

"No, never. Never."

"Let's go inside," he whispered roughly against her ear.

"The horse. We have to…"

"Damn," he said with a groan and a laugh. "A woman has to tell me to take care of a horse. I knew I was losing my mind. This is proof. We'll get Maggie situated, *then* go to the house." He nuzzled his lips against the hair at Carly's temple. "I want you naked beneath me, around me. I want to bury myself in you and never leave."

She shuddered against him. "Damn you. Take care of my horse."

He pulled back and grinned at her. "Your horse?"

"We're not married yet, buster."

More than an hour later, Tyler and Carly lay in his big brass bed letting their heated flesh cool while the winter sun streaked a pattern across the new Navajo rug on the floor beside them.

Tom and Smitty were probably still down in the mares' barn oohing and ahhing over Magnificent Cutter and grinning like idiots, knowing full well what Tyler and Carly were doing in the house. With any luck at all, Arthur, Willis and Neal wouldn't return from checking the cattle for a while yet.

"I love you," Tyler said softly in her ear.

The words spread through Carly like warm honey, golden and sweet. With his warm, wonderful weight pressing her into the mattress, she sighed. "And I love you."

"I know. Say it again."

"I love you." She grinned and narrowed her eyes while running her fingers down his spine. "Are you sure you're not marrying me just for my mare?"

"Honey," he said with a chuckle, "when I think of you, believe me, horseflesh is the farthest thing from my mind." He nuzzled behind her ear and set her skin on fire before pulling back to look at her. "The pickup, the trailer, the horse. What did you do, spend every dime you had?"

"Not on your life. Most of it, but I've still got a tidy little chunk left." She narrowed her gaze at him. "And you're not getting one penny of it back, so just forget it. I've learned to be greedy."

"Good," he said with a grin. "So what are you going to do with all that money?"

"Take you and Amanda—Arthur, too, if he behaves himself—to Disneyland the first chance we can get away. After that, I don't know. I'm feeling incredibly lucky these days. Maybe I'll dabble in the stock market. Invest in ice cream."

"What?"

"There's this wonderful little creamery down in Brenham, Texas, that makes the best ice cream. Or that chain of ice cream and dairy stores headquartered in Oklahoma. Then there's Swenson's. Baskin-Robbins. Ben and Jerry's. Yeah. I could—"

Tyler cut her off with a laughing kiss. "I don't care if you get fat off ice cream. Physically or financially. You do whatever you want. How does next weekend sound?"

"For Disneyland?"

"For a wedding date."

Before she could answer, they heard the back door slam shut.

Carly flinched. Judging by the heavy sound of the footsteps clomping up the stairs a few seconds later, it had to be Arthur. She tried to jump up, but Tyler held her down. "Oh, no, you don't, woman. I told you I'm not letting you go."

"We can't let him catch us—"

"Tyler?" A heavy fist pounded on the bedroom door.

"Too late," Tyler told her with a grin.

Carly moaned in acute embarrassment. And no little amount of dread. What would Arthur think of her coming back? What would he think of finding them in bed together?

"Tyler, you in there?"

"Go away, Dad. I'm busy."

"*Humph.* You alone in there?"

Tyler laughed. "Trust me, Dad. I haven't been this kind of busy when I was alone since I was fourteen years old."

Carly gasped and choked on a giggle.

"If you've got the driver of that fancy crew cab dually in there with you, I damn sure hope it ain't some bow-legged cowboy."

"Nope, I checked," Tyler called back.

"Get decent. I'm comin' in." The doorknob rattled.

With a shriek, Carly dived beneath the covers and buried her head.

The door flew open. "If you've got that Baker woman in here, I've got a question for her."

Tyler lifted the edge of the covers and peered beneath. "Are you that Baker woman? He says he has a question for you."

"Come on out from under there," Arthur demanded gruffly. "Hell, if I'm not embarrassed, you shouldn't be."

Outraged despite her embarrassment, Carly poked her head from beneath the covers. "If we're going to live under the same roof," she said to Arthur through clenched teeth, "you and I are going to have us a little talk. What do you want?"

Leaning casually against the door frame as though finding his son in bed with a woman in the middle of the afternoon was as common as beer in summer, Arthur removed a toothpick from his shirt pocket and stuck it between his teeth. He glanced from Tyler to Carly, then settled on Tyler. "Guess you ought to try and get a refund on that plane ticket."

"Dad," Tyler cautioned.

Carly peered at Tyler. "Plane ticket? Have I interrupted your travel plans?"

"Not likely," Arthur said. "Just saved him a trip, is all."

"What's he talking about?"

Tyler gave her a half smile. "I was coming after you next week. I couldn't stand it anymore."

"Oh, Tyler." Carly leaned toward him, her lips reaching for his, when at the last minute, she remembered Arthur. She drew back and glared at the older man.

Arthur pulled the toothpick from his mouth and pointed it at her. "I asked you once what your intentions toward my son were, and you never answered. Under the circumstances," he said, his narrowed gaze raking the disheveled bedcovers, "I'm asking again."

From the corner of her eye she saw Tyler's incredulous look.

"My intentions are strictly honorable," she told Arthur. By marrying Tyler, his family would become hers, and that included Arthur. But she'd be damned if she'd let him push her around anymore. "I asked him to marry me. I hope you don't have a problem with that."

The older man poked his tongue along the inside of his jaw and shifted his lazy gaze to his son. "You accepted?"

Tyler grinned. "I had to. She wouldn't give me the horse unless I did."

Beneath the covers, Carly pinched him on the thigh. Hard.

Tyler yelped.

Arthur squinted at the pair of them, then gave Tyler a sharp nod. "Smart move. Better hang on to her. She's the best thing that's happened around here lately. And the woman ain't bad, either," he added with a wink.

Carly stared wide-eyed and openmouthed as Arthur stepped into the hall and closed the door behind him. "Me an' the boys'll be headin' into town," he called from the other side. "We'll pick Amanda up from school and eat supper at the café. Probably won't be home till eight or nine. That's gonna be one happy little girl when she finds out about her new mama."

Stunned, Carly turned toward Tyler and blinked. "What happened to him?"

Tyler's expression turned serious. "He finally figured out how much I love you. He knows you're the only woman who can make me happy."

Carly's heart expanded. "Does he have any idea how much I love you?"

"I think your coming back here proved that beyond a doubt."

She closed her eyes. "I was so scared you wouldn't want me."

"Not want you?" Tyler wrapped his arms around her and pulled her on top of him. "Not want you? I *crave* you. I love you. I need you so damned much I nearly went crazy without you."

Carly's eyes misted over as she kissed him. "Then show me," she whispered against his lips.

"For the rest of my life."

* * * * *

Silhouette

SPECIAL EDITION

That's My Baby!

April 1997 **WHAT TO DO ABOUT BABY**
by Martha Hix (SE #1093)
When a handsome lawyer showed up on Carolyn Grant's
doorstep with a toddler in tow, she didn't know what to think.
Suddenly, she had a little sister she'd never known about...and
a *very* persistent man intent on making Caro his own....

June 1997 **HIS DAUGHTER'S LAUGHTER**
by Janis Reams Hudson (SE #1105)
Carly Baker came to widower Tyler Barnett's ranch to help
his fragile daughter—and connected emotionally with the
caring father and tenderhearted girl. But when Tyler's
interfering in-laws began stirring up trouble, would Carly be
forced to give up the man and child she loved?

And in August, be sure to check out...

ALISSA'S MIRACLE
by
Ginna Gray (SE#1117)

He'd told her that he could never have a child, and lovely
widow Alissa Kirkpatrick was so in love with enigmatic
Dirk Matheson that she agreed to a childless marriage. Until
the pregnancy test proved positive....

THAT'S MY BABY!
Sometimes, bringing up baby can bring
surprises...and showers of love.

TMBA-A

MILLION DOLLAR SWEEPSTAKES
OFFICIAL RULES
NO PURCHASE NECESSARY TO ENTER

1. To enter, follow the directions published. Method of entry may vary. For eligibility, entries must be received no later than March 31, 1998. No liability is assumed for printing errors, lost, late, non-delivered or misdirected entries.

   To determine winners, the sweepstakes numbers assigned to submitted entries will be compared against a list of randomly, preselected prize winning numbers. In the event all prizes are not claimed via the return of prize winning numbers, random drawings will be held from among all other entries received to award unclaimed prizes.

2. Prize winners will be determined no later than June 30, 1998. Selection of winning numbers and random drawings are under the supervision of D. L. Blair, Inc., an independent judging organization whose decisions are final. Limit: one prize to a family or organization. No substitution will be made for any prize, except as offered. Taxes and duties on all prizes are the sole responsibility of winners. Winners will be notified by mail. Odds of winning are determined by the number of eligible entries distributed and received.

3. Sweepstakes open to residents of the U.S. (except Puerto Rico), Canada and Europe who are 18 years of age or older, except employees and immediate family members of Torstar Corp., D. L. Blair, Inc., their affiliates, subsidiaries, and all other agencies, entities, and persons connected with the use, marketing or conduct of this sweepstakes. All applicable laws and regulations apply. Sweepstakes offer void wherever prohibited by law. Any litigation within the province of Quebec respecting the conduct and awarding of a prize in this sweepstakes must be submitted to the Régie des alcools, des courses et des jeux. In order to win a prize, residents of Canada will be required to correctly answer a time-limited arithmetical skill-testing question to be administered by mail.

4. Winners of major prizes (Grand through Fourth) will be obligated to sign and return an Affidavit of Eligibility and Release of Liability within 30 days of notification. In the event of non-compliance within this time period or if a prize is returned as undeliverable, D. L. Blair, Inc. may at its sole discretion, award that prize to an alternate winner. By acceptance of their prize, winners consent to use of their names, photographs or other likeness for purposes of advertising, trade and promotion on behalf of Torstar Corp., its affiliates and subsidiaries, without further compensation unless prohibited by law. Torstar Corp. and D. L. Blair, Inc., their affiliates and subsidiaries are not responsible for errors in printing of sweepstakes and prize winning numbers. In the event a duplication of a prize winning number occurs, a random drawing will be held from among all entries received with that prize winning number to award that prize.

5. This sweepstakes is presented by Torstar Corp., its subsidiaries and affiliates in conjunction with book, merchandise and/or product offerings. The number of prizes to be awarded and their value are as follows: Grand Prize — $1,000,000 (payable at $33,333.33 a year for 30 years); First Prize — $50,000; Second Prize — $10,000; Third Prize — $5,000; 3 Fourth Prizes — $1,000 each; 10 Fifth Prizes — $250 each; 1,000 Sixth Prizes — $10 each. Values of all prizes are in U.S. currency. Prizes in each level will be presented in different creative executions, including various currencies, vehicles, merchandise and travel. Any presentation of a prize level in a currency other than U.S. currency represents an approximate equivalent to the U.S. currency prize for that level, at that time. Prize winners will have the opportunity of selecting any prize offered for that level; however, the actual non U.S. currency equivalent prize if offered and selected, shall be awarded at the exchange rate existing at 3:00 P.M. New York time on March 31, 1998. A travel prize option, if offered and selected by winner, must be completed within 12 months of selection and is subject to: traveling companion(s) completing and returning of a Release of Liability prior to travel; and hotel and flight accommodations availability. For a current list of all prize options offered within prize levels, send a self-addressed, stamped envelope (WA residents need not affix postage) to: MILLION DOLLAR SWEEPSTAKES Prize Options, P.O. Box 4456, Blair, NE 68009-4456, USA.

6. For a list of prize winners (available after July 31, 1998) send a separate, stamped, self-addressed envelope to: MILLION DOLLAR SWEEPSTAKES Winners, P.O. Box 4459, Blair, NE 68009-4459, USA.

As seen on TV!
Free Gift Offer

With a Free Gift proof-of-purchase from any Silhouette® book,
you can receive a beautiful cubic zirconia pendant.

This gorgeous marquise-shaped stone is a genuine cubic
zirconia—accented by an 18" gold tone necklace.
(Approximate retail value $19.95)

Send for yours today...
compliments of ▼ *Silhouette*®
™

To receive your free gift, a cubic zirconia pendant, send us one original proof-of-purchase, photocopies not accepted, from the back of any Silhouette Romance™, Silhouette Desire®, Silhouette Special Edition®, Silhouette Intimate Moments® or Silhouette Yours Truly™ title available in February, March and April at your favorite retail outlet, together with the Free Gift Certificate, plus a check or money order for $1.65 U.S./$2.15 CAN. (do not send cash) to cover postage and handling, payable to Silhouette Free Gift Offer. We will send you the specified gift. Allow 6 to 8 weeks for delivery. Offer good until April 30, 1997 or while quantities last. Offer valid in the U.S. and Canada only.

Free Gift Certificate

Name: _____

Address: _____

City: _____ State/Province: _____ Zip/Postal Code: _____

Mail this certificate, one proof-of-purchase and a check or money order for postage and handling to: SILHOUETTE FREE GIFT OFFER 1997. In the U.S.: 3010 Walden Avenue, P.O. Box 9077, Buffalo NY 14269-9077. In Canada: P.O. Box 613, Fort Erie, Ontario L2Z 5X3.

COMING NEXT MONTH

#1111 THE 200% WIFE—Jennifer Greene
That Special Woman!/Stanford Sisters
Abby Stanford always gave 200% to her family, her job...even to making cookies! And when she met Gar Cameron she knew that if he married her, she'd be the *perfect* wife. But Gar didn't want perfection.... He just wanted to love Abby 200%!

#1112 FORGOTTEN FIANCÉE—Lucy Gordon
Amnesiac Justin Hallwood felt inexplicitly drawn to beautiful Sarah Conroy and her toddler son. Would he regain his memory in time to start anew with the woman and child who were so deeply a part of his past?

#1113 MAIL-ORDER MATTY—Emilie Richards
Matty Stewart married her secret crush, Damon Quinn, for the good of his baby girl. But when the infant's custody became uncertain, they had to decide whether love alone could keep them together....

#1114 THE READY-MADE FAMILY—Laurie Paige
Harrison Stone felt trapped when he realized bewitching Isadora Chavez had duped him into marriage to safeguard her younger brother's future. Could this newfound family learn to trust in their hearts—and embrace honest-to-goodness happiness?

#1115 SUBSTITUTE BRIDE—Trisha Alexander
Rachel Carlton had secretly yearned for her twin sister's fiancé for years—and impulsively posed as David Hanson's bride! Now she needed to captivate her unsuspecting "husband" on their week-long honeymoon before the truth came out!

#1116 NOTHING SHORT OF A MIRACLE—Patricia Thayer
Widowed nurse Cari Hallen needed to believe in life—and love—again, and single father Nick Malone needed to open his heart to hope again, too. But it would take nothing short of a miracle to join these two unlikely people together....

From the bestselling author of
Iron Lace and *Rising Tides*

EMILIE RICHARDS

When had the love and promises they'd shared turned
into conversations they couldn't face, feelings they
couldn't accept?

Samantha doesn't know how to fight the demons that
have come between her and her husband, Joe. But she
does know how to fight for something she wants: a child.

But the trouble is Joe. Can he accept that he'll never be the
man he's expected to be—and can he seize this one chance
at happiness that may never come again?

THE TROUBLE WITH JOE

"A great read and a winner in every sense of the word!"
—Janet Dailey

Available in June 1997
at your favorite retail outlet.

MIRA The brightest star in women's fiction

Look us up on-line at: http://www.romance.net

MER1

And the Winner Is... You!

...when you pick up these great titles from our new promotion at your favorite retail outlet this June!

Diana Palmer
The Case of the Mesmerizing Boss

Betty Neels
The Convenient Wife

Annette Broadrick
Irresistible

Emma Darcy
A Wedding to Remember

Rachel Lee
Lost Warriors

Marie Ferrarella
Father Goose

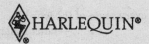 

New York Times **bestselling author**

LINDA LAEL MILLER

Two separate worlds, denied by destiny.

THERE AND NOW

Elizabeth McCartney returns to her centuries-old family home
in search of refuge—never dreaming escape would lie over a
threshold. She is taken back one hundred years into the past and
into the bedroom of the very handsome Dr. Jonathan Fortner,
who demands an explanation from his T-shirt-clad "guest."

But Elizabeth has no *reasonable* explanation to offer.

Available in July 1997 at your favorite retail outlet.

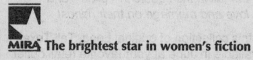

MIRA **The brightest star in women's fiction**